SHE'S THE ONE

WHO CARES TOO MUCH

S. R. CRONIN

ISBN-13: 978-1-941283-91-2

Cover design by Deranged Doctor Design
Editing by Goddess Fish

This book is a work of fiction and, with the exception of historical information, the events, characters and institutions in it are imaginary.

This is book is dedicated to the seven children of Peggy and John Cronin. No one in this story is meant to resemble any of them, yet collectively they have shown me how different seven siblings can be, all while sharing the common virtues of kindness and integrity. I'm honored to have become part of their family.

A special thank you also goes to my writers group for encouraging me to tell this story the way it needed to be told, from Coral's heart. Their input made this book so much better.

Warning: You Are About to Enter Ilari

Welcome to the thirteenth century in a universe almost identical to your own. The one major difference here is the existence of *Ilari.*

Ilari (el ARE ee) is a small hidden coalition of principalities in far eastern Europe. It has never been conquered thanks to its natural protection and the magic of its people. The lack of outside influence means that much will be new to you. But fear not, you have tools to help.

A map of *Ilari* is located at the front and back of this book. The back also has a description of the twelve nichnas (tiny principalities) that comprise *Ilari.*

Ilarians do not use any variation of the Roman calendar, as Rome never invaded their realm. Each chapter starts with a picture of the Ilarian calendar. The darkened area shows when that chapter takes place.

Ilarians use nine-day anks and forty-five-day eighths of the year. Each eighth begins with one of their eight seasonal holidays. Details are at the back of the book.

They have some unique words with no English translation. Those words are also given to you at the back of the book.

On the last page, you will find a list of the characters you are about to meet.

All of this information is also on the website *Seven Troublesome Sisters* at https://troublesome7sisters.xyz/ and can be downloaded and printed.

Ilarians of the 1200s have contact with the outside even though legend says interaction with others used to be rare. Ilarian scholars know facts about world history and have some idea of current events beyond their borders. What they know matches what you know because the world outside of *Ilari* is like ours.

However, the world inside is filled with surprises.

Enjoy your visit!

The Map of Ilari

The Year of Immense Concern

~ 1 ~

Hoping for Trouble

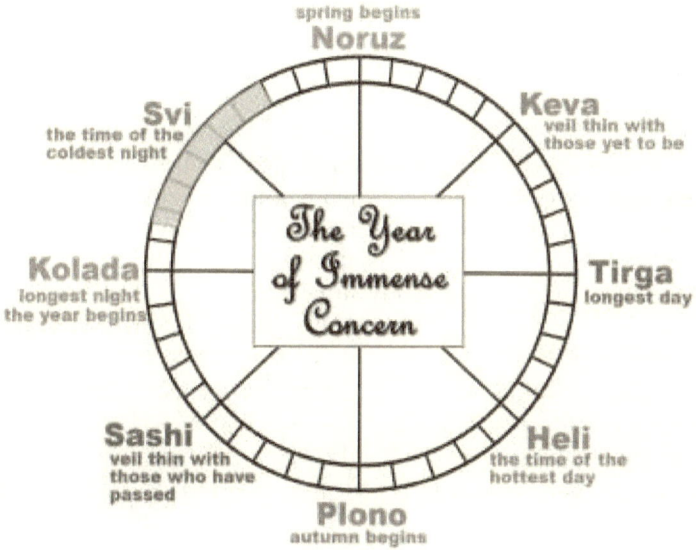

"What's your name?"

He stood in the doorway with a bright winter's sun shining low in the morning sky behind him. I squinted to see him better.

Why had a soldier come to our school? Questions formed in my mouth but his tone demanded a quick answer and the tension in his stance spoke of danger.

"Coral. I teach the youngest children here. What's happening?"

"We've had a report of vicious thieves nearby. Get all the kids into the barn, uh, Coral, and shutter the windows. Have them burrow into the hay. Keep them quiet. There's no time to waste."

Because my classroom sat at the front of the school, I'd been the one to greet this officer at the door. Now fear surged through me, and I wished another had met him instead. He saw me hesitate.

"Be quick. We rode here as fast as we could. We don't know how close they are."

I'd heard of such groups attacking other schools, of course. It didn't happen often; Ilari was usually as safe as one could hope. But once in a while a band of thieves crossed The Wide River, or came in through the grasslands of Bisu, prepared to grab everything of value they could before they fled our realm. Schools were easy prey and were known to keep coins on hand to handle their expenses. Teachers had died in such skirmishes, and children too.

I yelled to the teachers within earshot to tell the others to get their students to safety. Then I returned to my classroom and my little ones, who had heard everything. Only seven- and eight-years-old, now they huddled together and a few cried.

"No crying," I said in my firmest tone. "We'll be fine. The Svadlu are here. See all the nice brave soldiers out there to protect us? Now hush."

The room quieted. "We're going to play a game where we all pick up our things and see how fast we can tip-toe into the barn. Like bunnies." Some of the children giggled at the idea but they all did as I said, running on their toes behind me. A few of the braver ones made rabbit ears with their fingers as they ran.

The well-built barn was one of the finest things about our small country school. During the day it housed the teachers' horses, as well as those ridden by the older students, and by night it provided informal lodging for those who had to stay over due to bad weather or issues at home. It also served as a storage place, an infirmary for the sick, and a shelter during storms. I don't know what we'd have done without our barn.

Today the scent of anxious humans mixed with the smells of hay and horses as the barn filled with children. I looked around and saw six of the other seven teachers. Where was Sakina? Had word not gotten to her? Perhaps she'd been in the outhouse.

I had to find her. Yes, I *was* afraid of being caught outside when the thieves arrived, but what could I do? Sakina was my closest friend. Even if she hadn't been, I'd have felt responsible. I had been the one to sound the alarm.

I found her by the school door, hands on her hips, exasperated as she tried to get the attention of two older students too busy calling each other names to listen to her.

What? These two kids picked now to have a spat? Didn't they realize the danger we were in?

"You!" I barked it to the girl as I stepped between the two squabblers and put my face in front of hers. "Sit down. Now." She sat.

I turned to the other and let my eyes bore into his. "Stop talking. Walk into the barn and do not open your mouth." He glared at me but did as he was told.

My tone softened as I turned to Sakina. "You have your hands full with these two, don't you? Go get in the barn, and I'll bring this other one."

After the boy disappeared inside, I grabbed the girl by the wrist, gave her a look that said *don't say a word*, and led her to the barn door. The soldier who'd apprised me of the danger waited to close it behind me. Odd, I know, but I suddenly realized what an attractive man he was. To my surprise, he gave me a nod and smile of admiration.

"Well done, teacher Coral. My name is Davor. Once we repel these brigands, perhaps you and I could share some wine."

Really?

We spent the cold day hiding in the hay, with the children whimpering about their fear and how badly they needed the outhouse and how much they wanted food and water. I did my best to keep them calm, but as the day wore on, I thought I'd never been so scared and never would be again.

Then I wondered how I would handle it if more frightening things waited for me. If they did, I didn't want to know. It's easier to be brave if you don't know what's coming.

The brigands never attacked us. The Svadlu decided the thieves saw soldiers protecting the school and fled the realm with what they'd stolen from farms the day before. After an afternoon

3

of hiding, they allowed us to come out. We hugged each other in relief.

Davor sent most of his soldiers back to Pilk, leaving a few to stand guard through the night.

"Do all the children return home each day?" he asked.

"Most do. A few stay over for various reasons and teachers take turns spending the night with any left behind. With winter here, more will stay. Why?"

"I wondered if perhaps you'd be spending the night?"

"Not tonight."

"Oh. So does a new husband expect you home soon?"

"I'm single, sir." I felt the flush in my cheeks at his question. Of the seven girls in my family, I alone had been cursed with flaming hair and fair skin that turned warm and pink at the slightest embarrassment.

"I live with my parents. My family never knows whether to expect me or not, given the situation." I tried to force the heat back out of my cheeks.

"I see." His smile widened. "I travel with a tent befitting my station. I know it would be a tad peculiar, but under the circumstances, could a Mozdol offer a beautiful young woman…," at this he reached out and ran his fingers through my hair "… a toast to her bravery and her assistance during a difficult situation?"

A Mozdol? This man was more than a soldier, more than an officer. I'd been flirting with an honorary prince of the realm, a fighter who'd received this high honor for his bravery in battle. Oh my.

I looked closer. He was years older than I, his skin weathered by time in the sun. He was stocky and strong, although a bit short for a man. He had a full head of gorgeous shiny black hair, though, and dark eyes that spoke of mystery. I liked him.

"Well, sir …"

We both knew an unmarried woman like me enjoyed the company of men on the eight holidays of the year, as she sought a suitable husband. However, society considered it inappropriate to bed a stranger at other times. Lovers, of course, were permitted more freedom as they planned to wed, yet that hardly described my situation with this man.

4

I *could* avoid disapproval by bidding my fellow teachers farewell, disappearing awhile, then visiting this Mozdol's tent in secret. I *could* tell my family I'd stayed at the school. No one would be the wiser.

And I did have a good excuse. I'd been cheated out of my pleasure on the previous holiday. Two anks ago, my parents generously sent three of us sisters off to the great castle to a fabulous end-of-the-year ball. Saddled with seven unmarried daughters, they hoped at least one of us would find a mate while celebrating Kolada.

My mother had done her best. She packaged Ryalgar, our oldest, in a rich red gown that flattered Ryalgar's dark hair and accentuated her ample bosom. It worked. She caught the eye of a prince from Pilk, the richest nichna in Ilari. I watched them as they danced, and I liked him. He had kind eyes, and he seemed to care for her, and she for him. She could have done far worse.

I didn't fare as well. I landed in a fluffy pink frock that portrayed me more like a pastry than a woman. A hungry bumpkin from Gruen latched on to me and would not leave me alone. His breath stank of barley and his conversation was pitiful, yet his unwavering presence deterred all others.

In the past, I'd enjoyed the pleasures permitted on holidays as much as any of my sisters, if not more, and I'd looked forward to the joys of the night. But no amount of wine made this young man appealing enough, so before the evening ended, I sent him away, leaving us both annoyed and unsatisfied.

I figured I deserved a second chance. I'd consider a night with this Mozdol to be my own personal Kolada celebration. Surely the Goddess would understand.

Davor's men erected his tent for him before they left. Dark came early around Kolada. By the time I deemed it safe to sneak back to his campsite, I needed the candle he handed me to see the large interior filled with furs. Their softness invited me in.

"I'm from Lev, originally," he said as he handed me a small silver goblet. "This wine is from my own family's vineyards."

Could this have been more perfect?

I took a sip.

Although I enjoyed the taste of the full-bodied red wine, we didn't waste much time drinking. He undid the leather lacings of my bodice, and I appreciated his confident touch. How different from the bumbling boys I'd bedded so far. By the time his hand ran gently up the inside of my thigh, barely touching the parts of me only a lover touched, I knew I'd made a wise choice. I'd be visiting this man's tent as often as he wished.

I returned home the next evening, humming to myself as I rehearsed a tale of needing to stay at school unexpectedly. I figured if things went well with Davor, I'd invent a seemlier way for us to have become close. Until then, surely my little ruse caused no harm.

As I walked into the spacious stone building my family called home, I heard Ryalgar gushing to Mom about her prince and an invitation to come to Pilk to see him again. I watched the two tall, stately women as they leaned in close to each other, whispering and laughing. From the back, only the streaks of gray in mom's long dark hair distinguished her from her oldest daughter.

I knew Mom dreamed of a prince for Ryalgar. She dreamed of one for all of us.

I decided to keep news of Davor to myself. Ryalgar, only a year older than me, deserved some time to let my family focus on her happiness. If all went well, I could gush about my own prince later.

I spent the six workdays of the next ank wishing for more thieves to attack. I'd have been happy with any kind of trouble requiring the Svadlu to ride out to our Eastern Plains to save us, but through each long day, no danger came. Then I fussed and fretted my way through the three-day ank-break, unusually eager for the workweek to start again.

The following ank, as the first storm clouds of winter hovered low with a promise of snow, a lone horseman rode up to the school accompanied by a second mount laden with camping supplies. I went outside to greet him. My room was at the front, after all, but I also recognized his glossy black hair.

"I love camping on these plains during the first snowfall of winter," he greeted me. "But it's far more pleasurable if one shares the tent with a beautiful woman. Could I interest you in a cozy evening together?"

I'm sure the answer *yes* was written all over my face.

I saw Davor several more times as the winter wore on. He always surprised me at school and brought the supplies we needed for a romantic night. After a while, I stopped worrying he wouldn't come back. I could tell he was smitten with me, too, and I saw us having a future together.

I wanted that future, right? One with a prince as charming as the nights were long. I'd live with him in Lev, with lush grapevines growing outside my windows, and all my dreams would come true.

Why didn't this picture make me as happy as it should have?

****

Shortly after we celebrated Svi, the coldest time of the year, Sakina asked me a question as we walked to the barn together, each preparing for our ride home.

"Remember the day we thought thieves were coming to attack the school?"

Of course I remembered it. My life had become so much more interesting after that day.

"I've been wanting to ask you something ever since."

My heart pounded. Had she seen me sneak off to meet Davor that night? If so, had she noticed other nights as well? Had she talked to others about it? How concerned would the school be about such behavior?

"How did you ever get those two kids to stop bickering?" she said. "I deal with them all the time, and believe me, once those two get started, there is no way to shut them up. I've never taught two such difficult ones."

I laughed with relief. I hadn't thought about how I'd done it.

"I talked to them the way I talk to my own class. You know. Do it now."

"No, I don't know," she said. "I could say that all day and they'd ignore me."

I shrugged. She hesitated as if she was about to ask me an impolite question.

"Do you know what a luski is?" she said.

7

I did. "It's a make-believe magic person who can force people to do things by the way she speaks. You don't believe in them, do you?"

"It's not make-believe. My great-aunt was a luski. It's rare, but I know it's real."

"Are you serious?"

She looked completely serious.

"Wasn't it creepy having a relative who could make you do things?"

"No, because it doesn't work that way. It's an emergency tactic; they can only use it when it's important. I think you should find out more about it."

"Why?" Then I realized why. "Oh, wolf scump. Everyone keeps telling me I'm too tenderhearted. I'm *certainly* no luski."

"You don't get it," she said. "Luskies aren't monsters; they can be nice people, too. You should ask the Velka at one of their market stalls. I've heard they know all about luskies, and can tell if you are one."

"You think I should talk to the Velka?" Frankly, I found these women of the forest, the keepers of most of the magic in our realm, scary in their own right. I'd only spoken a few words with them and I didn't wish to ask a Velka if I was some kind of freak.

"No thanks. I've got enough problems right now."

And I did. I had all the problems I knew of, and a few more I hadn't discovered yet.

~ 2 ~

The Worries Begin

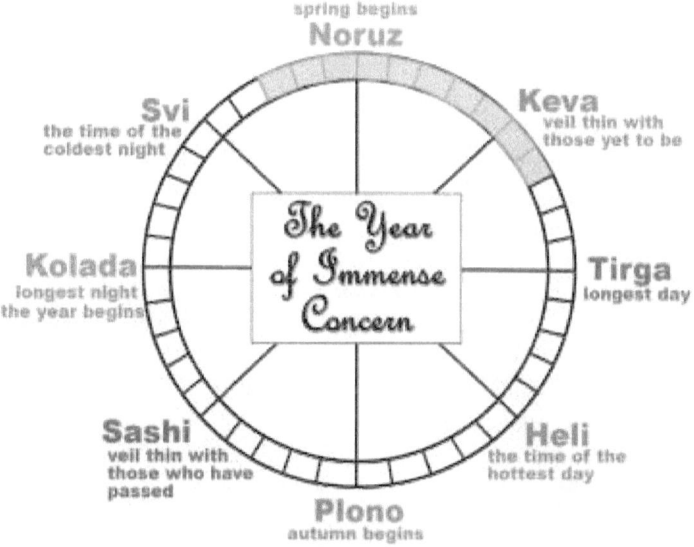

Not long after, during one of the worst storms of the winter, Davor proposed marriage.

The two of us drank red wine in his tent, huddled together under furs as the winds howled outside on a particularly brutal winter night. My lunch had been sparse, so I tore into the ham he'd brought for our dinner, paying more attention to the salty smokiness against my tongue than I paid to his words.

"Once I made up my mind, I was so anxious to get over here and do this," he laughed. "I should have waited for a calmer evening."

"Anxious to do what?" Had I missed something?

"Sweetheart. If you could leave the food alone for a bit, I'm trying to tell you I'd like to marry you."

"Marry me? You want me to be your wife?" I dropped the meat onto the furs beneath me.

He laughed again. "Yes, that's usually what marriage means. Look, I'll be honest with you. I've been getting pressure from the Royals for a while to settle down. I've hopes of becoming a Mozdol commander and they've gone so far as to imply my career advancement requires me to find a wife. Normally that kind of pressure would make me livid, but lucky for me, I've become quite taken with you. You may be a simple farm girl but you're one of the kindest women I've ever met. I think a man could do far worse, you know?"

"I don't know what to say."

And I didn't. This was the desired outcome, wasn't it? Yet perhaps his proposal had included a little too much honesty.

"Say yes," he suggested.

"I'm … honored. But this all began so strangely. My family doesn't know about you and I've never met yours. There's so much we haven't talked about…"

In fact, he and I had talked about very little. Talking wasn't a big part of our relationship.

He held up a hand to stop me, a trace of irritation creeping into his voice.

"I know these things. We'll do this slowly, Coral, as slowly as you need. You agree to marry me now, and we'll invent a more proper meeting and courtship we can tell everyone about. We'll discuss anything you want. But by spring, let's be planning our nuptials. Okay?"

"Yes. Of course, yes." What else could I say? I had my reservations and could have asked for time to think, but he looked so earnest and I didn't want to hurt his feelings.

Yet, plenty worried me.

He was from Lev, where vineyards thrived in picturesque hills and where the rich of Ilari spent their leisure time. He'd already invited me to meet his family but the trip made me nervous. He'd called me a simple farm girl. What would his family think of me?

And what would my unpretentious family think of him? Davor was a military man, nothing like my gentle, intellectual dad. Would the two of them have anything to say to each other?

And what of my mother? Over the years, she'd made it clear we weren't simply to marry. Our father was a respected soil expert in the farming nichna of Vinx, and she'd gone to great pains to ensure we learned everything from grooming to fine arts, polishing us enough to wed the best Ilari had to offer.

"But what about love?" I'd asked her repeatedly.

"It's just as easy to fall in love with a prince," she'd answered each time. I'd gotten the point by the time I was eight.

But Davor hadn't been born to a royal family. Rather, he'd achieved his status when a decree made him a Mozdol after his brave actions in a skirmish with a band of thieves. Being a Mozdol was supposed to be the legal equivalent of being a prince. Would it count with my mother?

On the plus side, I did believe in Davor's affection for me. He didn't think I was too nice and he didn't mind the bit of plumpness plaguing me. He told me my softness attracted him. And while I found my orange hair too bright, he adored it, running his figures through it every time he saw me.

Learning he was eight years my senior caused me concern because a man seldom waited so long to wed. I knew my parents would find this worrisome, too. He'd said his commitment to the Svadlu made it difficult to find a mate. I pushed for a better explanation and he told me he was still single because he'd been waiting for me. I knew *that* wasn't true, but it was a charming thing to say.

The next time we met, he urged me to make our courtship public.

"We'll largely stick to the truth. Say we met when I came to your school and we've written a few times since. Very proper. Tell people I've come to Vinx to court you and invited you to come to Lev so we can get to know each other better. Perhaps to celebrate Noruz? Women find the start of spring to be so romantic."

"No, not for Noruz," I shook my head. "My older sister hopes the man she's been seeing will propose to her while they celebrate the start of spring. I'd like to let her have her moment. Once she announces her engagement, we'll proceed. Please. It's just a few more anks."

He agreed, but I could tell he wasn't happy about it.

"Who is this person she's marrying, anyway?" he asked.

I froze. I'd kept quiet about the identity of Ryalgar's suitor for a lot of reasons. It seemed a private family matter and I didn't want to subject my sister to embarrassment if the relationship failed. Then, once Davor proposed, I feared he'd be insulted to learn he wouldn't be the highest-ranking son-in-law in the family. Now, I simply didn't want to have this discussion.

"He's just some man she likes."

"Well, that's good. I hope the two of them get on with it so we can do the same."

A few days later, life at the farm changed. Ryalgar retreated into her room in a flurry of tears and could be heard crying in there for days. She barely came out, and when she did, she wouldn't talk to me. I guessed she was embarrassed. I couldn't imagine what had gone wrong. Perhaps his family objected to her. But why?

Mom told the rest of us Ryalgar was ill, but we all knew better.

Good thing I hadn't brought up Davor. Perhaps her prince would reconsider. I wanted Ryalgar to have every chance to get her life together before I launched my happiness into the middle of her misery. So the next time I saw Davor, I begged him to wait a little longer.

"I'll tell my parents about you in an ank or two, I promise. In time for you to invite me to celebrate Keva."

"That's four anks away yet. I'm starting to think you're afraid to tell your parents about me."

"I am not."

"Then promise me this is the last delay, okay?" he said. "I'm not going to be able to keep these kinds of visits up much longer."

I felt a tightness in my chest. Was he thinking of ending it because I'd waited too long? He must have seen the look in my eyes.

"Look, honey cakes. I'd be willing to give you all the time you need to find your nerve, but things are changing for the

Svadlu. A band of thieves far worse than anything we've ever encountered has been swooping into farming areas like ours, taking everything they want. Traders tell us they only attack when it's cold, and they've been coming further west every year, seeking new areas to raid. They'll be here soon, maybe this year before the heat comes, or perhaps next winter."

"That's horrible."

"It's worse than you know. We've started to train for it and soon I'll have less freedom to take jaunts out to Vinx to spend the night with you. You need to tell your parents you've met a man and want to get married. You understand?"

I understood. No matter what happened in Ryalgar's life, I'd do it before Keva.

Then, Ryalgar did something I couldn't have predicted.

She announced she was joining the Velka, to become one of the women of the forest who lived without men. I couldn't imagine making such a choice. What was she thinking?

Clearly, she'd failed to snare her prince, and now she believed she'd never want another man. But I knew her heart would heal in time. All hearts did. I tried to tell her this, but she remained firm.

She only asked one thing of me.

"I'm going to enter the forest on the day of Keva. Please, Coral, be there to watch me go in."

At Keva? Bat scump. Everyone knew a new Velka's first lone journey into the woods was an important event, a ritual done on one of the eight holidays, such as Keva. Eerie as I thought joining the Velka sounded, how could I tell my sister no?

"Of course I'll be there."

Davor would understand. He'd have to. We'd start our courtship in earnest as soon as Ryalgar was gone, and then I could meet his family in Lev on Tirga.

On a beautiful sky-blue morning, halfway between the first day of spring and the summer solstice, all seven of us sisters set out on horseback dressed in our finest clothes. We wove flowers into our hair and wore them around our necks and on our wrists. What a pretty picture we must have made, seven young women covered in bright blossoms on a soft spring day. How innocent and harmless we must have looked.

Of course, everyone knows how dangerous we all proved to be, but on that happy day, no onlooker would have guessed it.

My father rode with us, but my mother felt too devastated by Ryalgar's choice to come along. She said her good-byes to her oldest daughter privately, at our farm, before we left.

As we approached the forest, Ryalgar seemed excited, not afraid or sad. She hopped off her horse and donned the overstuffed rucksack my father carried for her. She smiled, she waved, then she stepped in between the branches. Most of us had tears in our eyes as we watched.

I waited a day or two more, thinking Ryalgar would change her mind and show up at the front door, laughing about what an ill-advised decision that had been. I think many of my sisters hoped she would. Perhaps not all, though. Having the oldest girl in the family unmarried had put a damper on the rest of us, and I'm sure I wasn't the only one anxious to get on with my life.

Luckily for the remaining five, I had no intention of slowing them down. I planned to tell everyone about my lover, in a few more days.

But time went on and I said nothing. Why not? Was Davor right? Did I fear my parents' reaction? I didn't think so. I thought it had to do with my job.

Two years ago, when I'd finished with the advanced studies most young people in Ilari turned to before settling down, no wedding plans waited for me as they did for so many young women. Unlike Ryalgar, I hadn't wanted to take endless additional classes until the right man came along. So, I'd taken a job at the school and discovered I enjoyed teaching. The youngest children became my favorites to work with and I'd settled into my classroom, in no hurry for my life to change.

Getting married would change it.

Davor didn't handle the postponement well, and the first time I saw him after Ryalgar left for the forest, he didn't even kiss me when he greeted me.

"Why are we still sneaking around," he said as he threw his bags on top of the fur blankets on the floor. "I want to spend the night with you in a proper room."

I searched for something to say to soften his mood.

"They'll be no more delays. I promise."

He stepped closer to me, but all he did was shake his head as he ran his fingers through my hair. Then he stared hard into my eyes, as though he saw them for the first time.

"Your eyes are the same color as your hair," he declared.

"No, they're not. Nobody has orange eyes."

I laughed, thinking he joked with me, but his face grew angry at my laughter. He got a looking glass out of his pack, grabbed the back of my head, and forced me to look into it.

"See?"

I studied my blurry reflection. No, my eyes weren't orange.

"Why won't you listen to me?" he said. "I know your eye color better than you do." After he insisted a few more times, I gave in.

"Okay, I can maybe see a little orange." But by then his mood had turned more foul.

"So why haven't you said anything to your family during this past ank?" I understood his frustration.

"I wanted to make sure Ryalgar wasn't coming back."

"That's bull scump. You're scared of your parents. Get over it. I've got a horde of invaders to worry about, and you need to gain a little courage."

"But winter is well past. Do these men from the east remain a threat?" I asked as I poured us both some wine.

"Not till cold weather comes again, but it will arrive soon enough," he said.

After that we drank in silence, the beverage having become part of a ritual mating sequence we both knew well. After a few sips, he undressed me. He always liked having me naked for a while before he removed his garments. I touched him beneath his clothes. He touched me everywhere without mine. As we did what we usually did, I noticed he made less effort to ensure my enjoyment, but my body took its pleasure from him anyway and I was glad.

After we were done, he fell asleep snoring. As I lay listening to him, I started to cry and I couldn't seem to stop. Did I shed tears because of Davor's irritableness with me, or because the idea of invaders coming to steal everything from my people terrified me? Whatever the cause, I cried until my fair skin turned blotchy red and my eyes swelled so much it didn't matter what color they were.

The next morning, I felt nauseous. I thought all the crying caused it, but as I rode back to the schoolhouse, I did some math. Before last night, Davor and I hadn't been together for almost three anks. Twenty-seven days. My female time had been due an ank and a half ago and it still hadn't occurred. This happened sometimes, but today I needed to get off my horse because I couldn't keep down my breakfast.

As I retched the porridge out over a sweet-smelling clump of red clover blooms, I knew what the problem was. Prucking goat scump. I'd taken all the precautions. How in Heli had this happened?

~ 3 ~

Adjusting Expectations

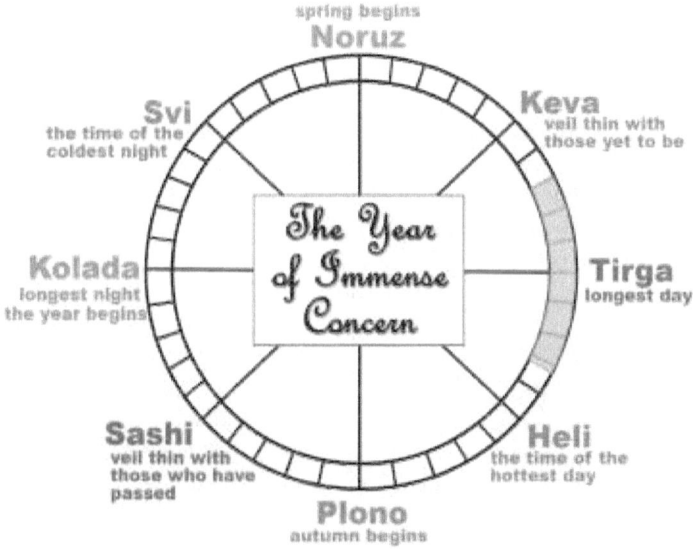

When I arrived at school a short time later, I washed my face and smoothed my clothes. I let two of the children climb onto my lap while I caught my breath. Other teachers told me not to be so affectionate with them, but I knew my little kindnesses did more good than harm.

Some of my students knew how to read when they arrived, but most didn't and few could count past ten apples, much less figure out what happened when you added apples or took them away. So I taught them these things, but I also played with them and listened to their made-up stories. You can only force children that young to study for so long.

Sitting on the bench I realized how much I wanted to keep my job. What a shame I had to choose between teaching and having a husband. Yet, everyone expected a new wife to move to her husband's nichna and care for him. Particularly a pregnant wife.

As Chessa, one of my favorites, snuggled in next to my hip, something else sunk in. If I wanted, I could have a daughter like her. Soon. The idea made me surprisingly happy.

The girl took my fingers in her two little hands and played with them as she spoke.

"Miss Coral," she said. "I want to be just like you when I grow up."

I sat with Chessa warm against my side, her words warming me on the inside as well. I knew plenty of women who'd stopped a pregnancy this early. I could easily do the same; the Velka had their ways. But as I put my hands over my belly, cradling what had begun, I knew I wanted the baby I could grow inside me. I wanted to be a mother, and it would be easier if I married Davor.

So, that settled it. Tonight, I'd tell my parents everything.

Dad listened as we sat in front of the fire talking, his slight frame hunched forward to catch my every word. He looked concerned but said nothing. Practical man that he was, I doubted my out-of-wedlock pregnancy disturbed him. Even with the Velka's best herbs, this happened on occasion. I guessed he didn't like having it all sprung on him at once. A suitor, a wedding, *and* a grandchild. A methodical man like him preferred life occur step by step. Yet when he finally spoke, he surprised me.

"So you'll be moving to Lev?" he asked.

My leaving home bothered him?

"I suppose so. We haven't talked specifics, but that's how it's usually done. Davor, he doesn't know I'm pregnant yet. We thought we had plenty of time to plan. Now, of course, we'll want to move things along more quickly."

My dad nodded. "Of course you will." He gave me the soft smile that often proceeded him telling me how much he loved me and my sisters. "I'm not sure I'm ready to lose another daughter so fast, but if you want this, Coral, then I'm happy for you."

My mother would lose a helper, yet she radiated joy at my news. Over the years I'd been her back-up, carrying the brunt of household chores and watching my youngest sisters while Ryalgar helped Dad. Of course, it had been years since the younger ones needed watching, but they all still came to me for comfort.

"A Mozdol is definitely a prince," she said. "You did it, Coral. You really did it. I can't wait to meet him." Then, with a bit of chiding. "You should have told me sooner. I would have kept it from Ryalgar, poor thing."

"Well, I was trying to make it easier for her."

"You've always been such a softie." My mother put her arm around my shoulders. "Well, now you've got a big strong Svadlu prince to look out for you and your child. Well done."

Then she hugged me like I'd discovered gold. Given the dowry that would be coming her way, I guess I had.

I wished I could let Davor know I'd told my parents. I considered sending him a message thru the Svadlu, who always had people riding from nichna to nichna, but my instincts told me he wouldn't be happy about that. Yet, I was nervous. School closed in Vinx for two anks while we harvested the wheat and the time for harvest drew near. Did he even know about the school's closing?

When he finally reappeared at the end of a school day, I was so relieved to see him and excited to share my news that I didn't notice how troubled he was. He suggested we dine at a nearby tavern and when I agreed without argument he raised an eyebrow.

"You no longer mind risking being seen together?"

"I don't." I'm sure I grinned. "I'm happy to be seen with you, and my family can't wait to meet you." He gave me a funny look and commented on how fast the weather had turned warm.

Once we were inside and seated, I studied his expression.

"What's wrong?"

"I counted on your continued timidity, frankly. I'm sorry you spoke with your family before I got this chance to talk to you."

"I thought you'd be happy!"

He took both of my hands in his. He seemed more sad than angry.

"Coral, I'm having second thoughts about us. For good reasons, mind you. I risk my life often. Being married to a Svadlu isn't for the easily frightened, or the overly emotional. Yes, I heard you crying the last time we were together and I'm not sure you're cut out for such a life."

Not cut out to be his wife? The suggestion infuriated me. *Who did he think he was, to say such things?*

He continued to hold my hands and look into my eyes as he spoke, willing me to understand.

"I'm sorry I got too caught up in the pressures on me and I didn't give this decision the thought it deserved. For the sake of your happiness, we need to reconsider."

He thought he'd do me a favor by breaking up with me?

"Perhaps I'm stronger than you think." It popped out of my mouth and surprised me.

"I don't see any evidence of it."

That comment hurt. I knew I could make this man a fine wife, but first things first.

"I'm pregnant, Davor. Before you ask. Yes, I'm sure it's yours. I'm five anks along now and yes, I want to keep it."

"Well. That does change things." He stared into the ale he'd ordered, sitting in silence for longer than was comfortable.

"How would you feel about my providing financial support without a marriage?" he finally asked.

"Awful. The child deserves to be born in wedlock."

At that, he put his head into both of his hands so I couldn't see his face, and he kept it there for so long that I thought about getting up and leaving.

When he did look up, he said "Okay then, this is how it's going to go. We'll marry. It's only right because I *did* propose to you, and of course that factored into your decision not to end it. My family isn't poor, and a Mozdol is well rewarded. Your family will get a nice dowry, and I'll see to it that you and the baby have all you need. You'll stay in Vinx. You can raise the child here, where your family can help you."

"You won't live with me?"

"Vinx is on the farthest edge of Ilari, Coral, and most of the time I'll need to be closer to Pilk, where the action is. Yet it makes no sense to bring you there, with me gone so much. Nor should you have to live in Lev. I'm there even less, and you don't know any of the Levish. So, I'll see you as often as I can, but you need to adjust your expectations."

I wondered what sort of arrangement he asked me to agree to. "This will be a real marriage?"

"Of course. We'll hold a legal wedding in Vinx, as soon as your family is ready."

"When do I get to come to Lev to meet your parents?"

"Uh. Give me a little time. My family is more socially conscious than yours, and they'll consider your situation more awkward than practical farm folks do. But don't worry. We'll work it out."

I believed him, though at the time I had no idea of the various things he'd be "working out."

When my mother came home from the market a few anks later glowing with happiness, I knew she'd shared plans for my upcoming wedding with anyone who'd listen. My dad and the farmhands harvested the wheat; adequate spring rains and a lack of hail storms left us with an ample crop. Once they put the wheat in storage, things would calm down on the farm and we'd plan my ceremony in earnest. It would be held at Plono.

"I spoke with the Velka in the marketplace," my mother said. This surprised me. Some of the locals were a little afraid of the Velka, and others who'd lost family members to them were sad, but only my mother seemed angry with them and had been for as long as I could remember.

"Did they have news of Ryalgar?"

"The two of them, selling their usual potions, told me Ryalgar was doing well, adjusting and learning their ways." She hesitated. "Under the circumstances, I guess we have to hope for that, right?

I nodded. There didn't seem to be a better answer.

"She's able to have visitors," my mother said. "Did you know that?"

"She told me. Are you going to go see her?"

"Me? Oh, definitely not. She's invited you to come, however, one ank from today. She'll meet you at the forest's edge where she went in. She's heard of your situation. I've no idea how. She wishes to speak with you about it."

I hadn't expected this. Would she be helpful with my pregnancy? Angry about my deception with Davor? Or appreciative of the way I'd tried to spare her feelings?

"Do you want to go?" my mother asked.

"Of course." I hesitated for a heartbeat. "Mom? Why do you hate the Velka so much?"

She looked at me with a raised eyebrow. I could tell she hadn't expected such a bold question.

"I don't hate them. But, under your circumstances, perhaps you *should* know the story."

"What do you mean?"

"They once failed me in the same way they failed you."

"What? You were pregnant with Ryalgar before you got married?" I don't know why, but this made me feel better.

"No. I misspoke. What I meant was, after I had my first three children, I didn't want any more. I mean, what woman would? Your father wanted a son though, so I agreed to try one more time."

This was fairly common knowledge in the family. Mom's reluctant fourth try for a son had yielded twin daughters instead.

"I went to the Velka after the twins were born and begged them to make sure those were the last children I ever had. I wasn't cut out to raise a big family. I sunk under the weight; I didn't think I'd survive. They promised me. They promised."

"Oh dear." I'd always assumed my next sister resulted from a more reluctant fifth try for a son. It hurt to know she was an outright mistake. "Poor you. Poor Dad. He didn't want you to end the pregnancy?"

"He begged me not to. I didn't blame him. We should never have been put in that horrible position." She smoothed her dress as if her hands could smooth over the conversation as well. "Your beautiful *wanted* child will have much love. Let's not ever speak of this other situation again."

****

Ryalgar met me as planned, and I followed her into the forest on the small donkey she provided. Watching the single thick, long braid of her dark hair sway across her back as she rode, I realized I knew the perfect Velka to ask about being a luski. Would Ryalgar laugh at my question? I hoped not.

At the end of our short journey, I discovered Ryalgar lived in a beautiful stone lodge filled with friendly women. She had a lovely room of her own, with fresh linens and a guest bed in which I could stay. Her existence lacked any of the oddity I expected.

I'd barely plopped my things in a corner when I burst out with the question at the front of my mind.

"Do you know what a luski is?" Asking about it made me nervous.

"Why?"

I tried to keep the flush off of my face. "Someone I work with said they thought I might be one."

She laughed. "Oh, I don't think so, Coral. I know a lot of people don't believe luskies are real, but we Velka know they are. I've learned it's a rare gift, though, and luskies are powerful women. Not that you're weak or anything, but …."

"Never mind." I'd grown tired of being told I wasn't strong enough and didn't want to listen to her explain why I couldn't have this talent. Was it so important to her to be the only one in the family with magic tendencies?

"You misunderstand me," she said. "I'm pretty sure motherhood, actual motherhood, is a qualification." She pointed to my still-flat belly. "You're not eligible. Yet."

I supposed I preferred that to being told I was too weak, but I dropped the subject anyway. She didn't bring it up again.

We sat on one of the Velka's many porches after dinner that night, listening to the crickets chirp as we sipped the rest of our dinner wine and enjoyed the scent of the wild lavender now blooming all around the lodge.

I'd already learned that the open forest housed over a thousand Velka, far more than people thought. This evening Ryalgar told me that while many lived in the lodges and cabins I'd seen, others preferred life alone deep in the woods.

"We're as varied as any other group. Who'd have thought?"

"Yet …. no men."

That was the next surprise.

Ryalgar told me that while the Velka welcomed no man deep in the forest, plenty of the women enjoyed male company, and not just for sex. Cabins near the forest's edge allowed fathers, brothers, friends, and lovers all to mingle. Ryalgar hoped Dad would come to see her one day.

Also, she was free to come and go as she pleased.

"By custom, the Velka seldom leave the forest, but obviously some of us have to come into the markets and others travel to the far corners of Ilari to provide help where we're needed. We're encouraged to be here most of the time because our power dissipates when we're gone for long. But I'll be at your wedding if you'd like me to."

"I'd like nothing better!"

She asked about Davor and I answered, feeling more comfortable sharing confidences as the growing darkness pushed against the last of the summery dusk.

"A soldier? He's not the sort I'd have picked for you. Do you love him?"

"I think so. I know I did at first. He's so tough, and yet he has more style than the farmers in Vinx."

Ryalgar didn't respond. Instead, she used the candle she'd brought out to light a second one that she gave to me. "I've made you a packet of things to take, to keep you and your baby healthy through the pregnancy," she said. "Promise me you'll use them."

"Of course. I'm sorry I didn't tell you about Davor when you were still with us. And I'm sorry about Nevik. I wished it could have worked out for you."

She smiled a strange smile behind the flicker of her candle.

"Perhaps it has. He's visited me twice now, and our time together is more precious than ever."

"How can that be? All of Ilari gossips about the princess he met from outside the realm and how the two of them fell madly in love. A wedding is expected."

"I know. Things are not always what they seem, Coral. Nevik is playing a role he must play. Please understand; my happiness depends on your discretion."

"Oh. You have it, of course." Suddenly Ryalgar's decision to live without men made a lot more sense. "Is *that* why you joined the Velka? So you could be the mistress of a prince?"

"No." She said it sharply. "I joined the Velka because they can teach me to develop certain powers I have. The occasional night with Nevik is a bonus and one that's likely to become less frequent. Aside from keeping up appearances with his new wife, there's this group of marauders moving westward every winter, stealing crops. Soon they'll threaten our realm."

At the mention of these invaders, I squirmed in my rocking chair. "Davor spoke of them, too. Frightening horsemen from the east."

"That's them. Nevik is the second son of the Ruling Prince of Pilk, so he's been put in charge of ensuring the Svadlu are properly trained to repel them. It will take most of his time until the attack comes and it could be as soon as this winter."

My stomach fluttered in fear. "Davor says that's why he'll need to keep a second home in Pilk. Most of his time will be spent on this, too."

Full darkness had come so we each stood, holding our candles high to make our way back inside.

"Then they must know each other," Ryalgar said. "Or if they don't, they will soon."

I nodded in agreement. "Oh, I hope they turn out to be good friends. Wouldn't that be nice?"

~ 4 ~

Almost Everything

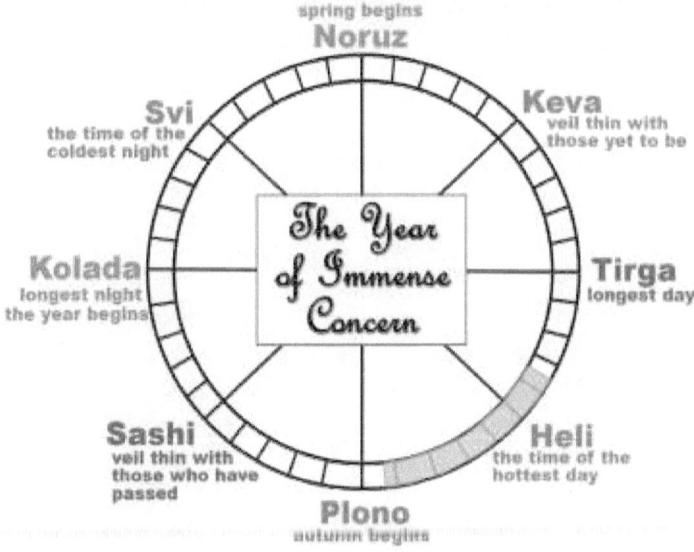

School resumed after I returned from my visit to the forest. There wouldn't be another farming-related pause in classes until the oats ripened in the fall. Davor had promised to come meet my family when we finished with the wheat harvest and he did.

He laid the charm on thick when he greeted my mother, and she melted under his flattery the way most people did. She hastened to prepare the guest room and then began discussing wedding plans with him. I'm sure she attributed his relative lack of interest in them to his gender. I noticed he never mentioned how excited he was to wed me, but if she noticed the omission, she hid it well.

Once my mother retreated to the kitchen to make sure the dinner was fit for a guest, he greeted my blushing sisters. Well, some blushed. Others scrutinized this older Mozdol who'd gotten their sister pregnant. Sulphur, the sister only a year younger than me, seldom paid attention to any man we courted. But tonight her unfashionably short blonde hair bobbed up and down as she nodded along with Davor's every word. I wondered why.

My father worked in the fields when Davor arrived. The oats had to be planted right after the wheat harvest, and my dad probably wished Davor knew more about grain farming and had waited another ank to come.

Maybe it was Dad's fatigue, but Davor failed to charm him. When he asked my dad to bless our nuptial plans, my father responded politely but I could sense no warmth between them.

Davor barely touched me the entire evening, even during the few moments when my family gave us time alone. He asked after my health, but otherwise had little to say. I went to my room feeling empty inside. As I got ready for bed, the desire to throw something at someone overwhelmed me. I settled for hurling my slipper at the wall before I flopped onto the mattress filled with a frustration I couldn't quite name.

Davor left early the next morning, before he and I had a chance to talk.

Back at school, I felt nauseous and out of sorts. Davor's visit to the farm had driven home the fact that he no longer wanted me. As I stood outside supervising the children's play, I stewed over the reasons why.

Had he really decided I wasn't fit to be a Svadlu's wife? If that was the only problem, I knew I could show him otherwise. But what if he'd fallen out of love with me for other reasons? What if he'd given me an excuse he hoped I'd believe? Perhaps another soft and sweet woman had taken my place in his heart.

The idea made me wince. If she existed, she couldn't have him. I wanted my child to have the life Davor could provide as a father. For the sake of my baby, I'd win the tug of war for Davor's heart.

"You doing okay?" Sakina walked over to me from the other side of the play area. "Problems in your classroom?"

Scump. She'd probably noticed my wild gesturing as I held angry conversations in my head. The other teachers all said she and I had the toughest jobs, me because I handled the scared little ones and her because she dealt with those who'd almost outgrown the school. Our shared challenges had strengthened our concern for each other.

"No. Thanks for asking, though."

She stood, waiting for more information. I relented; I probably should have told her already.

"Look, I've been keeping it secret for a lot of reasons, but I want you to know. I'm pregnant, and I'll be married by autumn. I'll be leaving my position soon."

She seemed sad at the idea of my going, but she said the right thing.

"That's wonderful, Coral. Congratulations. It's got to be that guy you've been sneaking off with, huh? You look so in love with him."

I had to laugh. "How many people know about him?"

"Pretty much everyone." She laughed too. "I'll miss you, but I wish you every happiness. You deserve it."

I thanked her. I thought I deserved every happiness too, even if it looked like I wasn't going to get it.

As the days wore on, Davor's lack of interest in me occupied my thoughts.

Yes, I'd probably waited too long to tell my family about him. I should have been less concerned with Ryalgar's feelings and more worried about my future.

Yes, continuing the pregnancy could have been a bad idea. Maybe I should have won his heart back first, and then gotten pregnant again.

Then I asked myself the hardest question of all. Did I still love him or did hurt pride fuel my anger? Perhaps my affection had cooled as well and I'd been slow to admit it.

Well, he *had* offered me financial support without a marriage. I could reconsider, raise a child without him, and find another husband. Some wouldn't want a wife with a baby, but others would welcome the proof of my fertility.

Yet, the wedding plans were so far along. My mother and sisters adored him. Would he be relieved if I canceled it? Or angry at me for hurting his pride? Perhaps so angry that he wouldn't support our child?

I'd fretted over my best course of action for days when he surprised me with a second visit to the farm. With the wedding only four anks away, I wondered where I'd live afterward. I could stay with my folks, though married women seldom did so. I hadn't figured Davor would look for a solution but he arrived one morning to announce he'd found a house for me he liked.

We rode to it slowly, in consideration of my pregnancy and the morning sickness that now lasted all day. When we reached the small cottage, I loved it as soon as I saw it because it had a big covered front porch and large trees. Davor had hired workers to fix it up, as it had been empty awhile, and he'd already arranged to have furniture made for it. Furniture for me.

"Best of all," he said "it's less than a ten-minute ride to your school. Do you think some of the older students, or perhaps your youngest sisters, would watch the baby for you while you teach?"

"You don't mind if I keep teaching after the baby is born?" This was far better news than I expected.

"Of course not. I won't be around much; you won't need to care for me. And I've heard you're uncommonly good with the little ones. I'll put in a word, let them know how strongly I feel about your getting to use your talents. I think if I twist a few arms…" he gave me that charming smile, "… they'll let you teach until you near your time to have the baby. Then you can come back after he's born, whenever you're ready."

Well. This made my decision easier. I'd once thought falling in love with a man would be the most important thing in my life, but it now appeared Davor and I didn't have to love each other for me to get almost everything I wanted. My own house. My own baby. A husband almost everyone else adored. The rare chance to keep teaching after my child was born. And my time to spend as I pleased.

Did it matter that I already knew our marriage would be a sham? It didn't, at least not nearly as much as I would have guessed.

I didn't expect Davor to stay, but he spent two nights at the farm. He made a noticeable effort to converse with my father, who made the same effort back.

"So, you must have been the one who named your daughters," Davor said, not knowing of the family controversies hidden in the topic.

"I named most of them." Dad wasn't going to give details. Mom felt otherwise.

"He started the whole thing off by naming Ryalgar after some obscure rock," she said.

"A perfectly lovely red mineral often found in mines," dad interjected.

"So I named our second daughter after the beautiful peach-colored necklace from Persia he bought me when we were married. The stone is the color of a soft setting sun."

"Coral is not a stone. It's organic. It comes from sea creatures."

Davor maintained a vacant smile as they argued.

"Then he got even by naming the next child Sulphur. Horrible name. Horrible smell. My sweet daughter."

Everyone turned to Sulphur, a strong young woman with hair the color of the stone dad had named her for. She shrugged. "I like my name. No one else has it."

My fourth sister, Olivine, joined us. She and her twin both had dad's slight build and gentle nature, but Olivine was more shy. She looked down and said nothing as she set another jug of wine on the table and added some sliced peaches and soft cheese for us to nibble on while we waited for the meal.

Later that night, Davor and I sat by the fire, listening to the dry logs crackle as they gave off sparks. The rest of the household had tactfully gone to bed. He held my hand, the friendliest gesture he'd exhibited so far.

"So how are things in Pilk?" I asked. A good wife is supposed to show an interest in her husband's profession.

"Eh. Politics." He gave a disgusted shrug. "As the Mozdol with the most fighting experience, I thought I'd be in charge of training the troops for this coming invasion. Then the rulers got together and picked some stupid prince to oversee what I'm doing.

Just because he's got royal blood; blood he's never shed a drop of."

"I'm sorry Davor. You don't need any Royal looking over your shoulder."

"You bet I don't. The men appreciate me, and they know I understand battle. Nobody respects this prince and the cushy life he's lived."

I was pretty sure this stupid prince was Nevik, my sister's lover. So much for the idea of him and Davor becoming friends.

"Is this the same prince everyone is talking about? Recently engaged to a princess from another realm?"

"Yup. Marrying a foreigner. Got only half his brain on the Mongols while the other half is occupied with what's happening between his sheets."

I said nothing. He got up to put another log on the fire and kept talking.

"I've been thinking about this invasion, Coral. If we get word they're getting close, I want to move you to safety until the battle's over. My baby too, if he's been born."

"What for? My little house couldn't be safer."

He looked annoyed with me again. "Surely you understand *something* about war. No place in Vinx will be safe. It sits on the only path leading from our entrance to where our riches lay."

"So what will happen to Vinx? And the people in it?"

"I don't know. We'll move those we can to safer areas, I guess. Don't get me wrong; we don't want to lose any Ilarians, but things don't always go as you'd like in a battle. I want you to be somewhere else when the time comes." He stopped, and he seemed to be counting on his fingers. "When exactly...."

"Right around Svi. The coldest night of the year."

He sighed. "The Mongols always attack in the winter. It could be this year. We'd better think about moving you to safety before you get too close to having the baby."

"But I want my mother there when the baby is born. My sisters."

He rolled his eyes. "Fine. We'll find a way. Tonight, let's just enjoy the fire."

I understood the conversation had ended. I reached back and took his hand again. He let me hold it, and we sat in silence. As he stared into the flames, I wondered what, or maybe who, he thought about.

When Ryalgar arrived at the farm a few days before my wedding, I welcomed having someone to talk to about something other than the upcoming ceremony.

I hung up the freshly washed bedding as she rode up. She gave her horse to Sulphur to tend to and hurried over to me, standing next to me behind the billowing sheets so we could talk privately amidst the smell of fresh soap and the loud flapping of the linens in the wind.

"I've learned more about luskies for you," she whispered in greeting.

"There's no need for that." Of all the things we needed to talk about, this power I didn't have sat low on the list.

"I'm not so sure. There's a persistent rumor that we Velka can recognize a luski, but it's not true. It takes another luski to tell. And it takes another to train a new luski, too."

"Why would this matter to me?"

"Because your friend could be right. I've learned not all luskies are mothers, not in the real sense of the word. The rare man has this talent. A few childless women do, too. It has to do with being a nurturer."

"So …."

"So, what I'm saying is, I was wrong. You could be a luski."

Hearing Ryalgar admit she'd been wrong constituted quite an event in our relationship. Yet … "I'm getting married in three days. I don't need this now."

She gave me a sympathetic look. "You don't have to do anything about it. I'm looking for a luski to talk to you. They're hard to find; most go to extraordinary pains to hide what they can do. But I'll find one."

I didn't know what to say.

"Thanks. I think."

~ 5 ~

Questions and Answers

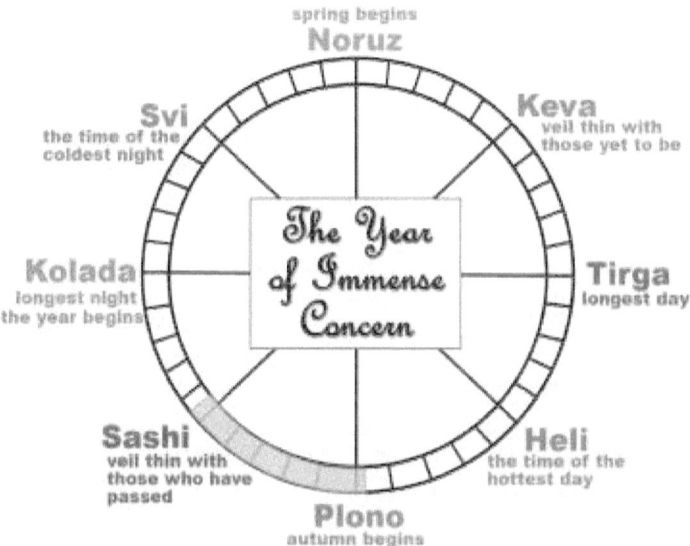

Davor arrived the day before the wedding, with his parents, a younger brother, and two of his best friends. My trip to Lev to meet his family had never materialized but I knew Davor had a second brother, a sister, several more pals, and other close relatives. I supposed some would follow later or the next morning.

Everyone in his party greeted me with warmth; these people had manners. His parents inquired about my health, and I surmised the child I carried interested them more than anything else about me. Honestly, Davor acted the least happy to see me of anyone. If he regretted agreeing to the wedding, it was too late to back out now. For either of us.

Thankfully, they were too many for us to house, so they all took lodging at a nearby inn. Before we parted for the night, he told me no others would arrive from Lev.

Really? His own brother and sister wouldn't attend? What an unbelievable lack of interest in our ceremony. Such a thing would never happen in Vinx.

I simmered at the news. My parents expected only two things of him regarding the wedding: a generous dowry and an ample showing of enthused attendees. They'd planned for at least twenty from his side, so now the seating would be adjusted. No parent wanted the humiliation of empty chairs at their daughter's wedding.

The next day, the group from Lev came to our farmhouse for an early morning breakfast, so we could travel together to the place my parents had rented. Mom oversaw a sumptuous feast, but I watched Davor's two friends and his brother exchanging smirks as they looked around our place. I guess we weren't fashionable.

Davor's mother kept pointing out how much she appreciated our "rustic charm" and a sharp glance towards Davor's younger brother punctuated her comment more than once. I knew the look. It meant *I told you to behave*. The brother ignored her.

Customs vary throughout Ilari, but by tradition, we follow those of the bride's family at a wedding. In Vinx, a Royal from the nichna always performs the ceremony. Because of my dad's stature as a teacher and scientist, the father of our Ruling Prince presided. Sakina squealed with delight for me when she learned of the honor and our other guests were all impressed.

Davor, however, seemed annoyed by it.

"Who would you have preferred to marry us?" I whispered to him once I recognized his frustration.

"Another Mozdol, of course. In Lev, a retired Mozdol would have been found; and great effort would have gone into securing the most senior man as an honor to me. It never occurred to me …."

Ah, well. One more thing we didn't understand about each other.

We made our way through the celebration with smiles pasted on our faces. I don't know what emotions lurked under Davor's façade but by the time we said our vows, disappointment had overtaken everything else within me. A woman looks forward to this special day her entire girlhood. No matter what had transpired between Davor and me, why couldn't our wedding have at least gone well?

Then one more incident challenged us. Before it got too late, everyone expected us to leave for our new home, where we'd both already moved some things. Custom dictated that before we left we walk together to each table and thank the guests for coming. This courtesy meant a lot in my community, yet when the time came, I couldn't find Davor. My family's search for him became increasingly frantic until one of his friends approached me.

"He's waiting for you in the carriage. He says he can't walk around with you. He, uh, has a little problem. He'll explain it when you get there."

When I demanded to know exactly what the little problem was, his friend told me Davor had no pants.

"What happened to the ones he was wearing? Never mind. Go give him yours. Right now. You sit in the varmin carriage without your pants while he joins me in thanking our guests. Do it."

The friend looked at me, then slinked off to give Davor his trousers. A flustered Davor appeared a few minutes later.

"This is important to me," I hissed. He said nothing, and we walked around the room together, our smiles more strained than before. Once we finished and got to our carriage, Davor returned his friend's pants, then pulled a blanket around his bare lower half.

"What happened to your clothes?" I asked.

"I spilled something. Don't ask me for details."

I dropped it, figuring the day had brought enough trouble and the specifics didn't matter.

"Don't ever order one of my friends around like that again," he added.

That annoyed me. I hadn't ordered anyone around.

"Your bargain included finishing this wedding," I replied. "Thank you for doing so."

We barely said another word to each other for the rest of the night, and when I woke up the next morning he was gone.

I spent the next two days helping my parents move my remaining possessions to my new home. I kept the tears away by remembering when I was nine, barely older than the children I now taught.

Our whole family had gone out together to celebrate a holiday. Mom held the hands of her six-year-old twin daughters, while Dad carried frail Iolite on one hip and held little Gypsum's hand. Ten-year-old Ryalgar, eight-year-old Sulphur, and I had been ordered to hang on to each other and stay close.

Vendors in the marketplace offered us tempting treats while couples fawned over each other and groups celebrated the day with wine and ale. A lone man stumbled into our path. As an adult, I recognize he was drunk and probably jilted by whatever lady he'd hoped to spend the night with. He tripped trying to avoid my mother and the twins. After he fell he looked up, furious at my mother.

"Get the Heli out of my way, you foolish pruska," he said.

Mom stood tall, glaring down at the man.

"And take your little pruskas with you," he added. "All of them." He waved his hand at me and each of my sisters. "Pruskas, every varmin one!"

My mother turned to my father, expecting him to defend his family's honor from what must have been a deep insult. My father was and still is smart, funny, and kind. But even as a child I knew he was no fighter. He let go of Gypsum, turned to the stranger, and with the sort of thoughtfulness he so often showed, he offered the man his hand.

"Let me help you up, dear sir. Clearly, the day has not gone your way. Get some rest this afternoon and sober up. Perhaps in a few hours the holiday will turn more to your liking."

My mother cried out in indignation.

The man took my dad's hand and stood, muttered something I couldn't hear, and stumbled off. My father turned to face my mother's wrath.

"Be reasonable, dearest. What would have been accomplished by arguing with a drunk who won't even remember the incident in the morning? Come now. Let's not let him ruin our celebration."

I remember how my mother's eyes narrowed and she said nothing to my father for the rest of the day. I saw the hurt in his face and felt sorry for him. Later, when I thought my mother couldn't hear me, I whispered in his ear that I thought he was the nicest man ever.

However, I was old enough to understand that I shouldn't ask my father the meaning of the word the man had used. Girls asked their mothers such questions, although I worried mine wouldn't respond well to my inquiry.

By the next day, though, my curiosity overcame my fear. As we sorted laundry, I asked.

"Mama? What's a pruska?"

She inhaled and the color went out of her face.

"Don't you ever use that word again."

"I won't, I promise. Just tell me what a pruska is."

The second time I said it she slapped me across the face. "I *said* never say it."

My parents seldom did that sort of thing, so I think the unfairness of the punishment upset me more than anything. I looked at her and before she could say anything more, I burst into tears.

"It's a girl who thinks men should be able to treat her mother offensively and her father need not do a thing about it," she said. "It's a girl who comforts her father when he acts like a scared bird and she thinks her mother isn't looking."

She hauled off and slapped me again, harder this time.

"And she's a who girl cries about it," my mother added, her voice filled with contempt. I was already sucking back my tears.

"That's right. You better straighten up, or you'll turn into one of those women who cares too much and weeps all the time."

I ran from the room and hid from Mom for the rest of the day.

Then a few days later, my mother and father spoke to each other again and she began to hug me and compliment me and give me little treats. I understood she felt bad for the way she acted to me and I didn't care. I didn't forgive her then and all these years later I still do my best not to cry in front of her.

My mother thought the house Davor bought was too small, but then again she thought it was meant to be a home for two adults and a child. I'd pushed my parents to move me soon after the wedding because I wanted to get back to teaching and it was a shorter ride from my new home to the school. My little ones had been put in with an older class in my absence, and that always caused problems.

I could tell my parents worried about me being alone, especially after Davor left so quickly. Both tucked small treats and extra provisions into the cart to help me get by and neither asked me why Davor hadn't stayed to help me finish moving.

Yet, I was hardly destitute. He'd left me a large handful of coins for buying food and supplies. It appeared he didn't have stinginess as a fault. The school also provided me with pay. It wasn't much and, in the past, I'd given most of it to my parents who fed and housed me. Now, I would use it.

For the first time, I realized they'd miss my contribution to our family purse, as well as the many chores I did. I'd never shirked my household duties, often filling in for sisters who were less industrious or at least less domestically inclined. So. The dowry compensated my parents for their loss.

This change in perspective made me feel better. If all Davor ever did for me was give me a healthy child, provide me with a house, and buy me my freedom to leave home, I could be happy enough with his contribution.

A little over an ank later, my sister Sulphur came to check on me. I recognized her short blonde hair atop her horse in the distance and felt annoyed because I'd been enjoying my time alone. I didn't need to be checked on.

However, once Sulphur tied up her horse, I saw she needed help. I'd seldom seen anyone so full of anguish, and certainly never my strong and sunny sister. She buoyed the rest of us up as we dealt with all of life's drama. I couldn't imagine her being brought down by drama of her own.

It took a bit of wine before she opened up that night in front of the fire. She told me of her desire to join the military of Ilari. I had no idea she harbored such an unusual dream but I did know that women had to go to extra lengths to get in.

She told me having a male sponsor helped; then I understood her fascination with Davor when she first met him. Of course he'd sponsor her. Then, after more wine, she confessed she'd already asked Davor to help her and he'd refused.

I wanted to chastise her for not coming to me first and letting me intercede but she didn't need a reprimand, she felt poorly enough. So instead I pointed out it could still happen. I don't think she believed me, but I intended to try.

Sulphur was a physical woman, tall and strong; the type who required vigorous exercise. So I kept her busy chopping and carrying wood and fetching water. I could do these things for myself but sensed that heavy work would help her cope. In the meantime, I put my problems on hold and tried to be positive for her. I managed until Sashi neared.

Adults traditionally celebrate all eight holidays with sexual activity as a way to honor the Goddess. New adults get a great deal of freedom during these festivities, while couples in love make extra efforts to be together. Married or not, if they can't be with their lover, they do without.

So, whatever problems Davor and I had, I still expected him on the holiday. He'd want to do what people did. But Sashi came and went, and he never appeared. Sulphur tried to make excuses for him. The training program to repel the Mongols was in full swing. He'd already missed a few days for the wedding. But she and I both knew he could have ridden in for the night if he'd wanted to.

Finally, three days after Sashi, we saw a horseman in the distance. Sulphur threw her bags onto her horse, determined to leave before Davor arrived. As she left, she promised to send another sister back in a few days to check on me.

As the horseman drew closer, though, I could tell it wasn't Davor. The rider was a woman, a tall, thin woman I'd never met. As she brought her horse to stop, she held her hands up in a universal sign of no harm intended.

I said nothing until she dismounted and tied up her horse.

"How can I help you?" I asked. She had fluffy hair starting to turn grey and soft eyes, but she made me nervous for reasons I didn't understand. I tried not to show it.

"Get me some water."

What a rude way to greet a stranger. Part of me wanted to tell her to get back on her horse and keep going, but another part of me felt strangely compelled to give her something to drink. I mean, despite the lack of courtesy, the request was reasonable. Of course her long ride had made her thirsty.

S. R. Cronin

I turned to walk into my kitchen to get a cup, then I understood.

"You're a luski!"

I steadied myself in the doorway at the realization of what this woman could do. She smiled at my perceptiveness.

"I am. A very good one, too. Your sister Ryalgar sent me here to answer your questions."

"I'm grateful. I do have a lot of them."

"Well then, it's good I have a lot of time."

~ 6 ~

I Think You Need to Eat

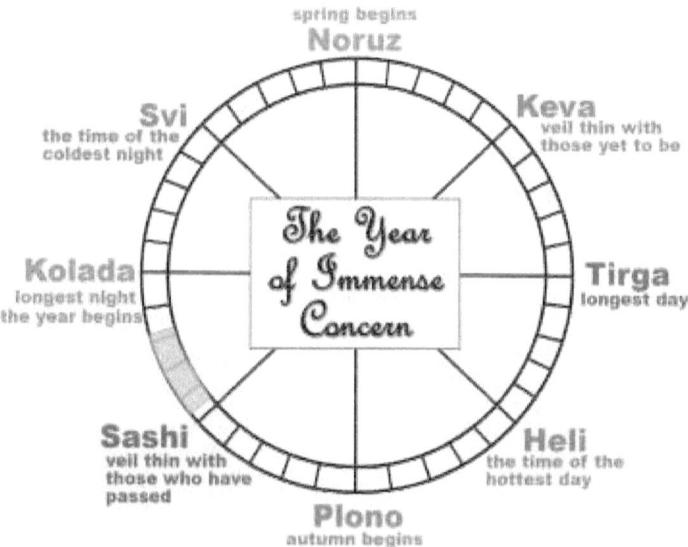

Despite being a luski, I learned that Ewalina had a normal life in Pilk as a single mother who made her living assisting the medical people in a place of higher learning. No one she worked with knew what she could do, but she confessed to being less guarded than many.

"The people in my world would at least let me explain the truth if my being a luski somehow came to light. Others face more superstition than I would."

She told me my sister Ryalgar had left the forest to travel around the realm to learn about the Mongols. People said the Velka asked her to devise a defense strategy for them. I had to smile. It sounded like Ryalgar wasted no time establishing herself as someone who liked to be in charge.

Ewalina had a close connection to the Velka, and Ryalgar sought her out while traveling and persuaded her to visit me. I appreciated that she had. At least I now knew being a luski was a real thing.

We spent most of the afternoon sitting in my front room by the fire, talking about people and life. I offered Ewalina afternoon wine and some of the little apple cakes I'd made to celebrate Sashi. She answered my questions while she ate.

I told her everything about me, perhaps more than I'd ever told any single human being. Certainly more than I'd ever told Davor. Before the afternoon ended, Ewalina decided I was a luski, despite not yet giving birth. Oddly, by then her proclamation didn't surprise me. I think I just knew already.

"Don't fault your sister for getting the facts wrong," she said. The gentleness in her eyes made me think she didn't fault people for much. "The development of this ability is more complicated than people realize because it comes from a variety of circumstances. Misunderstandings get perpetuated because of our secrecy. Plenty of potential luskies don't understand what they can do."

That made sense. How long had I been one without suspecting it?

"Once people do realize it, though, they inevitably come to the Velka for help," Ewalina said.

"Why? If it hadn't been for Ryalgar, that's the last group I'd have turned to."

By this time I'd started to make dinner, chopping vegetables for a simple stew. Ewalina offered to help, and while I worked on the cabbage she chopped an onion, a turnip, and two carrots with astounding expertise.

"Well, you have an unusual family," she said. "Ryalgar mentioned your mother's aversion to the Velka; I'm sure she colored your impression of them. Most people figure the Velka aren't afraid of magic, right? So they go to them with questions, and the Velka put them in touch with one of us. Let's face it. The idea of someone being able to compel you with their tone of voice is frightening, but it's also scary to think you can do such a thing to others."

I nodded without comment, feeling relieved that Ewalina's first task was getting me over my fears.

"Listen to me. This skill is grounded in the idea of an emergency, even though it doesn't have to be an emergency to use it. A luski speaks with the tone of a mother who sees her toddler about to touch a hot coal. She says 'stop' in a way that makes her child freeze. Everyone has been a child and still has a child inside. We all instinctually understand that particular timbre on a deep level."

"You call it a timbre. Like a musical instrument?"

"We do. We consider our voices to be instruments."

"Okay. So why can't I use my instrument to say 'give me all of your gold'?"

"You can. But you probably won't, because every adult also has a veneer of a rational mind that will turn on an instant later. It will override a command making no sense. People aren't children. You aren't their mother. There is no emergency. Giving you their gold is ridiculous, and they won't do it. What they will do is make a great deal of trouble for you for telling them to do so."

She smiled at my confusion. "So, you aren't so powerful after all," she said. "But suppose you do say 'stop' and say it in the way that commands. The rational veneer of another won't have enough information to override your instructions. The person will stop for you every time, while they may not stop for someone who isn't a luski. The time you gain may save your life or theirs. So please understand, this power is real, it's just far less dangerous than you've been led to believe."

I wasn't convinced. "What if my command isn't a good idea for them?"

"Now we're at the second half of how this works. Two strong opposing instincts come into play once a command is heard. The child inside them wants to obey you. When you speak as a luski, others will associate you with protection and affection, at least if they received some when young. The child inside will look for rational reasons to obey you."

I nodded. That made sense.

"Meanwhile, the adult inside instinctually resents being told what to do and will look for reasons not to obey." We both laughed at that.

"Which one wins?" I asked.

"It depends on the person, a little, and on the facts, a lot. The child is stronger in everyone, but not enough so to make an adult hurt themselves or do something they wouldn't normally do. When I told you to get me water when I first arrived, didn't you consider my request?"

"I did." I smiled as I understood. "I looked for reasons why it made sense to get you water despite your ill-mannered introduction. I found them."

"And that's the power we have. To get the child inside of someone to try to justify a command and obey it. If they can justify it, you will have made them do it. If they can't, it won't matter what you say."

"I was willing to give you water, but, well, not my horse Nutmeg. I couldn't justify giving her away. I love her."

"Nutmeg?"

Everyone asked about her odd name.

"I named her for this wonderful new spice for baking."

Ewalina chucked. "No, I couldn't make you give away your beloved horse. So you see why we luskies keep a low profile? We're scary, yet, at the same time, we're not always powerful."

That seemed like the worst possible combination.

"Could I at least keep someone from killing me?"

"Maybe. If they didn't really want to or didn't think you threatened them. On the other hand, if someone thought they had to kill you to survive, you couldn't stop them with your voice."

"Are there ways I can get better at this?"

"Of course. One can get better at anything. But no amount of improvement changes the basic rules. You understand that?"

"I do."

"Then why would you want to get better?"

I balked at being asked. I just did. Wasn't better always better?

Then I realized my motivation mattered to her, and it ought to matter to me. I gave it some thought.

"I'd like to get more confident, in case I ever need to use this to help me or someone else. And I'd like to get better at predicting how it will work."

Ewalina nodded. "Then I'll stay a few more days." She laughed at my suspicious look. "No tone there. I also want to help you get better at hearing it. It's so easy for a luski to get paranoid if she isn't good at recognizing the timbre for herself."

The next day was the first day of the ank so I had to be back at school. Ewalina made herself at home during the day while I taught. For the next few days, she did the cooking for the two of us, and did some cleaning and chopping wood for me, too. Perhaps she was bored, or maybe it was her way to be helpful.

Because dark came quickly as Kolada approached, we ate our dinner together soon after I got home each day, and then we sat in front of the fire and worked by candlelight. Often much of the night had passed by the time we stopped.

We covered inflection and intonation. Pitch. Cadence. Lilt. Accent. Stress. She liked to work with the sentence. "I think you need to eat."

I think you need to eat.

I *think* you need to eat.

I think *you* need to eat.

I think you *need* to eat.

I think you need *to* eat.

I think you need to *eat.*

I'd never considered how a simple sentence could be said so many ways, or mean so many subtly different things.

Every night she had me practice activating the feeling of an emergency within my head, so I could bring the timbre about at will. She taught me ways to turn it off and to make sure it stayed off in a particular situation. She had me practice detecting when she was using it, when she wasn't, and even when she was using it ineffectively.

"You'll meet luskies who have no idea they are one. They'll use their skill unknowingly."

"When that happens, do I need to tell someone about this person?"

She winced. "No. Absolutely not. There's no over-reaching organization to report someone to. No one polices us or even guides us. Keeping their situation to yourself is the kindest thing you can do for them."

"Should I tell them about themselves if they don't already know?"

This time she shrugged. "Maybe. We try to help each other as best we can, but it's a judgment call. You have to be sure you can trust the person you're helping. I came here because your sister insisted there is no one in the world kinder than you."

Really? Ryalgar said that?

"And because she hoped your potential skills could be useful in her search for ways to defend our realm."

Useful. Yes, that sounded more like Ryalgar.

"Do you think they could be?" I asked.

"Honestly, given the way this works, I doubt it. I told her so, too. But, you never know. Why not collaborate with her and find out? One last thing, Coral. We do have a rule, and it's important. If you get to know another luski the way you've gotten to know me, we revert to being strangers if we ever meet in public. Understand? It protects both of us."

"Of course. Best to avoid awkward 'how do you two know each other?' questions, right?"

"Exactly. When we bid each other farewell, we often say 'We part as strangers.' Remember it."

When Ewalina told me it was time for her to get back to her own life, I knew she'd taught me what she could. I hugged her and thanked her and asked her how I could repay her.

"I'll take a few coins for my travel expenses, but only if you have them to give. Other than that, be prepared to take the risk of teaching another someday. Good luck, Coral. We part as strangers." She gave me a slight bow of her head.

"Thank you, Ewalina." I dipped my head in response. "Yes. We part as strangers."

I carried myself differently after Ewalina left. Sakina commented on it, and I could tell other teachers and even some of the children noticed. I didn't make anyone do anything, but I spoke with more confidence. People listened more. I liked the change.

Meanwhile, my belly grew. My baby would be here in about 7 anks now, just over two full cycles of the moon. I used the herbs Ryalgar gave me to keep healthy but I worried none-the-less. I guessed all expectant mothers did.

Now that I knew Davor didn't consider my current location safe if the Mongols invaded, I needed a plan. I didn't want to go to Lev alone to have the baby amongst strangers. Possibly one of my younger sisters could come with me. Olivine and Celestine had finished their two years of advanced schooling this summer, and following what appeared to be a family tradition, neither of the twins had wedding plans. However, both of them kept busy with pursuits of their own. Would either do such a thing for me?

My only other real option was to see if Ryalgar would let me stay with her as my time approached. There wasn't a safer place than the forest, or a better group to midwife me than the Velka. The idea had merit.

On the next break from school, I'd ride over to the market. I could look for baby supplies and send word to Ryalgar to thank her for sending me a luski teacher. Then I could see if we could meet to talk about where I would give birth.

The next morning, as I headed to the privy, I saw another rider approaching in the distance. I took care of my personal needs quickly, and by the time I emerged from the little outhouse, the rider was close enough for me to tell it was Davor.

Never mind the plans I'd made. My husband was home.

~ 7 ~

Under One Condition

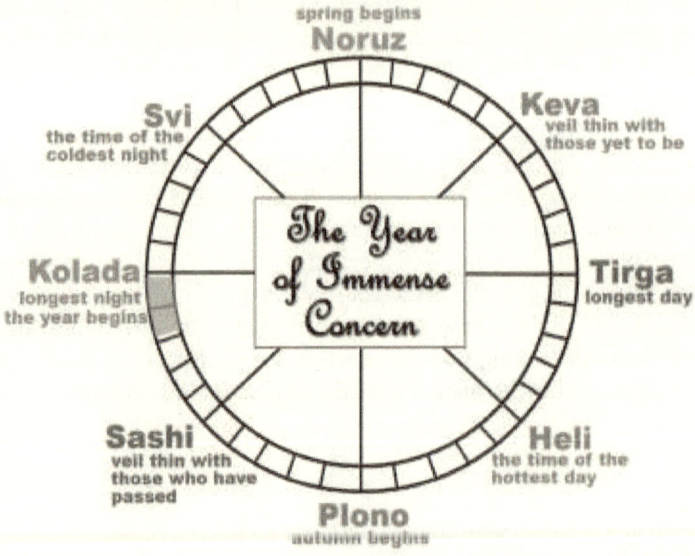

spring begins
Noruz

Keva
veil thin with
those yet to be

Svi
the time of the
coldest night

*The Year
of Immense
Concern*

Kolada
longest night
the year begins

Tirga
longest day

Sashi
veil thin with
those who have
passed

Heli
the time of the
hottest day

Plono
autumn begins

Davor greeted me kindly enough and insisted I head over to school to teach, as it was the sixth day of the ank and they expected me. He said he'd be fine having a day to rest. So I went, but by the time I came home, his mood had soured.

He'd spent time fixing minor things around the house, things he thought I should have taken care of. I had neglected the place during Ewalina's visit, between teaching all day and practicing with her every evening. He'd also starting drinking some brew from a jug he'd brought with him. It smelled strong. When he saw

48

me give it a sniff, he handed it to me to have a swig. It didn't seem the sort of thing a baby needed so I passed, pointing to my belly.

He shrugged. "Suit yourself. You're quiet tonight. Did your new lover wear you out?"

What? So that was the problem? He thought ....

"I'm two moons away from having a child! Are you crazy? I've no lover."

"Doesn't stop some women," he said, but he let it drop. Wisely.

Scump. He'd probably found evidence of a visitor somewhere. I could have told him the truth, but I was pretty sure he'd prefer my having sex with anyone to my having a guest teach me how to control people with my voice. Kind of control them, to be accurate, but I knew the "kind of" part wouldn't register with him no matter how many times I said it. So I let his accusation go unanswered.

I tried to put a decent meal together from the supplies I had left, and he made a fire. We sat down to eat together like a husband and wife, and I realized it was the first time we'd done so.

"You can cook," he said. He seemed surprised, and a little pleased.

His mood softened as he ate, and we sat together in front of the fire when we were done.

"You don't have to tell me about him," he said. "I shouldn't blame you for looking elsewhere. I haven't been much of a husband in the short time we've been wed."

"I knew what I was getting into." I could have left it at that, but I wanted to know more. "I'm curious," I said. "There was a time when you wanted me for your wife. What happened? Did I do something wrong?"

He laughed. "It's what you didn't do. I met someone while I was waiting for you to tell your parents about me. She made you seem like a scared little girl. Or an overly kind sister. Whatever. You were unable to grab the moment and go for it. It doesn't matter now. I'm in love with another, and she's worthy of me."

Ouch. I wasn't? Tears formed at his harsh words, but I fought them back. He valued strength? I'd show him strength.

"What's she like?" I don't know why I asked. I guess I thought the information would distract me from crying.

"She's from the mountains of Tolo. Those are tough people up there, you know? They struggle against the elements all their lives. She's a few years older than you. Widowed. Rugged lady. She'll wait for me for as long as it takes."

So. He hadn't found another version of me he liked better. He'd found someone totally different.

A new thought occurred to me. I wondered if he'd have tired of me no matter what I'd done. No matter what I was. Maybe he loved something new more than he loved any woman.

"You'll be wanting a divorce then?"

"Won't you? But we need to wait. Let the baby be born in wedlock, as you asked. Let me get through this rough patch with the Svadlu, too. This scump-head Nevik is making my life difficult. He thinks he's contributing, but he disapproves of everything a soldier is. The Royals frown on divorce, you know. They're not practical like the common people. He'd use it against me and I don't need that now."

"I'm happy to wait. So after the baby is born?"

"I'd like to get through this idiotic invasion first, too, and let the dust settle from that. Maybe I'll get a new medal, or better yet a commendation with a purse attached. That way, I can leave you well cared for until you find another husband. You're pretty, Coral, and plenty of men like women like you. Soft and sweet. It's not your fault you're not to my taste. You'll find another."

I distinctly remembered him praising my softness and sweetness not long ago, but I let that drop. To this day, I have no idea why I said what I did next. It just came out.

"I'll be the most cooperative wife, and eventual ex-wife, you could possibly have, under one condition."

"Name it, honey cakes." He seemed pleased with the congenial and non-emotional way this discussion was going.

"You sponsor Sulphur to join the Svadlu."

He slammed his fist down on the table and choked on the liquor in his mouth.

"That flaming pruska of a sister of yours?" he said as he stopped coughing. "No way."

I inhaled at the insult, but let it pass. I said it again. With intention. With meaning. Yes, now that he'd called my sister a pruska, I went ahead and used the timbre on him, encouraging him to find a way to want to do my bidding.

50

"You'll get absolutely everything you want from me if you do this. You'll get nothing but grief and trouble if you don't. So. Sponsor. Sulphur."

He looked at me like he considered it. I wasn't surprised. Maybe his rational adult brain needed more of a nudge.

"Your life will be so. Much. Easier. And, as a bonus, she's been training like Heli for years. She'll make you proud. You'll get to take credit for her accomplishments, too."

He *was* considering it, but the idea of a competent woman soldier seemed to take him back out of his comfort zone. Scump. I should have quit talking while I was ahead.

"Nah ...."

"Suit yourself." I walked away as I said it.

I hadn't negotiated much or I'd have understood the power of leaving. I made it all the way to the bedroom when he spoke up.

"I call the shots on absolutely everything else if I do this one thing for you?"

Was I willing to promise him so much? Oh Heli, he was going to call the shots on everything anyway. What was the difference?

"Yes, of course you do, dear."

"How bad can she be? Okay, you've got a deal."

From a purely practical point of view, Davor and I had an extremely productive visit. He spent the next day making more minor repairs to our home and ensuring I had an ample supply of wood. Laziness wasn't one of his faults. That evening, he brought up the intertwined issues of my safety and the birth of our child.

"So, I get to decide where you give birth, right?" He was making sure our agreement of the previous evening held.

"I suppose I could say my part of the bargain doesn't start until you meet your obligation."

He grimaced. "I plan to take care of this inconvenient sponsorship as soon as I get back to Pilk tomorrow. I'm leaving in the morning."

I nodded. "Okay then. So what location do you think is best for me?" I could tell from the tense way he sat, and the way he avoided my eyes, that he didn't expect me to like his answer.

"Good chance these savages don't make it as far as us this winter. But they could, and we can't have you here about to give birth if they do. We just can't."

"I understand that. Neither this home nor my parents' farm is safe." Did he think I was a dullard? I knew he thought Vinx would fall to the invaders.

"It's not that I don't want you and your mother, or sisters, to come to Lev." I could see the apology forming in his eyes. "My parents found you to be quite sweet, and they would do the right thing by you. It's just that, under our special circumstances, well, I've decided I don't want them to get too attached to you and your family. I'd like to keep some distance, Coral. It will make the whole thing easier in the end."

This was helpful. I'd been afraid he'd use our new agreement to *force* me to give birth in Lev.

"And my place in Pilk isn't a good option," he said. "I don't even know if I'd be nearby when the time came. We need you somewhere absolutely safe and I only know of one location that qualifies. You need to ask Ryalgar if there is any way you can go hide with the Velka until the baby is born and spring arrives."

Should I act like I was making a concession? I didn't want to play those sorts of games with my husband, even during a short marriage. No. Behaving in ways I didn't like was the *one* thing I wouldn't let him force me to do.

"I considered going to Ryalgar a few days ago, and hoped to convince *you* it was the best solution." I smiled. "I'm so glad we agree. The Velka may not take me, but let's find out."

He seemed a little disappointed that we both wanted the same solution. I supposed he looked forward to insisting I honor my promise. *Oh well.* We both knew he'd have plenty of other opportunities.

I hadn't seen the woman in the market before, and I hesitated to give her such a personal message. Yet, what were my options?

She stopped her work to listen to me but didn't become friendlier when I told her my sister was one of them. Perhaps she wasn't fond of Ryalgar. How unfortunate.

I changed my approach.

When I visited Ryalgar nearly half a year ago, she'd told me the truth about my grandmother, Aliz. All of us girls had been told

Aliz died long ago, soon after my grandfather's early death. In truth, Grandma Aliz had run away in her grief to join the Velka, leaving her grown children, including my father, behind.

My mother decided death was an easier explanation for her mother-in-law's absence.

I'd wanted to meet this mystery grandparent, but when I visited Ryalgar she'd been called away on Velka business. Ryalgar implied she held a position of importance and said I'd meet her next time.

Suddenly, Grandma became a solution to my problem.

"It's not Ryalgar I need to get a message to, though. It's my grandmother, Aliz." The woman immediately looked more interested.

"I need to speak with her about several things." I realized it was true. There was giving birth and being a luski and putting my sister into the Svadlu and the possible death of my whole family in Vinx if someone didn't do something. These were all fine items to discuss with Ryalgar, too, but she and I didn't always communicate so well. Perhaps this unmet grandmother could be of more help in sorting out the mess my life had become.

And, if she was someone important, perhaps her influence could buy me a safe place for the winter.

An ank later, a rider appeared in the distance as the sun set. This one was unaccustomed to riding a horse and had trouble controlling it. I'd never seen such a thing in an adult.

"These animals are impossible," she complained as she dismounted. The horse seemed as glad to be rid of the inept rider as she was to be off of him. "Give me a calm little donkey any day."

At my baffled look, she added "I grew up in the forests of Zur. We don't use horses there. I'm Joli, your sister's friend. I didn't get to meet you when you visited. Your grandmother sent me to tell you to make arrangements to leave your teaching post for the winter and to say goodbye to your sisters and parents over the next few anks. Three days before Kolada, you're to come to the same place where your sister entered and join us as a temporary resident. Bring whatever things you need to last until spring, and have someone with you who can take your horse home."

So. A woman once too scared to talk to the frightening Velka was about to become a temporary member. This would be interesting.

I hadn't seen Davor since we reached our agreement, and I hadn't heard from Sulphur either. I found that my advancing pregnancy left me more exhausted each day, and dealing with my classroom and my own care and feeding took all the energy I had. Was late pregnancy always so tiring? I tried to get information from the other teachers, but they were all single and knew little more than I did.

At the ank break before I would go into the forest, I gathered my strength and rode over to my parents' farm. I used to think of it as a short distance, but that morning it took forever.

My mother apologized for not coming to see me, or at least sending a sister to check on me, but so much had happened at the farm. Olivine packed to visit Ryalgar as we spoke, and Sulphur had applied for and been admitted into the Svadlu. My mom had sent the rest of her things off only a day ago.

"We hear they're trying to double the army from 200 to 400 before the Mongols attack," she said. Then she lowered her voice. "So they've lessened the standards a little. You know, letting in more women and older men and what not ...."

I felt insulted for Sulphur. She'd have qualified under any circumstances but I let it drop. Davor had come through, and I hoped he'd already come to appreciate Sulphur more.

Mom handled my news about giving birth at Ryalgar's lodge well. She understood the many ways it would be safest and, to be honest, I don't think she wanted to have me and a newborn at the farm all winter. My dad seemed sad, so I asked if he'd take me to the forest and bring Nutmeg back to the farm and care for her while I was gone.

"Of course. I'm getting good at this handoff."

Grey clouds covered the sky on the morning we left, and the air felt cold. Dad rode slowly, asking often if I needed to stop to rest.

"I'm a farm girl, Dad. I've been riding all my life."

"Every woman gets exhausted near the end, dear. I was there for your mother, for my younger sister, and I've watched many an animal give birth. Be gentle with yourself, okay?"

I smiled. I needed to hear those words.

Sulphur joined us on the way, so I'd have someone to go with me to the lodge. After we dismounted at the forest's edge, I gave Dad a long hug.

"Next time I see you, I'll have Ryalgar with me, I promise. And you'll get to hold your first grandchild."

An unknown Velka stepped out from between the trees and motioned us in. Sulphur and I made our way through the thick underbrush to the two donkeys waiting for us.

I couldn't get comfortable as I rode, and everywhere I looked the trees closed in on me in a way they hadn't before. Odd, given many of them had shed their leaves, showing bits of the gloomy sky above. Perhaps the extra bulk of pregnancy affected me as I struggled to breathe.

Sulphur talked with the Velka as we rode, but I made my way in silence to my new home, hiding my discomfort as best I could.

The Year of
Extreme
Distress

~ 8 ~

Every Ridiculous Alternative

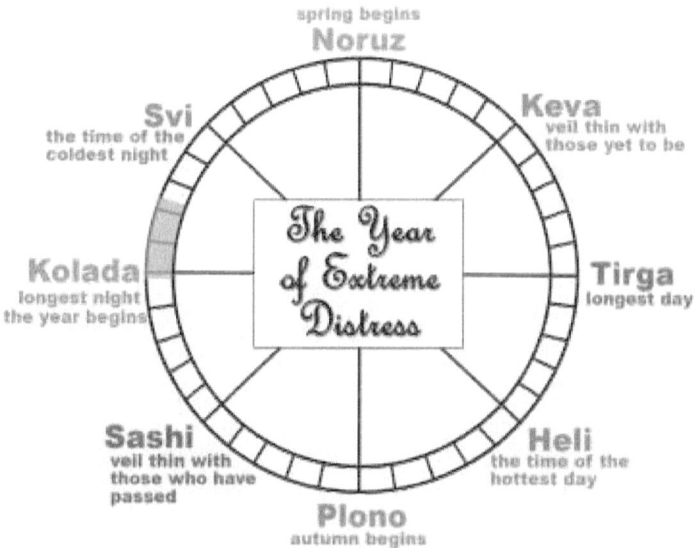

Our guide showed Sulphur and me to Ryalgar's room, where our sister Olivine already had made herself at home. I tried not to worry about the cramped quarters; this would be precious time together, despite my constant need to pee.

The day I arrived I learned that Ryalgar *had* gone on a research rampage, just as Ewalina said. She'd traveled around Pilk interviewing travelers, traders, and scholars, and claimed she now knew more about the Mongols than anyone else in Ilari. She probably did.

The first night, after others in the lodge had gone to bed, the four of us huddled under our blankets and she explained to us the reality of the danger we faced. For while Ilari's mountains, rivers, and marshlands protected us, as we knew, they also isolated us from everyone else. In fact, Velka legends claimed that long ago the Velka had combined their magic with our landscape to hide us completely from the rest of the world.

Today, traders knew of us and made their way in. The rare Ilarian traveled abroad and brought back tales, and occasionally even a mate. An infrequent explorer or refugee from elsewhere stumbled upon us as well. But most Ilarians rarely interacted with outsiders, so our army seemed large and fierce to us.

"We have a mere four hundred fighters, most of whom have never fought before!" Ryalgar's voice grew loud and Olivine reached out a hand to quiet her, pointing to the door.

She lowered her voice. "Four hundred soldiers is a pitiful defense for a realm our size. I think the invaders will expect resistance from ten times as many."

"Then we need to raise a larger army and train it," Sulphur said.

Ryalgar shook her head. "Few realms with large armies fend off these warriors on horseback, either. The Mongols ride in and conquer people before their soldiers have picked up their weapons!"

She told us how some among the Svadlu knew this and they had decided Ilari could increase its chances of surviving by drawing in its borders, jettisoning the least populated and less wealthy nichnas on the eastern side. Although no one could argue about the eastern nichnas being harder to defend, the plan gave up Vinx and left the Velka surrounded by enemies.

Ryalgar didn't favor this approach for all the obvious reasons, but her biggest objection was it wouldn't work. Not only would the eastern half of the realm be lost without a fight, but the Svadlu would likely be defeated defending the remaining part.

"You have to believe me," she said. "These invaders set their own terms, and the best arrangement involves living in servitude. Everyone I spoke with gave me different specifics about what is demanded, but the truth is most people choose to fight. Once they do, the Mongols kill them all and burn their homeland to the ground."

"Our Svadlu are too arrogant to surrender," I said. I had seen some of this arrogance first hand. "They think, or they want to believe, they can win this war with more recruits and extra practice sessions."

Sulphur argued with me because she believed in the Svadlu and was one of them. But she still had a mind of her own and she listened.

Every night after that, the four of us pulled our bedding together in the center of Ryalgar's room and while a single candle flickered against one wall, we worried together. Then we talked of crazy schemes to save our realm. Nothing is inevitable, right?

Could we slow down an army on horseback enough to give our defenders more time? Could we fight back while pretending to acquiesce? Vague ideas began to take shape as we whispered. It was easy to share wild notions in the dark with those we loved close by.

As each night passed, I wondered if Ilari's future would be better because none of us insisted we go to sleep instead.

Olivine and Sulphur left a few days later and I moved into a little cottage of my own. As soon as I settled in, my grandmother came to call.

She had the enthusiasm of a little girl as she took my hands in hers and introduced herself. She was a small and lively woman who wore her hair in these beautiful long braids wrapped around her head. She reminded me of my dad, and I liked her right away. And despite her absence for most of my life, she seemed to care about me, too.

"I'm so glad I got the chance to know you," I told her after we'd talked half an afternoon away.

A trace of sorrow complicated her smile. "Not half as glad as I am," she said. "May I come back to visit?"

"Often. Please."

And she did.

After that, three midwives also took turns checking in on me, giving me more herbs to take and sharing information about how the birth would go. Ryalgar didn't come by much, but I didn't fault her for seldom visiting me. I could tell her planning for the invasion overwhelmed her,

She did ask me if I'd like Ewalina, the luski who'd visited me in Vinx, to come to see me here. I wanted to say no. I had no energy for anything, but I saw the worry on her face.

She wants me to learn more.

That thought gave me strength and made me feel valued. I wanted to be more than someone to keep safe. I wanted to be part of the safekeeping.

"Please," I said. Ryalgar's smile lit up her face, and Ewalina showed up at my door a few days later.

"Always interesting to come into the forest," she said. "but honestly, I'm not sure I can do more to train you."

"I know. It's not training I need. I want to tell you my troubles." I ushered her inside and gestured her to a chair so she could warm herself by the fire as we spoke.

"I want you to believe they're your troubles too and I want you to help me think of every possible way we could aid my sister and every person who could help us do so."

To Ewalina's credit, she settled in beside my small fireplace, kicked off her shoes, and curled her long legs up under her skirt. Then she listened as I repeated Ryalgar's analysis. She started to argue with me about the certainty of Ilari's demise, but after I spouted back fact after fact, she gave up.

"Okay. Suppose I agree we're doomed. Then what?" I understood it wasn't an easy conclusion to reach and I respected her for being able to get there.

"Given we've nothing to lose, join me in thinking of every ridiculous alternative you can that would involve luskies."

She tried. Over the years she'd given a lot of thought to what luskies could and couldn't do, and her insights helped as we talked through the options.

"I've never heard the timbre work on more than one person at a time," she said. "It appears to be a specific interaction between two people."

"So that rules out shouting commands to their whole army."

"Or even to a small group of them. Also, it's a short term thing, always about a specific action. It's not like you could get one of them alone and then command them to never kill again."

"Just like you couldn't have commanded me to fetch water for every traveler who came by my cottage."

"Exactly."

"Well that rules out trying to turn each invader into a peace-loving farmer," I said. "I hoped for that option. So if the best we can do is get one person to do one thing, how do we help?"

"Well, to make any difference at all, we'd need a scump-load of luskies, and that's a problem. I know of twenty counting us, and most of them are deathly afraid of being found out. Some wouldn't use their timbre in public to save a life, and a few refuse to use it at all. Are we doomed?"

"No, only stuck. Go home. Keep trying to think of something. I'll do the same. Maybe there's a twist we haven't considered."

My mother sent Celestine to sit by my side through the birth. Celestine had to give up several chances to sing and play her psaltery to be with me, and I knew she wasn't happy about it. She didn't complain though. She brought in two sets of saddlebags stuffed to overflowing, unpacked and hung up her beautiful clothes with care, and then settled into the cottage to be with me.

When I asked about her music, she spoke of it, but her heart wasn't in her words. What else was on her mind? A lover perhaps? She'd always been a beautiful girl, with her curly coal-black hair and bright blue eyes, and she received more attention from boys than any of us.

She'd been sort of shy around males as a child though. Maybe it was having no brothers? For whatever reason, she tended to ignore boys, so their attention often turned to teasing, the way it does when a girl doesn't give enough of a response. When she was younger, I'd found her crying in the barn often, upset about how the boys picked on her.

"They do that because they like you," had never comforted her, and to be honest I never understood why it should. I'd quit saying it, even though it was true, and just held her when she cried.

Now, I wondered what sort of special man had stolen her heart? A kind one, I suspected. I knew she'd talk to me about him when she was ready. Given my mother's ambitions, I had to hope he was a prince, or close enough to one to satisfy Mom.

At first, I kept quiet about my newly discovered talents, but late one night, after a few goblets of wine, she and I ran out of things we were both willing to talk about. So I told her about being a luski. She responded with curiosity, not fear.

I hadn't considered how my ability to use my voice would pique her musical interest. She knew all about the timbre of various instruments and was fascinated to think there were vocal timbres capable of eliciting a deep subconscious response in the human mind. At her insistence, I tried to demonstrate. Not only was she not afraid, but she wanted me to keep trying to make her do various things. Why would this work but not that? I ended up showing her most of what Ewalina had taught me.

Finally, I had to ask. "Do you think you're a luski, too?"

"Oh, I know I'm not. My voice is my life. I don't think singers could be this thing, actually. It wouldn't be compatible with singing."

Interesting.

"Why work so hard at this luski thing now, of all times? I mean, shouldn't you be, you know, thinking about your baby?"

"I *am* thinking about my baby, Celestine. I'm scared to death about the world this baby is going to be born into, and in my small way I'm trying to help make it safer."

"With your voice?" Celestine was incredulous. "How? Why?"

I knew Ryalgar wanted to have the conversation with Celestine that she'd had with me, Sulphur, and Olivine, but Celestine had been here now for days and Ryalgar hadn't gotten around to it. It was time Celestine learned what we were doing.

She rolled her eyes when I mentioned the Mongols, but once I started in about Ryalgar's research I got her attention. Every one of us girls respected how our oldest dealt with information as if she had my dad's brains and my mother's drive. If Ryalgar said it was time to panic, it probably was.

By the time I finished talking, Celestine responded as I expected. As I had.

"What can I do?"

"You need to talk to Ryalgar." I knew she would.

Days ran together in the forest, with nothing to mark one from another, but the day after my conversation with Celestine, something happened. I got a message sent by way of a Velka who went to a market in Pilk. Davor had picked a name for our son. My baby was to be called Davot, after his father.

This made me angry on so many levels. I could be having a daughter. Was she not worth naming? And, if a boy, I'd be raising him. Shouldn't I pick a name I liked to say, given I'd be the one saying it day and night? "Eat your porridge, Davot. Put down that stick, Davot. Go to bed, Davot."

Then I paused. The woman who brought the message had used odd words. She said, "He wants the boy to be named Davot in memory of him."

In memory of? Was Davor dying? Probably not. More likely, Davor gave serious thought to his odds of surviving a fight with the Mongols and he didn't like his chances. He was scared. He wanted to leave a bit of himself behind when he died, especially if that death was soon.

I massaged this new understanding into my tight ball of anger and felt my tension relax. Davot wasn't a bad name, and I could use an affectionate nickname of my choosing.

Votto sounded cute.

I put my hand over my belly. "Votto? If it's you in there, everything's going to be okay. Your mama and your dad are both doing their best out here to make it so."

I think he believed me.

~ 9 ~

Sleeping Donkeys

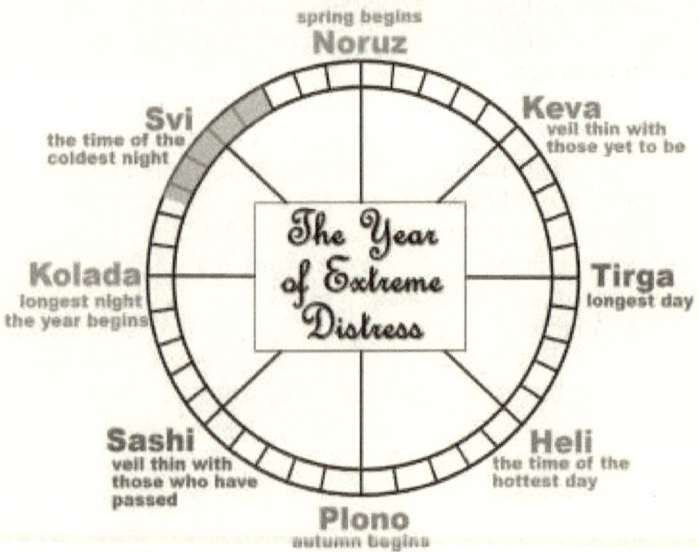

The next day another message came, this one from a Velka who'd gone to a different market in Pilk. She'd spoken with Ewalina, who sent word that she'd enlisted luskies to help us. Several women had hissed at her to go away when approached, but she'd still managed to recruit twenty-three of them scattered around the realm. The women ranged in ages from eighteen to seventy-eight; the lone man was a miner in Tolo. All agreed to come train with us because the Mongols scared them more than

64

frightened and angry neighbors did. What should she tell them? Could we use them?

I needed to send back a reply, and soon.

I got my answer later that day, by accident. I'd been trying all sorts of variations with my voice based on the wild ideas Ewalina and I discussed. I whispered instructions to unsuspecting people who could barely hear me. I shouted to those too far away to hear me well. In both cases, I got nowhere.

We'd speculated about trying to influence something not human, so I'd also given orders to rose bushes and pebbles. I wasn't surprised when they ignored me, but I kept looking for that advantage no one suspected.

My biggest hope had been to use my talents with animals. That success had obvious benefits given our enemy would ride in on horseback. For whatever reason, though, cats, dogs, donkeys, and squirrels all ignored me with equal aplomb. My timbre didn't resonate with them.

After hearing Ewalina's news, I decided to give it another try. Wouldn't it be wonderful if our small band of luskies could stop the Mongols horses in their tracks?

Little fluffy balls of white clouds speckled an otherwise blue sky on that day and the winter winds blew elsewhere, so I went outside for a bit of air. A tethered donkey stood nearby and he gave me a tired glance.

"Go to sleep, little donkey." I used my best singsong voice. I'd already discovered how humans tended to obey an order to rest, but this donkey ignored me. As I repeated it, Celestine rode up from the other direction, amused at my efforts.

"Go to sleep, little donkey," she sang along with me, laughing. The donkey gave her a quizzical look, then laid down in the dirt and closed his eyes. It would have been funny, but then her donkey did the same, stopping in the middle of the path, dropping to the ground, and coming rest on the hem of the lovely blue frock she wore. She gasped in indignation as her animal fell into a deep slumber while laying on her dress.

"You're a luski for animals!" I declared.

"I can't be. There wasn't an animal on our farm that ever did what I said."

"Did you try singing to them?" I thought singing could be the key.

"I sang to them all the time."

So much for that theory.

"So what made these two respond to you now?"

She stood up and yanked the edge of her skirt out from under the slumbering animal and studied the damage to her pretty clothes.

"I have no idea," she said.

"Then we need a lot more donkeys so we can find out."

It didn't take long for us to discover animals all ignored me whether I spoke, sang, or played an instrument when I gave my orders. I tried giggling, shrieking, whispering, and whistling for good measure. I couldn't deliver my message to them and get them to care.

Celestine met with a similar lack of success.

The only time they paid attention was when I used my luski voice, and Celestine sang along with me. It was like one of those clever little boxes you can only open if you hold down two buttons in two places at once.

Even with her and I working together, the animals seemed less inclined to obey than humans.

We began to attract people as we borrowed more donkeys and brought in whatever other pets we could find. Soon word reached Ryalgar. She arrived in our yard out of breath and flushed from running.

"Well done!" She hugged each of us in turn. "Show me."

We did our best, but by then our cadre of donkeys had gotten tired of being tired and the cats had all wandered off. Only the small dog continued to try to please us, now doing tricks even when we made no noise at all.

"This was all more impressive a while ago," I told her.

"I believe you. Obviously, we need to know how this works with horses. If we can make them lie down and stay down, then we've got the invaders right where we want them. Battle over."

"I doubt that's possible," Celestine said. "Horses are extremely loyal to their humans. It would be one thing to get a tired horse carrying a stranger to lie down, and quite another to get a well-trained horse to defy the wishes of its human partner."

Good point. I couldn't imagine Nutmeg falling asleep while she carried me.

Ryalgar agreed. "We have to try this on horses with riders they know. And then, we have to have to try this with bigger groups, with so many hoofs hitting the ground we can barely be heard."

"We need more luskies, then too," I said, happy to have my answer for Ewalina.

"And way more singers," Celestine added. "How many people in the realm sing well? Or does the quality of the singing matter?"

"We need more information about horses. Unless you think we can get hundreds of squirrels to stage an attack for us." Ryalgar looked at me hopefully and I shook my head. "Okay then, let's not waste time on other animals. We need to get out of the forest and run tests on the one creature that matters."

It was a great plan. Ryalgar and Celestine began working on it right away, making arrangements. In their excitement, they forgot one thing.

The day before we planned to meet the group of horsemen at the forest's edge, I found myself in a puddle of water. The midwives had warned me about this. It meant labor would start.

I started to clean up the mess, hoping a midwife would come by soon. It seemed they were always hovering around these days, but the next footsteps I heard were Celestine's as she came back from the lodge with food for us.

"Ick. What happened here?"

"You need to get one of the midwives. Quick."

"No! You can't have a baby now. You have to wait a few more days."

"She can't wait." Aliz walked behind her, carrying fresh towels and sheets for us. It was the sharpest tone I'd heard my grandmother use to anyone.

"Go get the midwife," she said to Celestine. "I'll help Coral get comfortable."

Before long I had Celestine, Grandma, two midwives, and Ryalgar at my bedside. Once it was apparent nothing important would happen soon, the conversation turned to the arrangements for testing horses.

S. R. Cronin

"We can do this without Coral," Ryalgar said. "We have other luskies coming; Ewalina has found over twenty who will help and she's bringing four of them." She turned to me, almost as an afterthought. "You can have this baby without us, right?"

"She can, but she doesn't have to." Grandma was firm. "Reports show all is quiet around Ilari. Yes, I read the Recorders' notes too. If we go without Coral, we waste the day trying to duplicate what Celestine and Coral did. Perhaps their bond as sisters matters. Or maybe Coral's specific voice does. Or maybe not but we won't know. We're better served to cancel and reconvene it in two anks when Coral and the baby are strong enough to travel. Less time wasted and less frustration on the part of the riders we need to help us."

I could see the struggle on Ryalgar's face. Up until now, she'd thought she was in charge, but now she understood she only got to run things when Aliz didn't disagree with her.

Wisdom won out over her pride.

"Yes, that makes perfect sense, Grandmother," she said. I, for one, knew how hard it was for my sister to say such a thing.

My labor was long, as most first labors are, but caring relatives and healers anxious to make me comfortable surrounded me. I knew others faced this painful ordeal with far less support. In the last passionate burst of pushing the baby out, I screamed, not a yell of pain but one of triumph. Producing this little human was one of the greatest achievements of my life.

I looked down at the bloody squealing mess in the midwife's arms and saw … Davor. A tiny Davor, with a burst of the same black hair on his head and most definitely a pizzle between his legs.

I was disappointed for a second, but as his little scrunched face turned towards me, I melted. He was Votto, and he was exactly who he was meant to be.

The midwife laid him on my stomach, nudging him toward my teats to suckle. I'd been told feeding him would help with the afterbirth and would calm him as well. It calmed me. I stroked his shiny hair as he fed, my fingers lingering over the silky touch, and when I looked up half the room had tears in their eyes.

"There is magic in this moment," Aliz said.

She was right. There was.

68

Two anks after Votto was born I was ready to ride. A mild winter storm had made its way through Ilari, and the Velka's weather forecasters determined we now had days of clear skies ahead. The time to experiment with luskies, singers, and horses had arrived.

During his first eighteen days, Votto established himself as a model baby. He fed with gusto, slept soundly, and gave everyone endearing looks with his wide eyes. There wasn't a woman in the forest who didn't adore the child. It seemed he'd inherited his father's ability to charm.

As for me, I didn't doubt I'd lay my life down for him. So I balked at the idea of taking him with me to the forest's edge for Ryalgar's research project. Why put a newborn in such danger?

"We can make a carrier for you," the women insisted. "He's too little to be away from you for hours. He'll be hungry. He can sleep bound close to your body as you ride. Trust us. You'll both be happier this way."

The fatigue from round the clock feedings left me little energy to argue with anyone. I may have been a luski, but in those first weeks after Votto was born, I pretty much did what other people told me to do. I was too tired to do anything else.

The contraption did seem to hold him well. He slept as we rode along the Velka's half-hidden donkey trail to one of the seven entry places into the forest. I'd never been to this one, located on the border with Gruen, midway along the forest's southern edge. I wondered what waited for us on the other side.

~ 10 ~

What a Horse Wants to Do

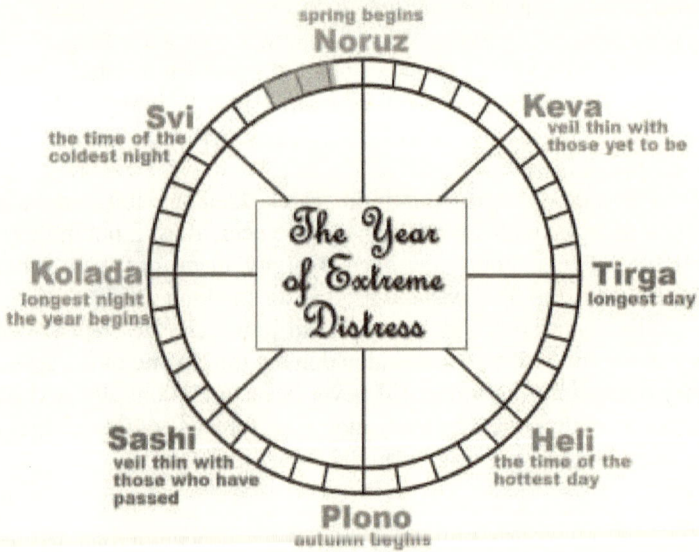

spring begins
Noruz

Svi
the time of the
coldest night

Keva
veil thin with
those yet to be

Kolada
longest night
the year begins

*The Year
of Extreme
Distress*

Tirga
longest day

Sashi
veil thin with
those who have
passed

Heli
the time of the
hottest day

Plono
autumn begins

Chaos took over before we arrived. I dismounted to see women, men, and animals milling about in mistrustful confusion. Five women huddled together, wearing costume-party masks that covered the upper half of their faces. I could pick out Ewalina's tall slender body among them and recognized her tufts of fluffy greying hair. I reminded myself she was a stranger to me.

My father stood with several of our farmhands and twice as many of our horses. The farmhands kept their distance from the masked women.

70

Celestine had left the forest the day after Votto's birth and she waited for us too, with several singers she'd brought so we could try more variations. The singers seemed leery of the masked women, but not as frightened as the farmhands.

I wondered. Should I hide my identity too? Of course I should, although a mask would provide little disguise with my bright red hair and at least half the people here already knowing me. Next time I'd bring one, along with a scarf or hood to cover my hair.

Ryalgar took one look at the commotion and didn't hesitate. She found a large rock to stand upon, held up a cone-shaped piece of carved wood my grandmother gave her to amplify her voice, and began to shout instructions. As she worked her magic of organization, my father walked towards me with his arms open wide to hug me.

"No." I barked it out with more vehemence than I meant and saw the hurt on his face. I knew Ryalgar had told him what I could do because she felt she had no choice. Now he'd overcome his fears to offer me this hug and I'd rebuffed him. I felt awful.

"I'd love to hug you, Dad, but look." I opened my cloak a sliver as he came closer.

"Surely you didn't bring a newborn out here with you?"

"It's okay. The Velka said he'd be safest with me. Come. Meet your grandson, Votto."

My dad came close and his scowl at my rejection softened as he peeked at the tiny human asleep under my cloak. He studied the baby, then gently touched the child's forehead without saying a word.

"He looks a lot like his father, doesn't he?" I said.

My dad nodded. "I hoped he'd have your beautiful red hair."

"Coral. We need you." My sister's voice broke the spell. I closed my cloak as I turned to do my part.

"Maybe he'll have your beautiful disposition instead," my dad added as I walked away.

We started out trying to make the animals go to sleep, the way we'd done with the donkeys a few anks ago. At first nothing worked, other than the luskies' singsong words making the farmhands yawn a lot. As the excitement wore off and we all got bored, a few of the donkeys took the opportunity to nap. We couldn't tell if it had to do with our efforts or not.

Eventually, a couple of the horses without riders nodded off while standing up, as horses often do. My dad told me years ago horses napped on their feet because they can't get up as fast as other animals.

"I think we're back to the idea of only being able to get a creature to do what it wants to do," the woman I knew was Ewalina told Ryalgar. "These donkeys and horses are tired, so now they're happy to comply with our suggestions."

My dad agreed. "When we started, everyone was full of anticipation. Animals pick up on that. No creature wants to sleep if something exciting is about to happen. It's not safe. Plus, they could miss the chance for food. They're not stupid."

Joli lowered her voice so only Ryalgar and those standing near her could hear.

"Why not do this napping thing instead of shooting their horses while they sleep? Use luskies to keep the Mongol's horses slumbering for days, with no arrows needed?"

"I wish," Ryalgar answered. "You didn't grow up with horses, did you? A sleeping horse can't hear your suggestion and it will wake up to eat. Besides, the Mongols would wake them. No, I hoped we could use this later on, to somehow bring the remaining horde to a stop. Now I'm having trouble seeing how it could help us at all."

Ewalina agreed. "This isn't a sleeping potion, that's for sure."

"Yeah," Joli laughed. "It's more like a sleeping suggestion. What good is that?"

"Then why not suggest they do something besides sleep? Something they want to do?" I asked. Everyone turned to me in surprise. "What else does a horse want to do?" I added. I guess it was a naïve question. Several of the farmhands responded with crude gestures and laughs.

Joli turned to them in irritation. "Besides that. Although now that you mention it ..."

"No!" Ryalgar said. "We are not going to try to get eight hundred horses into a prucking frenzy." Several of us giggled at the image and even the farmhands laughed and came in closer to listen.

"Could we make these eight hundred horses go wildly hungry?" Ewalina asked.

"I'm guessing they're too well trained for that," my father said.

"If you scare them, they'll be more likely to ignore their training. Act from their instincts." One of the farmhands had stopped smirking and was taking this problem seriously.

"You're right," Ryalgar said. "But I don't think you can scare them into eating. Or mating. How about just scaring them into bucking?"

"That's it," my dad said. "A well-trained horse will seldom throw its rider, but if you startle it enough and then add your people's mumbo jumbo, maybe …."

And so part two of Ryalgar's master plan was born.

In our enthusiasm, we threw everything at the problem. All the luskies chanting in their deepest voices "Throw your rider!" All the singers howling and screeching exhortations at the top of their lungs to do the same. Then we added a flaming torch a couple of the farmhands devised and the sudden sound of everyone else hitting anything they could find with a stick.

By mid-afternoon, several riders had hit the ground hard enough to sustain minor injuries but everyone grinned, and none more than those who'd been thrown by their own affectionate horses.

"It's going to take a lot more fire and noise for the numbers we'll be dealing with," Ryalgar said, "but at least we know it can be done."

"It's not something you can keep doing," Ewalina pointed out. "Already these horses are less inclined to respond."

"I know. This needs to be a one-time event. We'll place a blockage of some sort on the way to Pilk, then we'll do this once, as well as we can."

"And what will keep these thrown riders from getting back on their horses?" Joli asked. Then she looked at Ryalgar. "You have a plan for that, don't you? Of course you do."

Ryalgar smiled. "It looks like the cow herders of Bisu aren't the only ones needing training from the Svadlu. The farm folk of Vinx will need some, too." She looked around at the group. "Okay. Now we're going to try this with as many riders at once as we can. We need to make sure the sounds of the luskies and the singers can penetrate the noise because it's going to be so much louder with hundreds of horses."

I looked over at the farmhand standing next to me. He'd been thrown twice, and the sprain in his wrist would likely cause him pain for days. Both he and the horse standing next to him reeked of confusion and fatigue.

"Ryalgar?"

"What?" She wasn't happy to be interrupted.

"It's time to stop for the day." I didn't mean to say it as a command; I just knew one more attempt could push riders and horses beyond what was safe.

I could see the argument forming on her lips when she stopped and thought about my words.

"It *has* been a long day," she said. "And everyone needs to be home by dark. Good point, Coral. Sometimes my determination gets the better of me." She gave me a warm smile and turned to the whole group. "Change in plans. We'll meet again in two anks to look into the problems of noise. Let's see if we can gather more people next time so our testing can be more realistic."

Everyone turned away, grateful to be headed home.

As Votto and I rode back into the forest, I began to suckle him under my cloak. Had I forced Ryalgar into her decision? Had I nudged her into it? Or had she simply seen the wisdom in what I said?

I had no real way of knowing.

Three anks after Votto was born, his father sent for me.

"Your husband wishes to meet his son," the older Velka said "He didn't send word; he came to the marketplace in person to find out if you'd be well enough in one ank to ride to the forest's edge and meet him at the new wall being built between Gruen and Pilk. I told him I'd ask."

I was well enough already and the woman knew it, but I appreciated how she'd left the decision to me. I wanted to introduce Votto to his father, but Davor had chosen the same day Ryalgar had for her second experiment.

"Please tell him I'd like an extra ank for my recovery, and I'd like to give Votto time to grow stronger before we travel. Ask if I could meet him there in two anks instead. It will be Noruz then, and he and I could celebrate the spring equinox together."

Yes, I was trying to shame him into spending one holiday with me instead of with his new love from Tolo. I knew it was petty, but on some level I thought producing a son for him ought to buy me the status of being seen on his arm during a public occasion.

The woman gave me a knowing smile. "I'll convey to him your concerns for your health and your child."

An ank later I bound Votto to my chest and prepared for our second ride. In nine days he'd grown heavier. No surprise, given he fed all day. Others told me not to worry, every baby ate according to their own natural rhythm. I had to admit, the chubbier he became, the cuter he got.

Clouds hung low in the sky as we emerged from the forest, but the air was mild and still. Puddles of mud dotted a landscape still wet from melting snow. Everyone had worried about injuries last time, but today the farmers had done something about it. Many brought straw-filled wagons and we arrived to mounds of straw being spread to cover the mud and to lessen the impact of the falls.

This time I brought a mask of my own, and a scarf to cover my hair. Strands of orange popped out on every side, but at least my efforts made it clear I didn't wish to be recognized. I stood with the other luskies.

My father stopped his work spreading straw as soon as he saw me and headed my way. Unless I asked him to ignore me after today, he'd continue to make it hard to hide my identity.

Knowing Votto slept under my cloak, he reached his arms out towards me and I offered him Votto wrapped in his blanket. Dad took the bundle without hesitation and began making faces and noises as he held the baby, trying to get him to smile. When Votto finally gave my dad his first grin, both of us got tears in our eyes.

"Thanks, Dad, for all the extra people you talked into coming!" Ryalgar strode over to us, oblivious to the moment she interrupted.

"My pleasure," Dad answered. "People talk, dear. Everyone is scared about the Mongols. Nearly everyone knows you're doing something to keep the people safe. They wanted to come."

I looked around and counted at least fifty horses and riders. Celestine had been one of four singers for the first experiment. I don't know how she'd done it, but today she was one of forty, all warming up with vocalizing exercises. We'd had six luskies last time. This time we had fourteen, including a man who had to be the famed lone male luski from Tolo.

A dozen Velka had somehow brought two large gongs and a giant drum through the forest to this spot. Off to one side stood several reczavy from the edges of K'ba. The reczavy were known for their circus-like performances, many of which included fire. This group looked ready to start a blaze that would frighten any number of horses. I couldn't imagine who in my family convinced the reczavy to help us, or how in the world they had managed it.

Ryalgar took her position on the rock, the wooden cone in her hand. We began.

By our third attempt we knew a large number of trained horses could be startled and nudged into throwing their riders. Ryalgar had brought more of the cones she used to amplify her voice, and results improved when the singers and luskies both used them. Fire and noise worked best in combination, but if only one was used, fire was better. Smoke helped too.

Ryalgar had two more things she wanted to try before we called it quits. She'd been having the riders stay far apart, not wanting to chance anyone being trampled. She needed to know if the horses would behave differently if they were closer together.

And, she needed to know if the luskies and singers could change their song at the end, and encourage the horses to run far and fast once they dumped their riders. She decided to combine both questions into a trial run with unridden horses bunched together. Given the hassle of getting the horses back, this was a one-time experiment best conducted at the end of the day.

We were nearly ready to begin when a cloud of dust in the distance showed another group of riders coming to us. No matter who it was, being discovered wasn't good. Ryalgar didn't hesitate.

"All the Velka, into the forest. Take the gongs and drums. Luskies go with them. Disappear now." They all moved towards the trees except for me.

She turned to the singers. "Grab horses and wagons and head towards Pilk. You're just passing through. On your way to a show. You have nothing to do with us."

They obliged, with haste.

She turned to the reczavy, but they were already gone.

"How'd they do that?" She shrugged and turned to the farmers and farmhands. "Please make up something about what you're doing with fifty horses and all this hay. It doesn't have to make much sense. Whoever they are, just give them some answers so they'll move on."

Dad spoke up. "I've got this. You get out of here, Ryalgar."

~ 11 ~

An Awkward Meeting

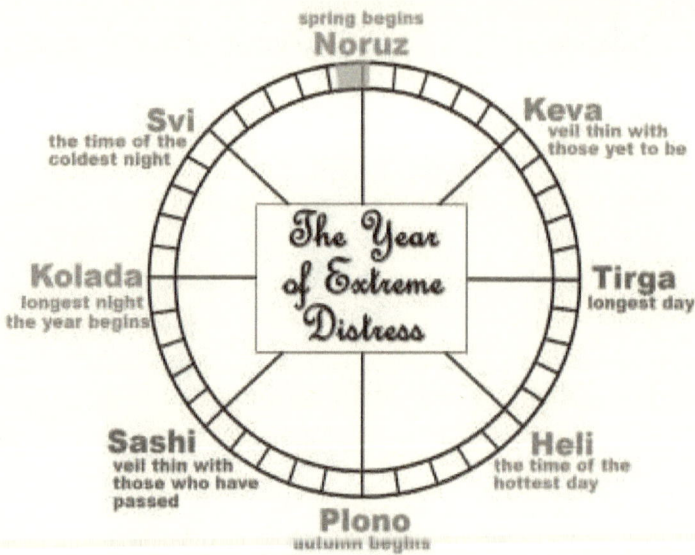

spring begins
Noruz

Svi
the time of the
coldest night

Keva
veil thin with
those yet to be

*The Year
of Extreme
Distress*

Kolada
longest night
the year begins

Tirga
longest day

Sashi
veil thin with
those who have
passed

Heli
the time of the
hottest day

Plono
autumn begins

Two days later the same older Velka who'd delivered Davor's first message came to my cottage to tell me my husband wished to see me immediately.

"He sent word instructing you to be at the new wall between Pilk and Gruen by midmorning tomorrow."

"That's odd. Should I go?"

She shrugged. "What do you think?"

Well, I had made a promise. Defying his brusque order would feel good but gain me nothing but trouble. So I packed a

78

few extra things in case he expected me to leave the forest and come with him to Pilk, then I walked over to the lodge and made arrangements for an escort,

He stood in the sunshine, leaning against the rock wall waiting for me. I handed the reins of my donkey to my escort, promising to let her know soon if she should wait or go. I left my pack with her.

Davor gave me no more than a fleeting smile before his eyes settled on my brown wool cloak. He wanted to see his son. I knew the Velka had passed reports along about the baby's gender and health, but as I took a groggy Votto out of his carrier, Davor studied the infant in my arms.

"You didn't lie to me at least," he said. "He's definitely mine."

"He is." Then because I thought I should add more, "He's a good baby. Happy. Healthy. Eats well."

Davor nodded. "You've done a fine job with him, Coral. He's more than I could have asked for. Because of that, I hate to do this to you now, but I don't have much choice."

Several bad alternatives ran through my head.

"What in Heli is your father up to?" he asked. "Fifty horsemen at the forest's edge doing some sort of training? Is he trying to start his own make-shift army to fight the Mongols? We do not need this sort of interference from our citizens."

That's what had upset him? I almost laughed in relief.

"I can't think of a man less likely to start an army than my father," I said, opting for a truth.

"I agree, but one of our squads came upon a bunch of men, horses, and straw in the middle of nowhere a couple of days ago, with your dad in charge. You need to go to your parents' house and find out what's going on."

Scump.

Was more truth my best option? I thought so. "He wasn't doing anything except helping my sister Ryalgar."

"What? The one who's a Velka? The one who asked me all the military questions when I met her at your wedding?"

"I didn't realize she'd done that. But yes, her. She's also the one who's given me a place to give birth and has seen to it your son was cared for and safe. That sister."

Davor took a deep breath. "I'm grateful for her help regarding my son. But let me assure you, if she's planning trouble of any kind from inside the forest ...."

I placed my eyes in front of Davor's. "The last thing my sister is planning is trouble."

"Then what is she doing conducting exercises with horsemen?"

"Trying to help you."

"Huh? What in Heli's name makes her think I need her help?"

"She's looked at a map. She's talked to people. She's pretty varmin sure the Svadlu will end up giving Vinx and the nichnas around it to the Mongols thinking they don't have a choice. She knows that will leave the Velka surrounded by enemies, and she thinks if she can help you, you'll have a better chance of winning your battle."

Davor burst into laughter. "Well, if that doesn't top everything. Now I've got old ladies and farmhands trying to help me. Prucking goat scump."

"Davor, there's no harm in what she's doing. I promise. If you talk to her, she'll tell you all about it. It's no secret people are afraid. They've heard stories. She's giving them something positive to do."

"Look, if they want to do something positive, why don't they join the Svadlu? We could use more men. More women, too," he added.

"She's coming at the problem in different ways. Not like a soldier." When Davor looked alarmed by this idea, I added. "It's nothing harmful. Nothing you'd object to."

He shook his head. "Okay, Coral. Because she's been so helpful with our baby, I'll give her a little leeway, but I need to know more. Tell her the two of you must come to Pilk for Noruz." I'm sure the enthusiasm showed on my face. "Not to celebrate with me. I'm sorry, honey cakes. Let her know she and I will have a serious conversation then, and it's going to be about what she is and isn't allowed to do as a citizen."

"I'll tell her. So does this mean you're now totally in charge of training the troops for the Mongol invasion?" I thought a slight subject change would be helpful.

He spat on the ground off to the side. "No, that idiot Nevik is still around. I've been taking him out for drinks lately, pretending I like him, so he'll give me less trouble."

Davor appeared to struggle with an idea as it crossed his mind.

"You know, I probably ought to bring him along to this conversation with your sister so he doesn't get his royal feelings hurt. Better warn Ryalgar a prince could be there; I don't want her flustered. Your family reflects on me now, and I can't have her making a fool of herself."

I swallowed hard. This was certainly getting complicated.

"I'll let her know. We'll make arrangements to travel to Pilk in a few days. Uh ...."

"I'm sorry, I don't have room for you at my house, but I'll make arrangements for a nice place where the two of you can stay. The three of you, rather. Bring my little man along, of course. I can't wait to show him off."

Davor looked hard at the baby, as he tried to figure out how to say goodbye to him.

"Would you like to hold him for a minute?"

"Heli no. I don't want to drop him. Maybe when he's older."

With that, I bundled Votto back into his carrier and walked to my donkey. In my head I prepared to give my sister the alarming news that in a few days she'd need to defend her budding plans to save our realm to both her secret lover and my grumpy estranged husband who happened to hate him.

Ryalgar took the news pretty well. She'd always been a pragmatic girl; maybe she realized we didn't have a better choice. I admit I didn't tell her everything; Davor's disdain for Nevik felt too hurtful to share.

As we headed to Pilk Central together, I again struggled to nurse an infant while riding. I wondered if she had any idea how physically difficult this was for me. When we got to the inn Votto became uncharacteristically fussy and I decided he was wise beyond his years. I needed a break from Ryalgar and so did he.

"The tavern's right down the street. I'll catch up with you, once I get him to sleep," I said. When she didn't respond, I added, "Go ahead. Go without me."

"You bet your sweet arse I won't." I couldn't believe her response, but this was no time for us to have words with each other. I swallowed my outrage at her rudeness and said nothing.

"Nice try, though," I muttered to Votto as I swaddled him in a fresh diaper and bundled him tight against me. By the time we walked to the tavern, he'd fallen asleep.

Ryalgar explained how her evolving plans to help Ilari depended upon the Svadlu abandoning the eastern nichnas, so she could deliver a greatly diminished foe to the doorstep of Pilk. Davor wasn't eager to admit she or anyone else could help the mighty Svadlu, but he understood a good arrangement when he heard it. Agreeing to Ryalgar's plans would reduce his liability and make his life easier. No one had ever called him stupid.

"This could be something we'd allow you to do," he conceded. "The Svadlu can explain how the abandonment of the outer nichnas is the best military plan for all, and everyone will be grateful to us when it ends well."

Yes, he'd claim the victory if she was successful. He'd also probably lambast her for her lies if she wasn't. Both made me defensive for the sister I'd been so annoyed with a short while ago.

Ryalgar opened her mouth to reply to him when the guard at the door shocked us all by yelling "The Mongols are here! The invasion has started!"

I thought for a second I'd dreamt it, but no, everyone around us began to panic. Ryalgar shooed the two men out of the room to handle their responsibilities. Then she grabbed my hand and pulled me through the tavern. We passed those hiding under the tables and made our way out to the street filled with frightened people.

Some Ilarians yelled for help, others pleaded for safety. A few looted newly-abandoned merchants' stands. The only thing missing from the chaotic scene was an actual Mongol.

"Where are they?" I asked.

"In Pilk center," a man said. "They're outside the offices of the Ruling Prince of Pilk."

I looked at Ryalgar, and she nodded in agreement as we headed towards the center of the town.

We never saw a Mongol, but we heard how a small delegation paid our realm a visit to demand tribute, insisting we provide it on the coming Kolada. After listening to several versions of the story, she and I returned to our room, waiting for Davor and Nevik to contact us.

They didn't that night, but the next morning Nevik came by to tell us the Royals and Svadlu had met the previous evening and agreed to our proposal. The official defense of Ilari would begin at the border of Pilk. They'd do their best to move the affected citizens to safety before the attack, leaving us free to use all of the outer nichnas to stage whatever shenanigans we wanted.

It made me sad Davor hadn't bothered to come with Nevik to share this news and to say farewell to his son. The pain grew sharper when I noticed Ryalgar and Nevik making eyes at each other, and casting hopeful glances my way.

Sure, I could take the baby out for some air and go for a walk. Sure, I could take my time.

At our final experiment with the horses, my dad had said my parents hoped to go to Pilk for the Noruz celebration to visit with Iolite and Gypsum, who were in school nearby. Ryalgar and I had planned to surprise them after our meeting with Davor and Nevik, as she knew the inn where they usually stayed. With the appearance of the Mongol envoys, it hadn't happened.

So after I left to give Ryalgar and Nevik time alone, I decided to find my parents. I got directions to the inn but early revelers already filled the larger streets while discarded food and trash made the narrower ones too stench-filled to handle. By the time I finally got there, my feet hurt. Then, when I asked about my family's whereabouts, an unhelpful proprietor told me he was too busy with the Noruz crowds to pay attention to the comings and goings of his guests.

After my long and uncomfortable walk, I saw no harm in coercing this man into doing his job. So I tried again.

"I'm just a daughter, seeking news of my family's safety in these trying times. Are you *sure* you wouldn't like to? Help? Me?"

Upon reconsideration, he decided he wished to help. It turned out I'd just missed three of them. Gypsum hadn't been there, but an older couple had left to take a daughter, an ill one, back to her school. "The ill one" had to be a reference to Iolite, who had a

S. R. Cronin

disease that turned her hair silver. Polite folks seldom referred to her condition by name, so I assumed he was being coy.

"You mean my sister, the frundle?" I said.

His eyes widened and he pursed his lips. "You said it, I didn't." What a childish response.

"Did they all seem well when they left?" I asked.

"Yes, I suppose. Perhaps a little distraught, but who isn't these days?"

I don't know why, but the proprietor's impoliteness, combined with not getting to see my family, put me further into a bad mood. I hated having to use my timbre for something as basic as getting information on my parents. Did my promise to use my gift wisely hold when I was dealing with an unhelpful idiot?

On the way back, Votto began to fuss. I stepped into an alley to feed him. My back hurt as I leaned against a stone wall and tried to ignore the impromptu outhouse the end of the alley had become. By the time I got back to my inn, my head hurt more than my back or feet.

Ryalgar and Nevik, however, couldn't have been more cheerful.

"Last night Davor asked me to see the two of you, and the baby, out of Pilk," Nevik told me. "He assumes you'll go back to Vinx now that the danger is past, and you'll resume teaching."

So, I was being told to return to my old life. Just like that.

Nevik fumbled with something in his pocket. "He, uh, he also asked me to tell you he sends his love, along with this small gift."

He handed me a leather pouch and I pulled a pretty necklace out of it. I knew Davor hadn't bought such a thing for me.

"He said to tell you he'll visit you at your home as soon as he can."

I looked at him, the necklace dangling in my hand, and the same irrational anger I'd felt at the proprietor surfaced. I was tired of people not telling me the full truth.

"Is he still with the woman from Tolo, or has he moved on?"

Yes, my voice encouraged Nevik to be honest with me.

He sighed and looked unhappy, but he answered.

"I didn't realize you knew those details. Yes, she lives with him, but he's been telling me he grows tired of her. I suspect he's found her replacement; she just doesn't know it yet."

"That's oddly comforting." I had to laugh for the first time that morning. "Maybe she and I can start a club for women Davor has loved. I wonder how many members we'd have?"

"I'll ride with you ladies as far as the Gruen wall," Nevik said in reply. He and Ryalgar both looked uncomfortable as we left.

~ 12 ~

My New Life

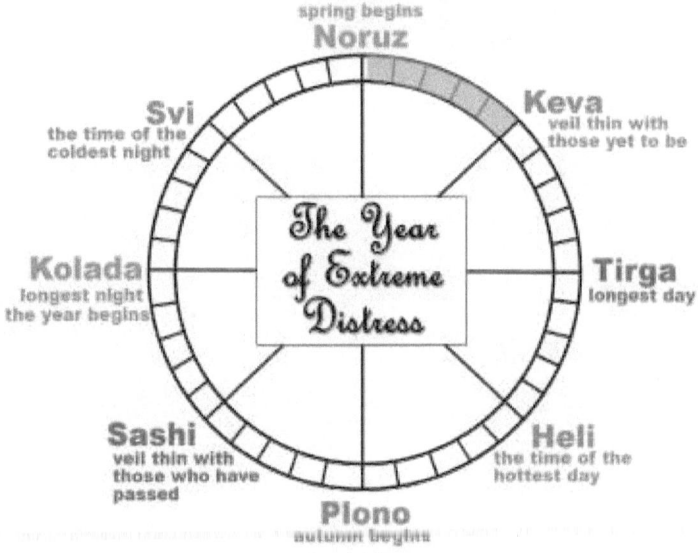

People always love the time between Noruz and Keva. Birdsong returns. The weather grows mild. The first flowers appear.

But in the Year of Extreme Distress, spring did more than fill us with hope. It served as a pause, a precious respite during which we enjoyed feeling normal as we complained about the little irritations of life and ignored the massive problems looming in the distance.

I felt fully alive again, now that I lived out on the open plains of Vinx where I could feel the wind blow and see the sun rise and set. I knew something inside me had held on to this land, keeping me from wanting to be a wife in Lev. Maybe I'd never be content living anywhere but Vinx.

The school hadn't expected me back until Keva, but they hadn't replaced me. My little ones suffered, crowded in with the more boisterous and advanced nine and ten-year-olds. The woman who ran the school liked the idea of my working a short shift in the morning and one again in the afternoon to give the youngest ones extra time and attention. The most responsible older girls would be allowed to take turns watching my baby while I taught.

Meanwhile, I'd become something of a celebrity. Sakina invited me to her parents' home for dinner so I could tell of my adventures. The other teachers and older students wanted to know about the home of the mysterious Velka and what it had been like living with them. Everyone held little Votto and cooed at him. Several older girls and three teachers confided in me that they loved seeing a woman allowed to teach after giving birth.

Not everyone agreed, though. Three of the teachers and several of the older students seemed disturbed by this exception to the rules. I guessed they felt I somehow threatened the grand order of things.

The parents of those I taught split along similar lines. Some went out of their way to tell me how glad they were to see me back. Others, including a few new mothers, barely spoke to me when they picked their children up. I felt certain my return to the school had been the topic of more than one heated discussion.

Other facets of my personal life must have entered into those conversations, too, because another change occurred. Before Votto's birth, the men of Vinx treated me with the proper respect given a married woman. Polite but never too personal. After my return, the men were friendlier. Sometimes, much friendlier. I had several offers to chop wood or make repairs around my home and a few went so far as to offer to be of service in any way at all. The inevitable you-know-what-I-mean look followed.

It made me uncomfortable. I was still married, even if I wasn't living with my husband. He served in the army during a time of turmoil and men in Vinx would normally have respected such a situation. It made me think the rumors went beyond "he doesn't live with her" and all the way to "he's cheating on her and everyone knows it, including her."

Most of these overly helpful men were married and even if their marriages weren't happy, I respected their matrimonial bonds and could ill afford to have their wives think otherwise. So I turned down every offer of masculine assistance with a polite but firm "no, thank you." If that didn't suffice I added, "My husband will be home soon and take care of all those things for me."

Although Votto slept well and fussed little, the combination of caring for him, my house, myself, and a bunch of lively seven and eight-year-olds twice a day wore me out. It would have been so *easy* to get both adults and children to cooperate with me and be done with it. But Ewalina had cautioned me against using my luski timbre to solve the minor problems of everyday life.

"On some level, people realize when they've been coerced. They don't like it, and if it happens often they won't like you, even if they don't fully understand why." She'd shrugged. "People aren't as foolish as they seem. All evidence to the contrary."

I'd ignored her warning while in Pilk but reconsidered my behavior at home. I knew I already walked a thin line, being allowed to work part-time and use older students for child care. Being allowed to work at all. Living alone as a married woman. I did not need the nice people of Vinx looking for reasons to dislike me. In fact, I needed them to be looking for reasons to like me *more*, particularly as rumors of my having a frightening power might start circulating once people at Ryalgar's practices noticed the bright orange hair under my scarf.

I resolved to keep even the slightest traces of the timbre out of my voice.

As the days grew warmer, the luskies and singers made plans to resume their practices despite the fear of injuries. We'd been lucky the first two times. Our thrown riders suffered no worse than bruises and a sprained wrist. The straw helped, of course, as did the skill of the farmhands. But we could ill afford to injure healthy young people by throwing them from horses. Could the animals throw off bags of sand instead?

I needed to confer with Celestine. Where was she these days?

Both twins had finished school and lived at home, and neither had a husband waiting in the wings. Olivine spent at least half her time in the artsy nichna of K'ba, painting and selling her artwork. Celestine split her time between K'ba, where she sang and performed with her psaltery, and Pilk, where many of the realm's better musicians made their home.

My parents realized my marriage with Davor would never last, and that Ryalgar was a Velka for life. Sulphur, who'd never had much in the way of boyfriends, would likely spend years in the Svadlu without marrying. As for the youngest two, everyone knew a frundle couldn't produce children, making it unlikely poor Iolite would ever have a husband. And Gypsum? Who knew what a rebel like her would do.

So, Mom must have pinned her hopes on the artistically talented Olivine and on the beautiful musician Celestine. How unfortunate. If I had to place a bet, it'd be that Olivine had an artist lover in K'ba and Celestine had a musician boyfriend in Pilk, and neither qualified as a prince.

I decided to take Votto to see his grandparents. He was nearly two-eighths of a year old and now he squirmed when I swaddled him close to me during a ride. He was a curious little guy, and he wanted to see the world. He also got heavier every day. I tried to adjust the contraption the Velka had made for me so he'd have more freedom to move and look around.

Mom saw me in the distance and yelled and waved. By the time I tethered Nutmeg, she had food and drinks ready. She took a fussy Votto from me and began to rock him. To my surprise, he quieted for her. I'd always known my mother didn't share the common female fondness for babies, but she made an exception for this little one.

My dad came in from the fields early, having seen me ride up, and we spent a pleasant evening together enjoying a spring sunset and sharing a meal of my mother's much-loved chicken pie. I learned they didn't expect Celestine or Olivine back for days. So over the rest of the ank break I napped, bathed, and cared for myself in ways I never could at home alone with a baby.

I dawdled as I packed to leave and a late afternoon spring storm blew in with a howling wind. The lightning and thunder

S. R. Cronin

scared Votto. I soothed his tears but couldn't imagine us riding Nutmeg home in such a squall.

"Stay with us through the next ank," my dad said. "I'll ride over to the school tomorrow before classes start, and let them know you and the child need a rest and you'll be back next ank. Your kids will be fine in the big class for six days."

He seemed so happy about having me and Votto around that I couldn't say no. So I didn't. Besides, staying for another ank made it certain I'd be able to confer with Celestine on our upcoming practices.

Over the next few days, I picked up in conversation that Ryalgar had agreed to help my father with something neither of my parents wanted to discuss with me.

When I asked my dad he said "Please don't try to guess. Just drop it. For me."

I agreed but I couldn't stop worrying.

Olivine was back at the farm by then, but she was preoccupied with her trainees and didn't want to speculate on where Ryalgar had gone.

"She sent word to me to hold the practice without her or Joli; I have no idea why Mom or Dad would know or care."

I moved on to my last resort. Mom.

"Coral. Why do you have to stick your nose into everything?"

"I don't. Stick my nose into everything. I just stick it into things involving the people I care about."

I noticed being a luski had enhanced my ability to stand up to my mom and I knew she didn't like the shifting balance of power between us.

"Has it ever occurred to you that you care about too many things?" she asked.

"I care about people, not things. And no, it has never occurred to me that I care about too many people."

I could tell I pushed her. Her face got that look, the one she'd had back when she slapped me for asking what a pruska was.

"Why won't you and Dad tell me where my sister is?" I wouldn't use my timbre on her, but I also wouldn't back down. "I care about Ryalgar. Where is she?"

"With the reczavy." My mother spat it out at me, almost like a slap.

90

Her answer made no sense. The reczavy were avant-garde people living on the fringes of society. They engaged in controversial sex. The more conservative in Ilaria condemned them as an unfortunate consequence of the promiscuity we permitted the tidzys around the holidays.

See. This is proof we need to reign in this behavior more. Look where it leads.

I knew Ryalgar's mind. She found intimacy with a stranger awkward and she felt at home with the Velka. She'd never join the reczavy.

"What's she doing there?"

Acquiescence showed in Mom's eyes as she finally told me the truth.

"Looking for Gypsum. We learned she dropped out of school two eighths ago, and her friends thought this is where she'd gone."

This made sense. It explained my father's embarrassment, too.

"Why send Ryalgar after her?"

"To see if it's true. To make sure she's okay. To beg her to leave."

I nodded and said no more. Once you have the facts, caring about people can mean walking away from further conversation.

Celestine arrived at the farm late in the ank, and I noticed both of my parents' frustration with her. She'd had been gone more than she'd been around, and had done a poor job of reassuring my parents as to her whereabouts. But she and I now shared a bond we'd never had. We could combine our vocal skills into something important.

I suggested we try to learn more, and she jumped at the chance. Olivine's group had left by then, and the barn was ours. It was full of bugs, mice, squirrels, a few cows, some cats, a goat, an old owl, a nest of swallows, a couple of lizards, a few rabbits, and some harmless garden snakes.

"What do animals want to do?"

We came up with a short list. Eat. Drink. Sleep. Screw. Amuse themselves. Groom themselves. Make themselves more comfortable.

"I think this covers humans, too," she said. I had to laugh.

We made ourselves a sort of sitting area in the barn, setting blankets, a couple of stools, and a small table amidst the hay. Then, over the next three days, as we ate, drank, and visited in the barn, we tried to get every creature interested in anything on our list. We discovered the insects and spiders could care less about us, and the snakes and lizards weren't far behind. We didn't impress the swallows but the old owl was susceptible. The rest of the animals responded to various degrees, each preferring some commands over others. The goat would munch on anything within reach within seconds, while the rabbits would start to have sex after only a few notes. It took no effort to get the cats to groom themselves, and was almost impossible to get a squirrel to do so.

"I don't know how this helps, but it sure is fascinating," Celestine said. "The smarter the creature, the more susceptible it is."

"I agree. It bodes well for working with horses. Animals don't get much smarter."

"We need to get back to practicing with them."

"Yes, but we also need to stop throwing people off before someone breaks a leg. Or worse. Here's what I think we should do."

She and I spent a happy afternoon plotting out ways to practice without putting anyone in danger, and ways to use fire better, and how to simulate the noise of an invasion. Now that Ryalgar was busy elsewhere, we got excited about our ideas because we thought we were in charge of these practices. It seemed reasonable, but we were about to learn we were wrong.

~ 13 ~

Another Person in Charge

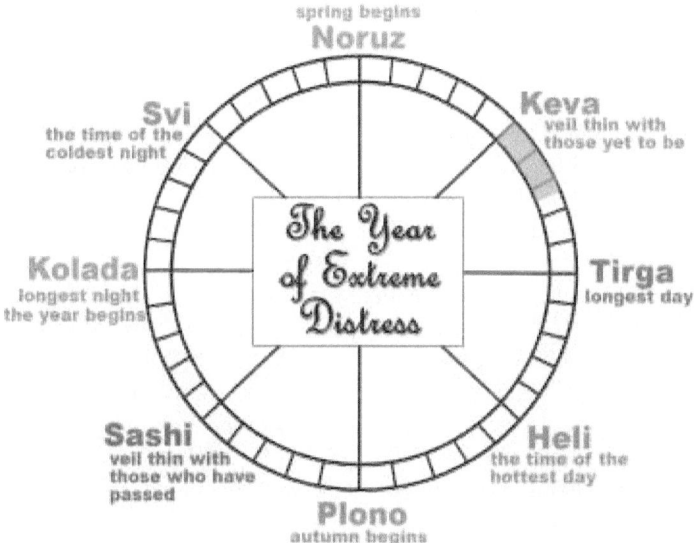

I'd been back at school for an eighth when an unknown horsewoman rode up to my cottage one evening. Days had grown long again with Keva past, and I sat on the porch rocking Votto and singing to him, hoping he'd fall asleep before dusk so I'd have time to tend to the flowers growing in my yard.

From a distance the rider reminded me of Ewalina, another tall, thin, and unknown woman who'd ridden up to my doorstep long ago. That had ended well.

"Hello." I greeted her with a wave. Any similarity to Ewalina ended as she got closer. This woman was younger and wore her brown hair wound into an uncommonly severe bun on her head.

"Who sent you?" I asked, hoping for news of a friend or relative.

She looked surprised I would question her. "Your sister, Ryalgar."

She dismounted from an excellent mare, young, large, and worth a good bit of coin.

"Your sister has put me in charge of you."

What? I was in charge of me, even though I had a husband who believed otherwise. I hardly needed my sister's friends deciding they ran my life too.

"I'm here to inform you of your training schedule for the summer, and when and how I'll need you. Here. I've written it all out so there'll be no confusion. Read it now so you can ask questions if you have them."

I stared at her. I didn't know where to begin, given her rudeness.

"Ryalgar said you could do this?" It was the nicest thing I could think of.

"Your sister and I have an arrangement. We're co-leading the Velka's efforts to stop the Mongols."

I didn't believe that. Ryalgar wasn't inclined to co-lead with anyone, and no one knew it better than me. If she'd been forced into this, she'd have gone out of her way to let me know about it.

I gave the woman a skeptical look. She tethered up her horse while we talked, and settled her bony backside into my other porch chair, uninvited.

"Please. Have a seat." If she caught my undertone, she ignored it. "My name is Coral..."

"I know your name."

"Yes, but I don't know yours."

She smiled as though she found me amusing, but said nothing. I *had* asked her name, by offering her mine. Didn't she understand how people interacted? I glared at her. "What's your name?"

She bristled at my scowl. "Let me warn you, I'm well versed in the powers of luskies, so don't try anything with me."

Ahh. That explained her brusqueness. She feared me.

"I wouldn't dream of it. I have manners." I gave her a smile sweet enough, I hoped, to make her wonder if I coaxed her. I did, but only a tiny bit. I wanted to know what she could detect.

"My manners aren't so good after a long ride. Forgive me. My name is Hana."

I glanced over the paper she'd given me, with dates and places listed in a bold hand.

"I have to work around my teaching schedule and, as Votto grows, I'll need someone to watch him, too."

"I've accounted for the teaching part, and it's a trivial matter for me to bring someone to watch Votto, and any other little ones, if we have to. Can you do this?"

I looked at the times and places she'd listed. I could.

"I'll be there. I'd like to talk to you about something else before you leave. Celestine and I are concerned about injuries. We want to look into using bags of sand instead of riders."

"Of course we'll use bags of sand. We're not throwing any more healthy Ilarians to the ground. And we'll only bring in the Reczavy at the end. As we move into the dry heat of summer, we don't need to be starting fires where we can't control them. Plus, I'd as soon deal with those people as little as possible. Point forward, our group will be sensible and well-disciplined."

I caught the implication that it hadn't been up until now.

"Fine."

I waited. Nothing happened. I *had* clearly said "before you leave" but she continued to sit in her chair, showing no signs of getting up. I hated to be rude but ...

"I need to get my little one to bed. Feel free to water your horse *before you leave*."

She looked surprised. "It's a long ride here and it's late. I thought at the least I could sleep on your floor."

I'd been raised to be hospitable, and even though my home was small and my child young, I'd have offered most people a spot for the night. But my instincts said *don't trust her* and I valued those instincts more every day.

"I'm sorry. I don't have the space and, with a baby this small, I don't let strangers in my house. I'm sure you understand."

She didn't look like she understood at all, and something in her demeanor gave me the impression she'd expected me to offer her my bed. Who was this woman?

"You've enough light left to get anywhere in Vinx. There's a wonderful little inn near the market stalls. Have a safe ride." I gave her a wave as I walked inside and closed the door behind me.

I worried she'd follow me in. If she thought she had a right to do so, I knew nothing I could say would make her leave. But *she* didn't know that. Her fear of me made me think she had a more grandiose idea of what a luski could do. She'd learn otherwise as she worked with us, but, for now, I saw the advantage in letting her think my abilities were stronger than they were.

I didn't have to dwell on Hana for long. A few days later Olivine visited, and a few days after that, Davor arrived.

I sat on the porch nursing Votto to sleep as he rode up, still hoping to tend to the flower patches I hadn't found time for yet. He rode in like he was coming home, without the wave and yell of greeting given by a visitor. I noticed it.

He tethered his horse and brushed the dust off his clothes as he walked over to me.

"Hi, Coral. It's good to be home."

Really? I'd probably spent a hundred and fifty nights in this house and he'd spent less than ten. Home?

"Has something happened to your home in Pilk?"

"Sort of." I waited. He said no more. "Did you sell it?"

"I never owned it, honey cakes. I rented the place because I always thought I'd build a home in Lev, on my family's land. Someday."

"Of course. Did your landlord kick you out, then?"

He laughed. "No one kicks out a Mozdol. I chose to leave, if you must know." His sigh was long and sad. "Remember the woman from Tolo I mentioned?"

"The one you want to marry after you divorce me? Yes, I remember her." He missed the sarcasm in my voice.

"She and I are not as well-suited as I once thought. My job is part political, you know, and I need someone with a certain amount of polish. Someone refined, who can enhance my reputation in Pilk, not destroy it. So she and I won't be marrying."

I had no idea what a soon-to-be ex-wife was supposed to say to that. *Good?* or *You poor dear?* or *Do you want me now instead?* or simply *Tell me what happened?*

I didn't say any of those.

"They are stubborn, those women from Tolo. I'll give them that. When we discussed how it was time for us to part ways, she wouldn't go. I mean, she refused to pack up her things and leave. I suppose I could have thrown her out by force, or called the Svadlu in to arrest her, but either would have looked horrible for me, and she knew it. So what could I do? She gets the place through Tirga, longer if she wants to keep paying the rent. Me, I have to find some decent lodging, and that takes time. Pilk Center is so overcrowded these days. Suitable rentals are not easy to come by.

"I see. So you'll be living here until then?"

"Mostly. I have a few buddies who can put me up when I have to be in Pilk, but yes. This house is my home for now."

Great. Hadn't Nevik said Davor found a new woman? I guessed the replacement lady was thoroughly refined, yet didn't have lodging to share.

"It's small, but hey, we'll make the best of it, right?" He gave me his most charming grin. "I could handle eating your cooking for a while. You do still cook, don't you?"

I nodded. The truth was I often didn't bother, opting for apples, cheeses, and bread I bought from the market. Experience showed Davor would not only fix things up around the house, but he'd also bring fresh food with him. Good food.

While he chopped wood, I could make dinner. It wouldn't be that bad. As an added plus, his presence would stop some of the tongue-wagging in Vinx, and discourage the last few would-be suitors to back off. I was willing to bet he'd tire of the arrangement before I did.

Davor stayed at the house three out of five nights that first ank. We shared the bed because there was no other place to sleep. Votto and I took the side against the wall, and I turned towards Votto and nursed him the first night as Davor came to bed. I hoped it made my lack of interest clear. Whether it did or not, he made no move towards me, sleeping soundly in his clothes and remaining on his side of the bed.

After the first night, the smell of a man nearby wakened urges I thought were gone, at least as far as Davor was concerned. I knew I was as entitled to seek my pleasure with him as he was with me, but my instincts told me the mere suggestion of desire would unnecessarily complicate my future. I refrained, and if he had any similar thoughts, he refrained too. I suppose having a baby in the bed with us helped.

My first practice session under Hana's command, if that was the right word for it, was scheduled for the ank-break after Davor arrived. I hoped he had plans, but no, he'd be around all three days.

"What could *you* possibly be practicing with the Velka that would be of any use?" he asked as I prepared to go. I was excited because he'd offered to watch Votto if I left the baby well fed and I returned before noon. My body ached for the freedom of riding Nutmeg at a gallop, and I hurried to make my exit before he changed his mind.

"Why, of course, I'm included because I'm a …"

Pruck. I'd never told Davor I was a luski. I suppose Ryalgar could have told Nevik …. but Nevik could hardly afford to discuss anything Ryalgar told him with anyone.

Did I want to tell him now and get it out of the way? Did I want to tell him ever? I wasn't sure of the answer to the last question, but I knew I didn't want to complicate getting out the door now. So I lied. No, that's not quite true. I told him several truths that in no way answered his question.

"They're working on ways to control horses. I'm good with animals. I grew up on a farm. I rode every day to teach school, remember?"

"Hmm. That's not a bad approach when your attackers are all mounted, I guess. I hope you ladies and all your tricks are wildly successful. See you by noon, honey cakes."

Off I rode, as fast as I could, with the wind dancing through my long hair and the sun on my face. I even screamed a few times, as loud as possible, because there was no baby to wake and it felt so good.

Hana did have Ryalgar's flair for organizing, I had to give her that. She also had a more cautious approach with people and animals. Despite our rocky interaction at my home, I had no quarrel with how she conducted our practice session.

We had a dozen horses who'd never been exposed to our luski-singer entreaties, a couple of dozen singers, and six of the luskies we'd recruited. I noticed all but two of the other luskies opted to not wear their masks with this smaller and safer group, so I didn't either. It was easier to work without the silly thing on my face and a scarf on my head.

Hana paired each luski with four singers and gave each team two horses and two heavy bags of sand. Then she told us to figure out what we could.

She walked around observing and asking questions, stopping us all several times to share bits that one group or another had discovered. We learned and gained confidence in what we could do. She had little to say to me, but she said nothing hostile. I concluded she took her responsibilities seriously and wanted no trouble. I was all for that.

Only one thing bothered me about the entire session. Hana seemed to lack curiosity about the singers and their role. Most of her questions concerned the luskies and exactly how they did what they did. Did she think she could teach herself to become a luski?

I wondered if I could find a way to visit my sister in the forest. Soon. I wanted to talk to Ryalgar and learn why she'd agreed to share her responsibilities with Hana. I really wanted to share my observations about Hana's fascination with luskies. Then again, maybe Ryalgar already knew.

~ 14 ~

More Good Sense Than Most

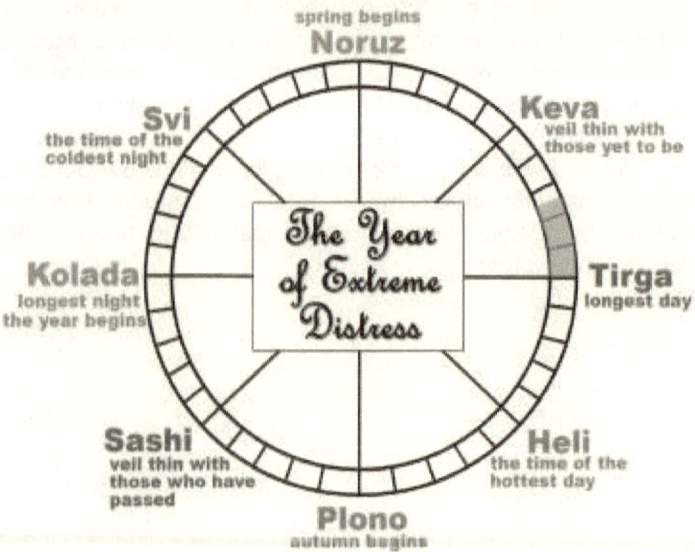

One morning on the following ank-break, Sulphur came to visit. Davor had left the day before, saying he'd be in Pilk the next few days. I reassured Sulphur with that news as she tended to her horse. She laughed.

"I picked this day to come because I knew he had big meetings going on in Pilk. But really, he's gotten used to me, and he doesn't treat me so poorly anymore."

She looked better than she had when she'd visited half a year ago, back when she was desperate to join the Svadlu. She even looked better than when I'd seen her in the forest before Votto was born, when we argued about who should be protecting Ilari.

I guessed being a Svadlu agreed with her.

We exchanged pleasantries while I brought some breakfast wine and pastries out to the porch. I sensed she struggled with something on her mind. As she took her first gulp, she came out with it.

"I came here because I need someone I can tell a secret to."

What was this about? Military secrets? Davor? Svadlu betrayals?

"I need someone I can trust."

"You can trust me." I said it without thinking, which is always an unwise thing to do.

"Iolite's left school. No one knows it yet. She finished her studies early and now she's somewhere safe where she shouldn't be disturbed."

"Why? Why not?" Given the various frailties that came with Iolite's condition, my parents would be worried sick if they knew she was anywhere but on campus.

"Especially by Mom and Dad."

I didn't have to reply. Sulphur saw my horrified look.

"She's working with the Svadlu and being incredibly brave, Coral. And this is her choice. No one else in the family knows, but if something happened to me … I could get sent into a skirmish, and things could go poorly. I want you to keep Iolite's secret safe. Just in case."

Goat scump. I didn't want to know this secret.

"I can't bear this," I said. "I'm too worried about her."

"And I'm worried about you," Sulphur replied. "You and everyone else with a part in this inane defense scheme."

"Do you know what part I'm playing?"

"Celestine and I talked. She told me you can do something downright frightening with your voice, something most people consider to be no more than a scary myth."

"I'm not a scary person."

"Coral, you're the least scary person I know. If anyone in this whole realm should be allowed to boss people around with their voice, it's you. I just wouldn't want too many people to know. I made Celestine promise not to tell anyone else."

"I'm being careful. Davor doesn't know. My friend Sakina is the only teacher at school who I've told. Dad knows because he gets us the horses for us to practice with, but even he thought I should wait to tell Mom. How do think Mom will handle it?"

She winced. "I'll keep your secret, from Davor, Mom, and everyone else. You'll keep mine?"

We raised our goblets in a salute. We had a deal.

Davor's ongoing presence accomplished much. The woodpile grew high, the cupboard stayed full, and he and I ate well. I also got more smiles from the mothers of those I taught, and fewer smiles from the fathers. Given my situation, that was for the best.

Only one gentleman, married and with an eight-year-old daughter, continued to eye me with interest. I avoided his gaze. My fondness for his daughter Chessa made it particularly awkward. Earlier in the year, the mother brought the child to school. She was a quiet woman who seemed sad most of the time, though she'd always been friendly to me. I hadn't seen her in a while and I hoped this man didn't contrive to bring his daughter so he could interact with me.

As Tirga approached, I noticed a change. I hardly saw the father either, because Chessa spent most nights at the school. Parents seldom did that, preferring to use the option for emergencies. I decided to ask the little girl why.

"I haven't seen your mother in a while. How is she doing?"

"Not good. Daddy says she's too sick to take me to school anymore, so that's why he has to bring me."

"Oh dear. Did he say what kind of sickness she has?"

"Not good. He keeps calling it 'not good.'"

My heart melted for this man I'd casually classed as annoying.

"Has she seen a doctor?"

"Lots of them. Daddy keeps bringing people to the house. Doctors, Velka. They all agree. It's 'not good.'"

I couldn't believe I'd been so insensitive.

An ank-break began that day, so all the children had to go home. I made a point of seeking out her father as classes let out.

Our wheat ripened early that year, so I knew we'd be taking our two- ank break for harvest soon after Tirga.

He ran up to me, apparently relieved I gave him eye contact for once. Now that I didn't feel I had to avoid his gaze, I took a longer look at him.

He was younger than I'd thought; he must have married early and had Chessa soon after. He had a serious face, not sad like his wife's but more like he'd been carrying worries for too many years. His dark eyes held an unusual intensity, and had an almost metallic glint to them, as if they were made of iron ore.

"I've been wanting to talk to you, but you always seem so busy," he said.

"I'm sorry, but by the end of the day, I'm tired. I have a small baby of my own you know."

That amused him. "The whole nichna knows. Look, I don't know if my daughter has told you, but my wife is ill. She's failing and there seems to be nothing we can do for her."

"I only learned of this today. I had no idea."

"Yes, well, it's happened fast. She was healthy at Noruz. We never expected anything like this."

"No one ever does."

"We moved here from Faroo a few years ago. It's a long story, but we left with both of our families angry at us so we've no one nearby and no one coming to help. Chessa adores you; she talks about you all the time. I, I don't know how to ask this, but I don't want her there when her mother passes. I think it would be so hard for one her age, you know? Old enough to understand, but not really, and no other relatives around to comfort her. I wondered if …. I know this is a huge favor … I wondered if Chessa could visit you, maybe spend a night or two. When it gets near the end."

Oh my. That's what the man had been trying to speak with me about? I felt like the worst human ever.

"Of course she can. My place isn't big, but I'll make room. She's welcome whenever. For as long as you need. I'm so sorry."

His smile was genuine. And appreciative.

"My name is Janx. If it hasn't, uh, happened already, maybe could I send her home with you when we break for harvest? I could bring along some clothes and things when I bring her to school?"

So, this was going to be more than a few days, wasn't it?

I didn't know how I'd finesse this with Davor, or with Hana, or with my training schedule, but I'd think of something.

Davor returned to the cottage that evening with excellent news. He'd managed to find a new place in Pilk, better than the one he'd had. I didn't ask for details other than how soon he'd be moving.

"Aren't you going to miss me? Even a little?"

"I will." There was no reason not to tell him the truth. He made for a decent roommate, handling more than his share of the chores. In many ways, having him there was easier than being alone. Now that we weren't really husband and wife, or even lovers, we'd kind of become friends.

He'd even become a passable father, having grown more comfortable caring for Votto. I'd noticed his affection developing for the baby and, maybe more importantly, the affection the baby developed for him. He must have been thinking along the same lines.

"I'm gonna miss the little guy, you know."

"And he'll miss you. You should come back and spend time with him. It'd be good for both of you."

"You wouldn't mind if I dropped in just to play with him?"

"You're his father."

"I wanted to talk to you about that. Once this Mongol invasion is handled, and we're divorced, you're going to want to remarry, aren't you?"

"I don't know. I like my independence, but I always saw myself having a family. Not as big as the one I came from, of course, but, you know, a few kids."

"Remarrying is the best way to do that."

"I agree."

"So, this new guy. He'd become Votto's dad?"

"His step-dad, yes. Don't worry, I wouldn't consider marrying a man who wouldn't love and care for Votto as if he was his own."

"Yeah, okay. But then, I don't get to be his dad anymore?"

"You're always his dad. Nothing can change that, and I'm not going to raise him with a lie. He'll know who you are, and he'll know we didn't stay together, but, okay, he probably won't know why. Children don't need those kinds of details. He will know what his true relationship with my new husband is, though, if there is one."

"So I could still come to see him?"

"Of course you could. You'd have to be a monster before I'd feel otherwise. Better yet, as he gets older he could come to visit you. Spend time at your place. Maybe even...." A sigh escaped before I could draw it back in. "Maybe even get to know that new refined wife of yours and be a part of whatever sort of family the two of you make."

"You know something? For a lady who cries so varmin much, you've got more sense than most. I could have done far worse picking a girl to get pregnant."

I don't know why, but his words sent me straight to the edge of tears. *Pruck it.* I turned away so he couldn't see my face.

He stayed through the ank-break, though I don't think he'd been planning to. Having good-bye sex with him crossed my mind more than once and, based on the occasional looks we exchanged, I suspected it crossed his. Perhaps he struggled with faithfulness to his new polished lady of Pilk. Did he feel loyalty of that sort? I really didn't know. He hadn't felt it with me.

I couldn't imagine I'd ever be foolish enough to fall back in love with him, but a little passion under the covers while Votto slept would be one of the few ways it could happen. Bad idea. So I kept my distance.

I attended an uneventful practice session under Hana's watchful eye, and he played with Votto a lot for a few days. As he prepared to leave on the afternoon before the eve of Tirga, he kissed me on the cheek, the way one would a sister.

"Take good care of my little guy. Like you always do."

I watched him ride away with a bittersweet melancholy. I'd miss him, even though I was glad to see him go.

~ 15 ~

What Sort of Monster

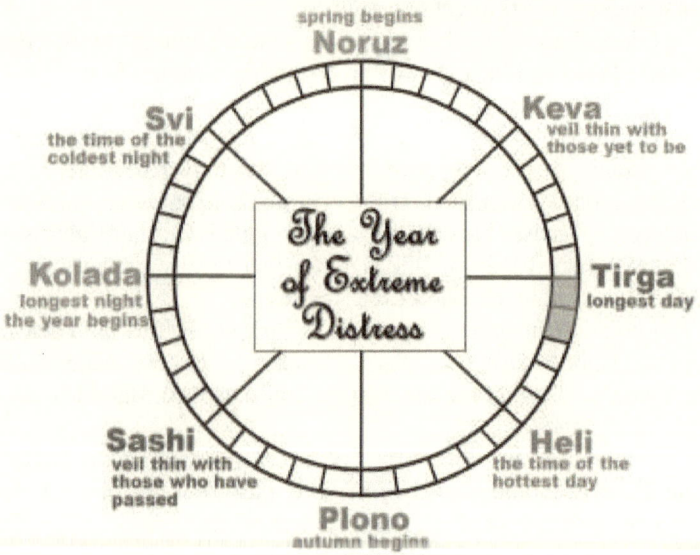

spring begins
Noruz

Svi
the time of the
coldest night

Keva
veil thin with
those yet to be

*The Year
of Extreme
Distress*

Kolada
longest night
the year begins

Tirga
longest day

Sashi
veil thin with
those who have
passed

Heli
the time of the
hottest day

Plono
autumn begins

Chessa came home with me four days later. She spent a night at home first, presumably to say goodbye to her mother, though I doubted her father presented it that way. He brought her to school with enough things to last her indefinitely, gave her a long hug as tears rolled down his cheeks, and turned her over to me, muttering "I'm sorry, I don't know how long this will be …"

"Send word?" I asked. He nodded, too choked up to speak.

I'd always found Chessa adorable, and she seemed equally fond of me, but as her father left she had that child's sense of when things aren't right.

"Why won't Daddy pick me up today?" she demanded. "I need to go home to be with Mommy." And she did. Yet, her father wanted to spare her pain, and he probably wanted some time alone with his wife, and then time to grieve. I couldn't begrudge him any of those.

"Your daddy says your mommy needs rest now. Come. We'll have fun at my house. You'll get to play with my baby. He's starting to crawl. It's so cute."

She looked torn. Getting to play with a crawling baby was a treat, but not tempting enough.

"No. I want to go home to be with my mommy." She talked louder. If she got more upset, other children and teachers would intervene. Neither she nor I needed that.

"Hush," I told her. "Hush." I used the oldest mothers' timbre in the world, the voice to soothe a distraught child, as I encouraged her to find the calm within herself. "It'll be okay."

"No. It won't." She looked at me with defiance in slate-colored eyes identical to her father's and I knew the truth of what I'd been told. If she didn't wish to be soothed, I could say nothing to quiet her.

Then, as she stared at me, her eyes softened. She found the calm inside herself with no help from me.

"Daddy asked you to do this, didn't he?"

"Yes, Chessa. He did. He loves you and loves your mommy, and he's trying to take care of both of you as best he can."

She nodded and started to cry. "I don't want my mommy to die."

"Oh sweetheart, who said she's going to die?"

"Everyone. They all whisper it so I won't hear, but I do. I know what 'it's not good' does to people."

Adults can be so stupid.

"Will she die before I see her again?"

And one more stupid thing is to lie to a child who knows better.

"Probably. Your daddy asked me to watch you because now he has to work harder to take care of her. You want him to do that, right?"

Her answer was to throw her arms around my waist, hide her head of shiny black hair deep in my skirt, and wail. We had plenty of people noticing us now. I ignored them and patted her head. Then, I let myself cry with her. I know, I know. Crying along isn't always the best response, but on that day, it was.

Some people will intervene if a child is in tears, others will stand and stare. But if a grown woman cries, people get away fast. I knew; I'd cried plenty at school over the past year. The crowd dispersed, and I bet many of them guessed the little girl comforted me.

"Come on," I whispered to her. "Let's get to class and show everybody how brave we can be. Okay?"

She nodded, and we did.

The following ank-break I had to take both Chessa and Votto with me to the luski practice. I hoped Chessa would keep an eye on Votto, and not ask too many questions. She did neither. I could tell she made the other luskies nervous; two more put their masks back on once it was obvious the little girl tried to figure out what they did.

"This isn't working," Hana said.

"You told me you could provide child care."

"And I can. But you haven't needed it the last two times, so today I didn't bring anyone. And I've never seen this other child before. Who is she?"

"A student of mine. I'm helping out her family."

Hana looked to the sky as if pleading with the spirits for patience.

"You have serious work to do here. This is no time for you to take on charity projects. What is the matter with you?"

Something about Hana brought out my most argumentative side.

"Nothing is the matter with me. Next time have child care like you promised, and we won't have a problem."

"Are you using the timbre with me?" I could hear the irritation in her voice.

I hadn't been. "Maybe." I said, watching her anger grow. This woman had a problem with what luskies could do. She had a problem with not being sure she was in charge.

As the second sister to Ryalgar, I understood that dynamic. Don't get me wrong, Ryalgar was far more likable than this lady, but she preferred to be in full control, too. I'd spent years learning how to hold my own against such a woman.

"You'll never know when I'm using it," I said. "Best not to piss me off."

She turned towards the other luskies. I suppose she wondered if they'd overheard our discussion.

"You'll never know when they're using it either."

I knew there was a bit of a taunt in my voice. I wanted it there.

She glared at me and walked away.

After practice, Celestine caught up with me.

"Hey, big sis. What's with you and the lady in charge?"

I shrugged. "She has some issues to work out. How come none of you singers are the least bit afraid of us? Are you sure you people aren't all luskies too?"

She knew I joked, but she answered like I didn't.

"Well, we sort of are, in that we know the power of sound. We use it to evoke emotion all the time. The sorrow of a flute. The drumbeat of war. The pleading love of a softly plucked string. How can you be scared of your own language?" Then she added, "Hana is a little scared of all of us, isn't she?"

"I think so. She's pretty fascinated by us, too, though. What do you think she's up to?"

Celestine laughed. "You're so paranoid. I don't think she's up to anything, other than trying to make us better at throwing the people who want to kill us off of their horses. That's a good thing, so stop worrying. She is doing a decent job, and you should give her a break."

"I suppose. Maybe she doesn't like me because I'm Ryalgar's sister."

Celestine gave me a strange look.

"I'm Ryalgar's sister, too."

"Right. Of course." *What was I thinking?*

"And she seems to like me fine. Maybe ...."

I gave Celestine a don't-say-it look, but she said it anyway.

"Maybe *you're* the problem. Just saying."

What were sisters for, if not for pointing out things like that?

The summer turned unusually hot and still, and the winds that cooled off the plains of Vinx barely blew. The next day I left early to avoid the heat, riding with both Chessa and Votto on Nutmeg as we set off for my folk's farm. I knew harvest had started, and my father would have little time for me, but I could visit with my mother, and perhaps distract Chessa with the outing. Votto had gotten the hang of crawling, and I couldn't turn my back on him now. Having another set of eyes on him would be helpful, too.

My real goal, though, was to learn where Olivine was and arrange a way to see her, either at the farm or elsewhere. Of the seven of us, she'd always been the least emotional, perhaps because painting meant more to her than any crisis in our family. Sometimes I envied her detachment.

When you're having problems with one sister, that's what you do. You involve another sister. I needed Olivine's objectivity in figuring out if Celestine was right about Hana.

Mom prepared lunch for the workers and didn't see me ride up. I'm sure my surprise visit flustered her and having a strange child with me didn't help. Good thing a cute baby can ease any awkward situation. Mom and I both used Votto to avoid other topics as she cooed at him and asked after every detail of his well-being.

She pretty much ignored Chessa, which I found discourteous, but Chessa either didn't notice or didn't care. I suspected our farmhouse was grander than any home she'd ever been in. After she asked Mom if she could walk around and look at things if she didn't touch any of them, my mother softened a little and agreed. She asked with such politeness. After that, Chessa entertained herself.

I learned I'd just missed Olivine, but she planned to be back the first day of the next ank-break to hold an archery practice. Then, I helped my mother serve lunch to Dad and the workers, and she softened a little more. She'd always appreciated my helpfulness. After we'd eaten, I fed Votto while she pulled out some old dolls and gave them to Chessa to play with. With Chessa occupied, Votto asleep in my arms, and everyone else back in the fields, she and I could no longer avoid each other.

"You've changed," she said. "Perhaps marriage? Motherhood? Your career in teaching?"

She was right, I had. But I wondered how she saw it.

"In what way, Mom?"

She stood, while I sat holding Votto. Mom had always had a regal posture, with the height and full body that made a woman imposing. She looked down on me now.

"You're colder. More argumentative."

Okay. I hoped she'd say I was better at standing up for myself, but I guess she saw it differently.

"Maybe it's all the time you've spent with Ryalgar lately," mom added. "She always was more confrontational with me."

Votto stirred in my arms and I stood up, thanking him silently for his good timing. "I'm going to go lay him on your bed."

When I got back she surprised me by wanting to continue the conversation. This time I leaned against the wall, so I could look her in the eye.

"What exactly is it your sister has you doing with this Mongol thing?" she asked.

"What has she told you?"

"She says you're good with horses. I suppose you are, you're great with Nutmeg. She's got Celestine and other musicians trying to get these animals to do what she wants, and you're helping out."

"That's kind of true." I could have left it there. I probably should have. But I didn't.

"Do you know what a luski is, Mom?"

She sucked in her breath. "Some make-believe monster used to scare children."

"No, she's a woman, usually a woman, who can control people with her voice. Sometimes. A little." I cocked my head to one side. "Do you think luskies are real?"

"Certainly not."

I smiled. "I am one."

She stared at me as if I'd grown horns out of the top of my head, like one of the goats in the barn. "That's ridiculous." She turned as if to leave the room, not wanting to spend time on such nonsense.

I didn't want to demonstrate. I knew, deep down, she'd never forgive me if I did. So I just said "Maybe. Ryalgar thinks I'm one, at any rate, and it's how she's using me to help."

"Well, putting that sort of nonsense in your head would certainly explain the changes I've noticed," she said looking at me over her shoulder. "I'll have words with Ryalgar about this." I supposed she would.

Votto started to cry, and I ran into the bedroom to scoop him up before it occurred to him to crawl to the edge of the bed. I kissed him on the forehead to thank him for rescuing me.

"We'd best be going."

"Of course. Let me help you gather your things."

I'd already said good-bye to Dad; Mom got me packed up in record time. I knew how she worked, though. She'd think more about the luski thing after I was gone. She'd start to remember a few times when, maybe, it could have made sense. She'd ask a few questions. She'd probably confront poor Dad, and he'd confess that he'd known for a while.

Then she'd be mad at us all because no one had told her sooner. Then she'd figure out why we hadn't. Then she'd want to talk to me and tell me it was okay and she still loved me no matter what sort of monster I was.

I hoped we'd get to that point before Kolada.

~ 16 ~

Getting to Know Each Other

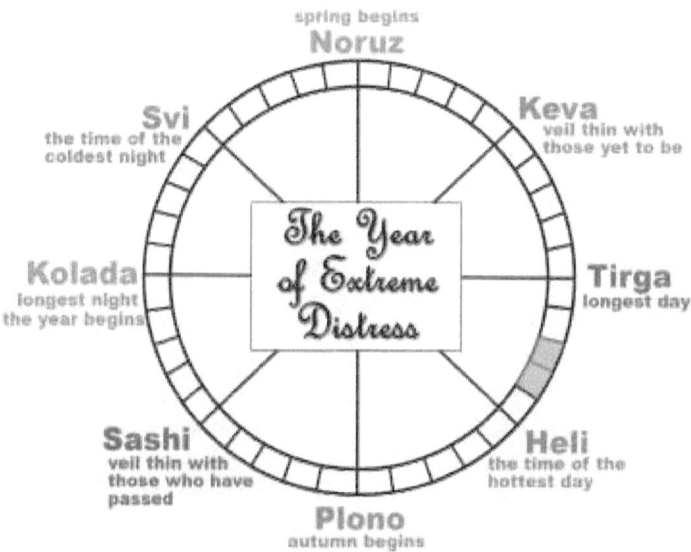

When Chessa and I arrived back at my cottage, a note from her father sat scrunched under the door. "Please bring Chessa home soon." I read it and looked at her. She knew, in that way kids do.

"It happened. Didn't it?"

"I think so. Your daddy says he needs you. Let's get you home."

She was calm, almost a sleep-walker, as she put her things into her bag. When she thought I wasn't looking, she pulled one of the small cloth dolls from my parents' house out from inside her dress and put it with her other things. Had she stolen it and hidden it in her clothes? I considered confronting her, then decided she had enough to deal with. She could keep the toy for now.

I put some grapes, bread, and smoked meat in a bag so she'd have something for dinner. Then I got us back on Nutmeg, thankful Votto enjoyed riding as much as I did. I hoped he'd never outgrow it.

When I helped her off my mare outside of her home, Chessa whispered "Can I stay with you again sometime?"

"Of course you can."

"Good. Thank your mother for the doll. Tell her I nursed her when we rode, just like you nurse Votto."

Janx saw us dismount and came outside, his face red and his eyes bleary. Family should be around to help under these circumstances. How could I leave this man alone?

"Your wife?"

He nodded. "I've gotten to know my neighbors better, with the practices we're having." He made a sound somewhere between a laugh, a cough, and a sob. "Learning how to capture Mongols is one way to make friends. But ... they came to help me. We, we buried her in a beautiful spot. I'll take Chessa there tomorrow. I wanted her last memories of mother to be ..."

He leaned on his porch rail as though he hadn't the strength to stand unsupported.

"I understand. Can I help somehow? I've brought food. I could put out a meal for you before I leave."

"Please," Chessa answered. He didn't say anything but he didn't have to. As I laid out the food I doubted he'd eat but I hoped she would.

"I'll check on you tomorrow if that's okay."

He nodded.

Then I remembered. With the on-going harvest break, Hana had scheduled another luski practice in the morning and warned us it would probably go all day. She'd been right when she said I didn't need a charitable project right now. But, what were we fighting for if we couldn't be bothered to care for each other? I'd find a way to take a break and check in on Chessa.

Something felt different when I got to the practice the next morning. Votto had needed a last-minute diaper change and I arrived late. An apology formed on my lips when I noticed there were no singers, no farmhands, and no horses.

The luskies all sat along a bench, at least twenty of them, probably every luski still willing to help. Half had removed their masks. Ewalina had hers off, the better for me to see the worry on her face.

"Glad you could make it," Hana said as I walked in. I heard her sarcasm. "I've instructed everyone to remove their face coverings. A few hesitate, but I trust they'll comply. I'm glad to see you didn't bother to put yours on."

I'd left my mask at home in my rush to get out of the door after Votto's delay, but she didn't need to know that. When I sat on the end of the bench with the others and didn't respond, she ignored me and addressed the group.

"I've long suspected you can do more than you let on. I don't blame you. Nobody wants to frighten their neighbors. However, we must trust each other. Today I want to get to know more about each of you, and I want you all to get to know more about each other. We're going to share stories. What have you been able to do in the past with your voice? What surprised you? What did you find challenging? I want every member of this group to help the others, so each of you can become the best luski you can be."

"As a matter of custom, we don't share personal information," Ewalina said. "It helps us maintain our anonymity. Whenever we leave each other, we promise to part as strangers."

"Well now, custom doesn't hold here, does it? We're about to go to war, ladies and gentleman. The old way of doing things is gone."

Several of the people exchanged uncomfortable looks. Those of us on the ends scooted to the edges to give everyone more room.

"I don't see why," an older woman sitting at the other end said. "I was promised we wouldn't be doing anything involving people, or I'd never have agreed to this."

"Me neither," said the man from Tolo. "She," he pointed to Ewalina, "she said you needed us to help a bunch of singers get horses to throw their riders. I got no problem doing that. I'll help you all day. But that's all I signed up for."

"That's all you *thought* you signed up for," Hana said. "In fact, we need you for more. Ilari needs you for more."

"Like what?" Several luskies said it.

"Like, we're looking into using you to get the Mongols to follow the wrong road. To get them to pause for the night to let their horses graze. To get them to be more docile once we capture them. You luskies have a wealth of uses, a potentially huge part to play in our success. Please. Let's not be meek. Now is the time to be bold!"

I knew Ryalgar wasn't looking into any of these ideas. She and I had talked, and she understood the limits of what I and the others could do. Also, the limits of what we *would* do. Controlling crowds of Mongols with our voices was not on either list.

I raised my hand. "My sister Ryalgar never mentioned any of these ideas."

When Hana turned to me I saw anger in her eyes, but her voice stayed calm.

"Your sister Ryalgar is not in charge of this operation. I am. I say what we *are* considering and what we are not. Do you understand?"

I wanted to argue with her, to tell her she mistook my sister's intentions, but I didn't know for sure. Maybe Ryalgar had told this woman she could do anything she wanted with the luskies.

If I disagreed and was wrong, she'd probably kick me out of the group and not let me defend my homeland. Or she'd hate me point forward and make my participation miserable.

And if I was right? Then Ryalgar would have words with her to reign her in and then she'd either kick me out of the group or hate me point forward. It was pretty much the same outcome either way.

But if I kept my silence, I could learn more.

"I understand. Completely." I said it loud with a heavy dose of encouragement for her to believe me because she wanted to. I knew the other luskies would pick up on my timbre and I counted on them to know it was a signal to do the same. My tone said *this woman could be dangerous. Let's learn more.*

Luskies get plenty of practice hiding who they are and what they think. I saw acquiescent nods around the room and veiled understanding in most eyes.

"Excellent," Hana said. She patted the tight little brown bun on her head in satisfaction, making sure it stayed in place. "Let's start by letting me learn more about each of you."

The morning dragged on in discomfort as we all revealed personal details about times we'd used our timbre and how effective it had been. I suspected many lied, at least in part. I know I did. The half-truths made me feel less vulnerable against the eerie intensity with which Hana sought information.

When we broke for lunch, I told her I had an errand to run. I hoped Janx's neighbors brought the customary food to his house, even though he wasn't a man of Vinx. Even if she had food, though, I worried about Chessa. She didn't know these neighbors, and her father could only spend so much time comforting her.

"Does this errand involve the child you've taken on as a charity?"

I didn't argue, although I objected to both her tone and her words.

"It does."

"Then let's have a short conversation now while the others eat, and you'll be free to go for the rest of the day. How does that sound?" She said it so pleasantly.

"Perfect. Thank you."

"Oh, don't thank me yet. Coral. You and I need to reach an understanding today. I can't have you running back to the Velka, back to your sister or your grandmother, every time I do something you don't like. War is a serious business. That sort of nonsense gets in the way of our defense. Do you understand?"

I took a breath. *Answer carefully.*

"Of course. I have no intention of doing that."

"Excellent. Because *if* you did, I'd have no choice but to make sure there were consequences, ones severe enough to ensure others don't cause me similar problems. Discipline is important in a wartime situation. Don't you agree?"

"No. Honestly. I don't."

"Coral, one can't maintain an army without absolute obedience. Now, how do you think your school would react to learning about what you can do with your voice? How do you think your fellow teachers would feel once they heard about how you tried to manipulate them?"

"I've never done such a thing."

"What do you mean? You told me two such stories earlier this morning."

Oh scump. I'd enhanced a couple of stories that could be construed that way.

"I don't think my first move would be to talk to your school, though. I'd go to your husband instead. I bet he doesn't know you're a luski, does he? I know Davor. If I asked, he'd keep quiet about you, for my sake and yours. But, I'm positive he'd never want his son raised by a luski. He's not so fond of powerful women. Perhaps you've noticed?"

"Don't threaten me." I put all the timbre I could into the words, but I knew it would have no effect. Hana wanted to threaten me and believed she had every right to do so.

She smiled, as though she'd saved the best news for last.

"You do know he's having an affair with an old friend of mine, don't you? Ketevan. She's a lovely lady, so don't you worry. She'll do a fine job of raising little Votto. He'd have all the advantages with her, too. Probably miss your milk at first, but hey, he's old enough to get by on gruel now, isn't he?"

My hands went straight to my breasts. I swear, my milk started to flow at the thought of losing my son.

"You wouldn't!"

"I would, because it would be best for Ilari. After that, you'd behave, doing everything I asked. Otherwise, I'd have to involve your school next, and then you'd lose your job as well as your child. That would be unnecessarily harsh."

My insides felt like icicles as I came to understand this woman held power over me.

"Good. I can see on your face that we've reached an understanding. See, it didn't take long. Now, go be nice to whatever poor little child you fancy. Oh, tell me, do you fancy her father, too?"

"Certainly not! The poor man's wife just died."

She laughed. "Ah, so you're just the woman providing comfort. I see. Well, either way, I'm sure they wouldn't be as fond of you if they knew your little secret.

She handed me a piece of paper, modified from the one she'd given me earlier.

"Read it over. We'll be having two sorts of practices from now on. At one set, we'll work with the singers to achieve our assigned objective. At the other, it'll be luskies only as we look into ways we can thwart the invasion in unanticipated ways. It never hurts to exceed expectations, right?"

I managed a numb nod.

"Good. We'll look to the future, too, as we contemplate how to make the Velka, and Pilk, and all of Ilari better when this is over."

"Better? Or more to your liking?" I let myself say it.

"You're right. More to my liking."

It concerned me that my question didn't even bother her.

I rode Nutmeg slowly as I left, stroking Votto's hair and inhaling his soft baby smell. I didn't think I could live without him. That meant I couldn't ever be the cause of Hana's receiving direct trouble from the Velka. I couldn't challenge her in any way. I had to do everything she asked. That or lose my precious son.

Could I could find a way to warn Ryalgar without Hana knowing the warning came from me? Would she assume any warning had? Maybe. But would she retaliate if she couldn't be sure? Maybe not. She only had so many ways she could destroy my life; I had to hope she wouldn't want to waste one.

Could I convince Davor that being a luski wasn't a big deal? Or the people at my school? Or Janx and Chessa? Maybe, but I couldn't afford to count on it.

Could I find another way to stop Hana? I had no idea how. My life exhausted me. I barely had the energy to wash myself or time to clean my clothes. I'd given up cooking and all the flowers in my yard had finally died from lack of care. I spent most of my time chasing around a half-year-old who seemed to crawl faster than I walked.

How in the name of all that was sacred could I thwart a blackmailing mastermind determined to control all the luskies in the realm?

Once home, I laid my sleeping baby in his crib, then patted down Nutmeg and gave her water and an apple. The only good news about today was that I no longer needed to find Olivine to ask her if she agreed that Hana was harmless. Hana had shown she wasn't.

Too frustrated to sit, I got up and walked around my dead flower beds, kicking at rocks until my toes hurt, even though I knew the dumb rocks could do nothing to stop Hana.

~ 17 ~

Throwing a Rock in the Dark

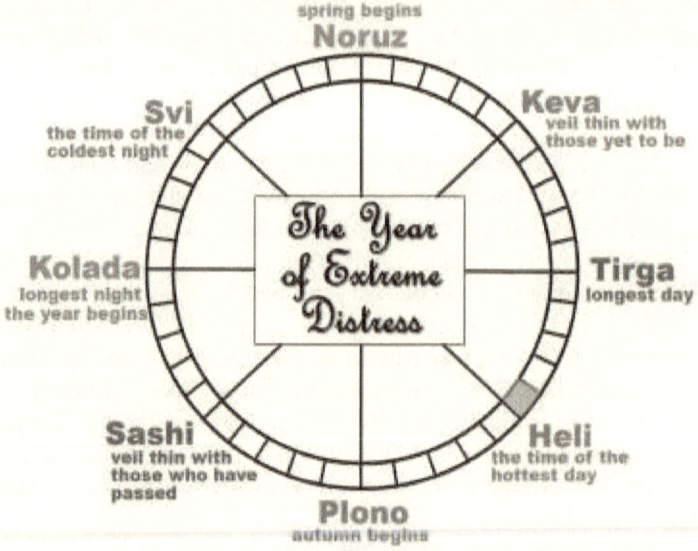

Between my frustration and my fatigue, I didn't make it over to Chessa's house until the next day. I arrived to see Janx chopping wood in the front yard and Chessa playing with the doll she'd gotten from my mother. She talked to it the way I talked to Votto as I went about my chores.

"What happened to you yesterday? You said you'd come back."

"I know. I'm sorry. Things kept me from coming over."

"What things?"

"Complicated grown-up things."

She scowled. "I hate complicated grown-up things."

I looked outside and saw the vehemence with which Janx swung his ax. I could only guess at the reasons he and his wife had landed so far from home, leaving him without the woman he loved, and with no family and a child to care for.

"Have you eaten breakfast?" I asked Chessa.

"Not yet. Daddy told me to eat the things the neighbors brought. Said we had to finish them before they spoiled."

"He's right." I looked at the food on the counter. "Here. Eat the meat first. It won't last long. I'll make you a plate."

These two needed help, and they were going to need it for a while. Could I find the time to give it? Votto squirmed in his carrier, reminding me my own life wasn't without complications.

Then a thought made me freeze. Would they even accept my help, if they knew the truth about me?

Ewalina had done a thorough job of making me comfortable with my talents when I first learned of them. I hadn't realized what a favor she'd done for me. Thanks to her, I understood my limitations and the boundaries I had to set. I knew no one could tell what I was, or what I was doing, except for another luski. I felt safe from the prejudice of others.

Then Hana upended my sense of security, thinking she could harness my talents to serve her ambitions. Now I was scared. Of everyone, and perhaps most of all of myself.

What was it Davor had accused me of being when he claimed I was too timid to be his wife? Easily frightened and overly emotional. Was I? Possibly. Sometimes. But to stop Hana from taking away my child, ruining my life, and destroying my homeland, I was pretty sure I could find a way not to be.

My willingness to do anything to stop her included using my talents as a luski to their fullest. If she forced me into the horrible choice of becoming her servant or becoming a monster, I'd choose monster.

I looked at Chessa and sighed. When this was all done, perhaps I couldn't be anyone's friend, ever.

"Why are you so upset?" she said.

Children. So perceptive sometimes.

"A bad woman is trying to get me to do bad things for her."

"I hate it when people act that way."

Really?

"You know people who do that sort of thing, Chessa?"

"Oh yes. My grandparents tried to make my mommy and daddy do bad things for them. Mommy and Daddy wouldn't and they keep saying ... they kept saying ... 'we made the right choice.' Did you know not doing bad things when people ask you to is called making the right choice?"

"Yes. I do know that."

Maybe I'd underestimated this little family. If we all lived through Kolada, perhaps Janx and Chessa *would* understand my situation.

Votto and I rode to the farm at the start of the next ank break so I could talk to Olivine. I no longer needed her opinion of Hana, but I hoped she could help me with my more complicated situation.

Dad saw me in the distance and waved from the furthest field. I wished I could warn Mom of my arrival because she didn't like surprises, and our relationship didn't need any more strain. Then Dad turned, and within seconds one of his farmhands galloped to the house to tell my mother there would be company soon.

I rode slowly with Votto; he usually nursed or slept as we traveled. By the time I reached the house, Mom had drinks waiting on the porch and a smile on her face. We sat together in the shade as the morning had already grown warm.

"You didn't bring that Chessa girl with you today?"

"Her name is Chessa, not 'that Chessa girl.' No, she's with her dad."

"He's not from around here, is he?"

"No. He said he and his wife moved from Faroo a few years ago."

"I thought so. The child looks like she's from Faroo."

"What's that mean?"

Mom shrugged. "They kind of have a look, you know. Like the Edsers have theirs. Scrudites too, of course. You know when you meet them."

She gave me a hopeful smile. "Farmland in Vinx isn't easy for outsiders to come by. He must have arrived with coins in his pocket."

"He told me they lucked out and found a small place belonging to an elderly childless couple. It's not much, but you're right, they must have had some means when they arrived."

"So. What else do you know about him?"

I caught her drift and I didn't like it.

"He's not a prince, Mom. I'm sure of that."

She gave a nervous laugh. "Yes, dear. One doesn't have a *second* marriage to a prince. However, a man of some means is better than a man of none, true? Oh, don't look at me that way. I know you and Davor won't stay together, and I don't blame you. He's a charming man but such a disappointment. We should have been more concerned he hadn't found a wife already. You're far too good to put up with a philanderer."

How could I stay mad at Mom when her hopes for her daughters were such a confusing blend of ambition, affection, and pride in our family?

"I'm sorry you had to learn of his bad behavior, Mom."

"Me and half the realm. Don't worry, dear. No one in Vinx faults you in the least. Any male who doesn't appreciate your beauty and sweet disposition is an idiot. I thought perhaps this man from Faroo is *not* an idiot and could provide for you. It's easier to raise a child with some help, you know."

She took a closer look at my face. "You're interested in him?"

"I could be someday, but not now. He just lost his wife, and I'm concerned about us all surviving past Kolada."

"Oh, yes. That. I thought Ryalgar had our defense well in hand. Your father sure has spent a lot of time helping her."

"She, Dad, and Olivine are concentrating on one part of her plan. It's called 'The Snakes.' I'm guessing it's going well, though I hope to talk to Olivine today. There's another part, called 'The Goats.' The ...."

I hated to upset my mother but I was going to have to say it

"... the reczavy are designing it and I have no idea how it's going."

"The ... those people? Oh my. Why in the world is Ryalgar trusting them with anything?"

"I don't know. What I do know is *my* part of it ..."

"Yes. The part using luskies. I've learned more since we last spoke."

Well, she couldn't say the word reczavy, but at least she managed to say luski.

"I'm glad you know more. We call my part 'The Lions.' The Lions are doing well but we've hit a little complication."

A germ of an idea sprouted in my head. It probably wouldn't lead anywhere, but I had little to lose.

"I'm sorry to hear it. Your father's been helping your group too, I understand."

"Yes, but the complication doesn't involve him. Just me."

"I see. Does this complication concern what you can do?"

I didn't answer her question but asked another.

"Mom, has anyone ever tried to force you to do something by threatening to take away or hurt people you loved?"

"Good heavens, no. People don't behave that way. Does someone you know act like that?"

Again, I ignored her question.

"What would you do if even talking about this threat to another could mean losing what you cared about most?"

"I'd say nothing to anyone. Obviously."

"Then you'd be wise, Mom. You are wise. I appreciate that about you."

I stood up and kissed her on the cheek.

"I'm going to go find Olivine. Do you mind watching Votto?"

I walked away knowing the gamble I'd taken. Mom was smart, and she had a devious streak my father lacked. She wanted to protect me. If she could think of some sneaky way to alert Ryalgar all was not well with me, she'd use it.

I wasn't naive enough to think I'd solved my predicament. Turning Mom loose on the problem was like throwing a rock at someone in the dark. You weren't sure who or what it was going to hit, but it was better than doing nothing. I needed to do more.

I paused on my way to the barn and watched.

Olivine leaned against one side of the building, her bronze hair blowing loose in the wind. Men and women with bows and arrows surrounded her. I hadn't seen her in two eighths and archery had changed her physique. She'd never been strong, but now her flimsy blouse half hid visible muscles as she stood like a tigress. I wondered if she knew of the change.

The large barn doors stood wide open and inside I could see women relaxing, lounging on the hay. They must be Ryalgar's famed oomrushers. My oldest sister was absent today, and her Velka friend Joli had taken charge. As I walked over, Joli dismissed everyone for lunch. She and Olivine greeted me, and Joli stood talking with us as though she was our sister too. It was a little thing, but it irritated me. Today I needed to talk to Olivine alone, yet I couldn't afford to raise suspicions by asking Joli to go away.

I hoped to say something to Olivine akin to what I'd told my mother, prompting Olivine to look into Hana's behavior without involving me. I thought I could have done it if Joli left but she didn't. She insisted on eating with us, sharing her fresh grapes and smoked fish, and telling stories as she ate. If she noticed my lack of interest, she ignored it.

Finally, as I gathered up the trash from our picnic, Joli turned to talk to another.

Olivine didn't wait but whispered in my ear. "You okay? You seem a little off." When I didn't answer, she added. "Joli gets a little over-enthused, but she means well. I wish Ryalgar handled this sometimes, though. How is it having Hana coordinate your stuff?"

I froze. I'm sure my eyes widened, and I know I gulped.

"That bad, huh?"

I shook my head. "I'd *never* want it to get back to Hana that I was anything but happy."

"Come on. There's no reason to be so afraid of the woman." Olivine stuck her elbow out towards me in a friendly nudge. I gave her another look. She read my expression. "There is?"

"I would *never* say such a thing. I have way too much to lose."

"Oh." Olivine was no dullard and she understood the workings of the Chimera better than Mom. I'd taken a bigger risk with her, but confiding in Olivine was more like throwing rocks in a dim light. I had a better chance of striking something I wanted to hit.

I wondered how many rocks I'd have to throw before I got the result I needed.

~ 18 ~

A Quick Trip Alone

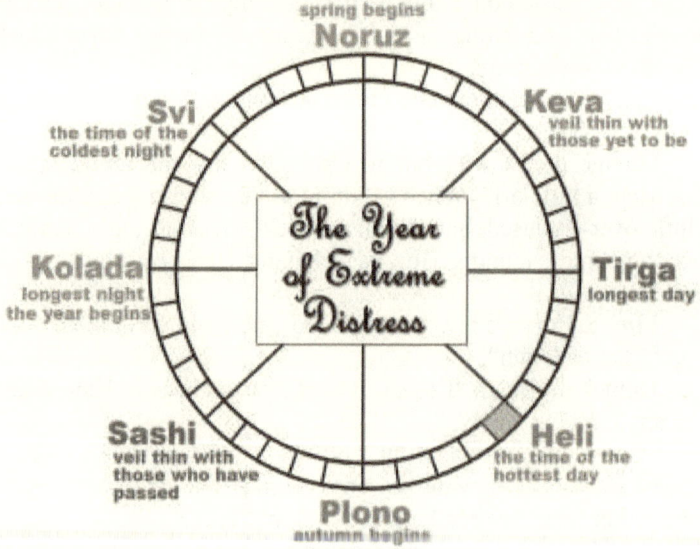

Every other day for the next ank I made the short ride over to Janx and Chessa's place in the evening, bringing a homemade dish. Chessa refused to sleep at the school now, claiming she had bad dreams when she did. One night I brought her back to my place so she could ride to school with me in the morning, but most other days she missed classes. Her father couldn't seem to get up early enough to make the ride.

I thought it was okay. She was a bright girl; she'd learn the material later. Now, they both needed to grieve together.

On the first day of the next ank-break, I rode over to my parents' farm, anxious to see if the seeds I'd planted with Mom and Olivine yielded anything. When I got there, though, mom paced the floor, too upset to sit.

Days ago, my parents had journeyed by coach to Iolite's school to see why she hadn't responded to their many letters. They knew she ought to be nearly done with her studies and would need a carriage to get her things home. Once there, they learned she'd finished earlier than most and already left. Everyone at the school assumed she went home.

Mom thought Iolite tried to travel back to the farm alone to prove her independence. Perhaps had a spell while traveling. They asked the Svadlu to search for her, hoping some kind couple had taken her in and she couldn't remember who she was. When the Svadlu said they couldn't find her, Mom became so distraught she went to my Grandmother for help. Now the Velka searched, too, and so far, they hadn't found her either.

My heart hurt. I'd promised Sulphur I'd keep her secret of Iolite's whereabouts, and of the brave assistance she provided the Svadlu. But I didn't think Sulphur thought through how worried the rest of the family would be if this happened. How could I not tell them?

Yet, how could I?

"Mom, Votto is more than half a year old. He'll do fine on cow's milk and gruel for a night. I need to ride to Pilk. Today. Without him. Would you care for him overnight?"

"Oh, Coral. Please don't do that. If something happened to you, with Iolite already missing …"

"Mom. I'll be fine. I'm going there to talk to my husband. You said the Svadlu looked for Iolite. I want to make sure they did everything they could. I believe I still have a little influence, so let me try to intervene."

Her face softened. "I didn't realize that was your errand. But don't you have your own practice thing to go to tomorrow?"

"I can miss one."

Her raised eyebrow let me know she understood my lack of eagerness to attend.

"What about these people you're caring for? Will they be okay?"

"Chessa and Janx? They'll be fine. They're both resilient."

"You better get going then, so you'll have plenty of light."

I needed to have words with two members of the Svadlu, and I had no idea how to find either one. I also didn't know how Davor would feel about my showing up and honestly, I didn't care. Whoever he was with, or whatever he was doing with her, didn't matter. I just wanted to know if my sister was safe. If she wasn't, Davor's problems were just beginning.

If she *was* okay, I needed to find my other sister. Sulphur would need a ridiculously good reason for me not to tell the rest of the family about Iolite's safety.

I expected to find the Svadlu headquarters deserted on an ank-break, but I couldn't have been more wrong. A man at the entrance directed visitors and helped several others before he got to me. When I expressed my surprise at the activity, he looked hard at my country clothes.

"Those from Pilk know our fine soldiers don't rest these days. We're always here, always preparing. How can I help you, miss?"

"I need to speak with my husband. He's with the Svadlu."

"We don't interrupt our fighters when they're training, ma'am. Can't this wait?"

"No, it can't. We've a family emergency."

I'll never know if he would have helped me, with or without my use of the timbre, because Davor walked into the foyer then with a group of men. I swear he turned to me to check me out, only to realize who I was. Then I think he considered ignoring me but thought the better of it.

"Coral. My dear. What in the world are you doing here?"

"I need your help, Davor. Do you have a minute?"

Nice big strong guy. Helping out the little missus. What could he say?

"I'll make time, dear. Come this way." He turned to the half dozen men with him.

"Gentlemen, I'll catch up with you."

He led me into his office, the place where he spent his days. I'd never seen it, but orderly maps and stacks of written materials didn't surprise me. He took his job seriously.

He gestured me to a chair then pulled out a jug from inside his desk. He followed it with two small mugs but I shook my head.

"I need to know where Iolite is."

He shrugged and poured himself a few sips.

"I've no idea."

"Bull scump. I know she's with the Svadlu, and my family is worried sick. But I promised ... someone ... I wouldn't tell the others she was with you."

I needn't have been so oblique. He figured it out right away.

"For pruck sake, why did Sulphur have to go and tell you?"

"She's worried she'll get killed and no one will know where Iolite is."

He had to laugh at that. "Guess your first skirmish does tend to scare you that way. Okay, you're the keeper of the secret, so I can tell you this much. Iolite has spent time with the Svadlu, but her mission with us remains highly confidential, at her request as well as ours."

"Why would she want that?"

"Her time with us was ... difficult. However, she left here with her boyfriend and I have no idea where they went."

"She has a boyfriend?"

He laughed again. "I think your family has fallen out of touch with this sister. Yet, I'm sure the dynamics with her are complicated."

That had to be the most sensitive thing I'd heard Davor say.

"Will the Svadlu help us find her, now that you're done with her?"

"I'd be glad to, but I understand others gave their word that we'd do no such thing. The promise was intended as a thank you, to give her and her boyfriend time to work some things out."

Well, so much for demanding the Svadlu release her.

"My parents are worried sick."

"I'm sure they are. Your best hope, Coral, is to find Iolite through methods of your own and persuade her to come home. I'm no longer involved."

"Do you know where I could find Sulphur?"

"Now that one I can help with. She got asked to fill in supervising fortifications along Pilk's eastern wall. It's too late in the day to ride out there now. Do you have a place to stay tonight?"

"No."

"I'm sorry, honey cakes, I can't have you stay over. But I'll walk you down the street to an inn and treat you to a night's stay. Say? Where's my little man tonight? Did you leave him home alone?"

I had to laugh. No sane mother would leave a half-year-old baby alone overnight, but I guess Davor didn't know that. "He's with my folks."

Davor said good night to me at the door of the inn. I felt sad, at first. Alone in Pilk and nothing to do. Then I realized I didn't have a baby with me or a chore needing to be done. Davor offered to pay my bill in full. The inn served food and drink.

I heard musical instruments playing in the front room and wandered in to hear the music. It sounded much like Celestine's performances. One musician played a flute, another plucked a stringed instrument and the third drummed while a man and woman harmonized with their voices. Pretty stuff. Then I looked closer at the man and woman. These singers were part of The Lion; we'd practiced together before. Maybe they knew Celestine.

I sought them out when they took a break.

"Celestine's sister!" The woman recognized me, or maybe just my hair. "Come drink with us when we've finished"

I did. By then they'd sent word to friends and several more singers from the Lion joined us, and two luskies as well. Although I'd never seen either without a mask, the combination of their hair, bodies, and voices let me identify them.

It surprised me to see luskies socializing with singers, but I supposed the hours of practice combined with the worries we shared had melted normal caution. Neither luski wore a mask, but why would they? Here they were merely people having fun with friends in a tavern.

The tall blonde one whispered to me. "Has she threatened you, too?"

"From what we've been able to find out, she's bullied every luski in the group," added the other, a shorter and stouter lady with greying hair. "She has an uncommon talent for discovering the right threat for each of us."

"Yes," I said. "She did and she found the best threat for me."

"We can't let her do this," the blonde said.

"We can't."

The singers at the table appeared to have heard these stories already, as several nodded in sympathy.

"We're lucky she doesn't need *us* for anything," one singer said.

"Why can't you people make her stop?" one singer asked.

"I wish we could. We're a fraction as powerful as people think we are," I said.

"Then fake her out somehow," said the man who played the drum.

"Not a bad idea," I said. "She does want to think we're more powerful than we are. Getting people to act on their desires is what we do best."

"Then it's how you stop her," the female singer said. "Make her as frightened of you as you are of her."

I considered. "We could end up making everyone more scared of luskies if we're not careful."

The tall blonde woman touched my arm. "I'm willing to do anything. I have so much to lose."

The other luski agreed. "I'll deal with the consequences later."

"You're sure? Because I have an idea for how to scare her and I have the connections to set it in motion."

I don't know what she'd threatened either of them with, but neither hesitated. "Please. Do it." They said it in unison.

Early the next morning I set off for the massive wall being built along the border between Pilk and Gruen. Stories had circulated the realm of how the Svadlu intended to make their stand against the Mongols along this barrier while all the nichnas outside of it would be evacuated and left undefended by our army. In those abandoned outer nichnas, Ryalgar's Lion, Snake, and Goat would be allowed to harass and reduce the Mongol hoard any way they could.

The wall had come to symbolize the upcoming conflict. It instilled fear in those behind its protection as well as in those whose homes lay on the wrong side of it. Every citizen of Ilari who looked at this colossal barricade of stone and mud shuddered.

I found Sulphur directing several young people adding rocks and filling to the top of the wall. A taller wall was better. She waved at me from a full five heights above me.

"I'll be right there."

Once she'd made her way down one of the many rope ladders, she greeted me. "So, you got away from the baby for a day? Having fun on the loose by yourself?"

It would have been a nice outing if my breasts hadn't been hard as rocks by then, filled with so much unused milk that riding a horse was painful and all I could think about was getting home to Votto and sweet relief.

"We have to talk about Iolite. The entire rest of the family is worried sick about her," I said in greeting. "What were the two of you thinking when you planned this? What did you expect?"

"Wait a minute." She held up her hands in protest. "Don't go putting any of this on me. I didn't plan anything and I had nothing to do with her helping the Svadlu. They brought me in at the end when they started to worry about our parents trying too hard to find her."

"I believe you." Sulphur's inability to lie was a legend in my family. "But then why are you hiding her now?"

"I'm not. Others promised her privacy, for reasons I don't know. I'm honoring their promise."

"You're not going to tell me, are you?"

"I can't tell you. Go ahead and try to make me. You'll see. I simply don't know."

Her question annoyed me. "I thought you understood. I can only make you tell me if you want to."

She shook her head and laughed. "I thought *you* understood. I absolutely want to tell you, but I can't because others won't tell me."

Why did Iolite want to stay hidden? Whatever her reasons, shouldn't I respect them too?

"Is giving her this time she needs so important?"

Sulphur nodded. "I think it is."

"Well then, I'll tell Mom Iolite is safe, and I'll insinuate she's involved in something super-secret with the army. I'll beg her and Dad not to tell anyone else for the sake of our realm. It'll buy Iolite some time and, by then, I hope she'll be ready to explain her whereabouts to everyone."

Sulphur agreed. "Want to go get an ale together?" she offered.

An ale sounded great. If my chest hadn't hurt so badly, I'd have jumped on the chance.

"I need to get back home. Next time."

~ 19 ~

Growing Teeth

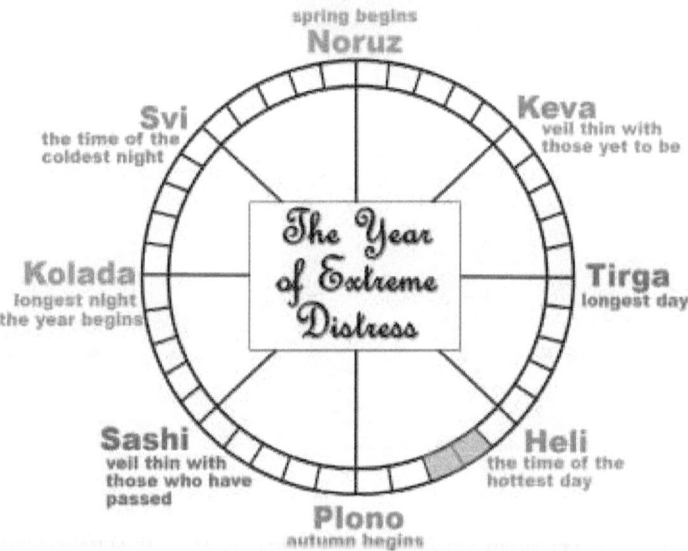

The unusually warm summer made us all lethargic. It got so bad my school held classes only in the morning and most of us did our chores early in the day or at dusk and rested in the heat of the afternoon.

I yearned for mid-day naps, but Votto's teeth grew in, and the pain in his mouth made him cranky. I went to the market to get clove oil from the Velka and was surprised to find Joli, Ryalgar's best friend, working at the Velka's stall.

"We're all having to take a turn these days," she explained. "What with all the fear in the air, Ilarians can't seem to get enough of our remedies. What can I help you with?"

I asked for her best treatment for sore baby gums. I hadn't intended to do more, but I probably wouldn't get a better opportunity to put my luski-saving plan into action.

"Since you're here, can I get you to share a message with Ryalgar? A confidential one?" Of course, Joli looked pleased at being asked.

"I need her to know that, well, by custom luskies don't interact much."

"I think she knows that."

"I know she does. But this whole Mongol thing has forced us to spend more time together and get to know each other. I ran into other luskies in Pilk and ended up drinking in a tavern with them."

"Wow. You? Out drinking? That is news." She grinned.

"Yeah. I know. While I was there, though, we discovered something Ryalgar should know. You and Grandma Aliz, too, of course. We, um, we thought we had certain limitations on how much we could persuade someone."

"Yeah. We know that too."

"And you know working with singers lets us influence animals, something we're unable to do on our own."

"Right. Tell me something I don't know." She spoke kindly enough, but other customers were looking at us with impatience in their eyes. I blew out a short puff of air. Here went nothing.

"Well, we found out when we work together, just luskies, no singers, and there's more than two of us, those old restraints with other humans don't apply so much. In fact, if you get several of us together, it looks like we can make a person do almost anything. Maybe even harm themselves or others. They don't have to want to do it, either. It's scary how much more power we have as a group."

"Are you nuts? It's wonderful. You people could get the Mongols to all kill themselves! Forget this other nonsense we're working on. You can stop the whole invasion for us."

Okay. I hadn't fully thought through the ramifications of my lie.

I searched for a way out.

"Uh, yeah, but it's like we can only do one person at a time, and it takes quite a while. It's more like a whole group of us can gang up on one lone person."

"Oh. Too bad. Doesn't seem like it would have much of an application in battle then."

"No, but we'll keep looking into it, just in case. I mean, because we've always been so secretive, we've never worked together before. Who knows what we'll find out if we keep experimenting? I wanted the top of the Velka command to be aware. You know, in case anything comes of it."

She paused, considering. "Does Hana know about this yet?"

"Oh, I'm sure she must." The lie slipped out easily. "A couple of the luskies from Pilk said they'd let her know. She'll like the news, I think."

"I bet she will. Okay. I appreciate this, and I'll pass it on to Ryalgar. I'll catch-up with Hana about it as well, just in case."

All the way back to my cottage I kept thinking *yes, please talk to Hana. Please.*

Next, I had to get back to Pilk without Votto. That meant I had to leave him with Mom. That meant I had to talk to Mom.

The last time I'd seen her, I arrived at the farmhouse after my conversation with Sulphur along the giant wall on Pilk's border. I'd done my best to balance news of Iolite's safety with a good bit of mystery about the wheres and whys of her situation. I'd been helped by my own bulging breasts, desperate to feed Votto, and his ravenous hunger for the only substance in the world he considered to be real food.

Because I could only feed him at one teat at a time, the other began to spurt milk as soon as he latched on, leaving my clothes soaked and a mess on the floor. It was easy to be vague about Iolite in the middle of such commotion.

This time, Mom would have more well-thought-out questions for me.

Luckily, I had another distraction in my back pocket and her name was Hana. I wasn't eager to go there, but these were desperate times.

"I'd rather not know details of what you can and can't do as a luski," my mother said. "It's taken me many days to accept you are one and to realize I love you anyway. You'll always be my daughter, no matter what sort of monster you are."

Yup ... pretty much what I'd expected.

"But Mom, I'm afraid I'm being turned into a worse monster. Hana ...."

"Oh, her. She's been in and out of here since the start of all this. I don't particularly like that woman, and I don't think she has Ryalgar's best interests at heart."

"She doesn't. She's been pushing us in ways that make me uncomfortable. All the luskies I know have a strong moral code and inherent restrictions on what we can do. She's trying to get us past those things, to turn us into actual monsters. I think it's power she's after."

"Does this have anything to do with the conversation you and I had? One where you intimated you'd been threatened?"

This seemed as good a time as any to tie it all together for Mom.

"Yes. She's threatened to expose me as a luski."

"What? I thought you said the Velka promised to hide your identity through all this."

"They did. They promised every one of us that, but she's threatening to selectively ignore the promise and expose each of us to the one person we'd least like to have the information. In my case, if I don't do what she asks, she'll tell Davor."

"Oh, dear. He's not the sort of man to handle that well, is he? How pathetic of her."

"It's worse." It embarrassed me to tell Mom the next part, but it also felt good to tell her the truth. "Davor's latest girlfriend is a friend of Hana's. Some woman from Pilk named Ketevan."

Mom sucked in her breath, offended on my behalf. I guessed she thought I shouldn't have been exposed to information about whom my husband slept with.

"Hana says once she tells Davor about me, Ketevan can convince him he should take his baby away from such a monster. This woman, his woman, would get to raise my child!"

My voice went to a high pitch with these last few words and, pruck it, my eyes welled up with tears. My mother looked aghast, and I thought she'd slap me for crying.

Instead, she said "We have to stop her. What can I do?"

Alright Mom.

I took a deep breath and regained my composure.

"We need to make people scared of her, not us," I said. "We need to start rumors, slow and careful rumors, about how luskies are moral and caring and our talents are rooted in a desire to save lives, not hurt people. But Hana is so ambitious she's seeking ways to corrupt us. We need people to know she's the frightening one. Not us."

"I see. Well, there's been plenty of speculation about these plans of Ryalgar's. Some insist there's magic involved, and others say it's nonsense, and she's using nothing but clever illusions. I've heard more than one story about the part luskies are playing."

"It doesn't surprise me. People talk."

"Then it won't surprise you they talk to me. Given most of my daughters are involved, folks have the crazy idea I could know something," She actually grinned. "I've been very quiet. Out of respect for Ryalgar and out of concern for all of my daughters' welfare. I suppose, even out of hope this crazy scheme works and saves our lives. Meanwhile, every day your father throws all the energy he's got into this, with the same hope."

"It's funny, Mom. I hadn't even thought of this from your point of view. Or his."

"Well, up till now my part has been to stay out of the way and not cause problems. But if you think a few well-placed rumors would help, I'll see what I can do."

Wow. Better than I'd hoped.

"Anything else?" she asked as pleasantly as if she'd just offered me a pastry and wanted to know if I'd like some fruit with it.

"Yeah, there is. I need to ride over to Pilk today and spend the night. I have to talk to the other luskies without Hana around, and it's the only way I know to do it."

She winced. "That cute baby of yours cried almost non-stop when you were gone last time. And look what a mess you were. I'm not sure you two are ready to be apart."

"I've been working on it the whole ank. He's been getting some gruel and cow's milk every day and I've been nursing him less. He'll do better and so will I. I promise."

I galloped out of there, lighter with no baby attached to me but burdened instead by all the provisions my mom insisted I take. I stopped at Janx's little farm.

"Coral!" Chessa called to me from their front porch, as I hopped off of Nutmeg.

"Hey, young lady," I responded. "Don't you think it's time you started coming back to school?" I was happy to see her too, but getting concerned about her absences.

Her father came outside, looking healthier than he had in anks. He'd cleaned up, gained back some of his weight and the glow of his skin spoke of time spent outdoors and not grieving in bed.

"I've been meaning to talk to you. I know I've been selfish, but it's helped to have her around during the day, and it's hardly seemed worth the effort to take her to school just for morning classes. But she's falling behind and it's not fair to her. Next ank, I promise I'll have her there, at least most days."

I knew Chessa needed that, and not just for learning. Playing with other children would help her, too. What could I do to ensure Janx kept his promise?

"They've suspended the option to sleep at the school until the heat passes. If it would help, she could spend a night or two each ank with me instead."

"Yes!" Chessa said.

"No, I wouldn't want to be a bother." He said it at the same time.

"The truth? I can get a few chores of my own done while Chessa keeps an eye on Votto. I'd consider it a favor if you could spare her. We'd exchange babysitting for her dinner and little extra tutoring to get her caught up?"

"Yay!" Chessa said. "I'm old enough to babysit."

"Not really." Her father smiled at me as he said it.

"You can do me another favor," I said. I turned to my heavy rucksack. "I don't want to lug all of this to Pilk, but my mother insisted on sending it with me." I pulled out some smoked sausages, bread, and fresh-picked pears. "Perhaps you'd take some off my hands?"

"Dinner!" Chessa's enthusiasm bubbled over again and I wondered when she'd last had a real meal.

"The food from the neighbors *has* sort of trickled off," he said. "I've also promised I'll get better about making regular meals for her. Kids need that."

As I readied myself to leave he added "So, you're off to Pilk to see your husband?"

His voice was casual. The question was reasonable. But it brought me to a complete stop.

"No. Though he and I must speak from time to time, we seldom see each other. The rumors you've probably heard are true."

"I didn't mean …"

"It's okay. It's an appropriate inquiry of a woman who is offering to watch your child." I recognized I'd become more formal. "My husband and I are estranged. We've agreed to divorce after Kolada, after this horrible invasion. Until then, we lead separate lives."

"I see. I'm sorry for you both."

"Enjoy the dinner."

As I turned to go, he added, "You're one of the kindest people I know. Thank you."

I used the rest of the ride over to Pilk to clear my head. To be honest, I did find Janx attractive. My mother spoke the truth; he and Chessa had the more russet skin tones, deep black hair, and iron-colored eyes common among Faroojers. I wasn't drawn specifically to his appearance even though he looked better now that he took care of himself again. No, the intensity of his eyes drew me in most. This man had stood up to his own family, choosing a more difficult life to do what was right. The power of that decision showed in his gaze.

I also knew he and his daughter offered the promise of a life I'd never have with Davor. Chessa would provide Votto with a ready-made sibling, and there'd likely be more children as well. I knew I wanted that.

I thought Janx liked me, too. Not only did he seem to find me pleasing, but I was a ready-made solution to several of his problems. Chessa needed a mother. His life and his farming would be easier with someone to do the chores a woman usually handled. My life, of course, would be easier with a male to do the same.

We Ilarians were practical people. We married to make our lives simpler as well as to share affection and sex. Although many of my sisters had quarrels with the traditional division of labor, I found it a reasonable system, perhaps because my talents and interests were well-suited to it.

My mom's tacit acceptance of Janx and her acknowledging one marriage to a prince was enough, helped. I'd have her blessing. My father, as always, would be content with whatever made me happy.

But Janx and I had obstacles as well. He'd loved his wife and would grieve for a long time. Chessa liked me now, but I hadn't stepped in to replace her mother and it could be another matter if I did. How would I handle a child turned resentful?

Meanwhile, my priority through Kolada had to be my role in Ryalgar's scheme, in her Chimera. She'd convinced me the lives of those I cared about depended on my success as a powerful luski. If the Chimera failed, any plans for after Kolada were moot.

But if we succeeded .... I still had problems. If I couldn't lessen Hana's control over the luskies, my future would be a mess. Even if I stopped Hana, I could end up such a pariah that Janx wanted nothing to do with me. Perhaps all men would want nothing to do with me.

A lot needed to go right before I could consider a second marriage.

~ 20 ~

Too Hot for Clothing

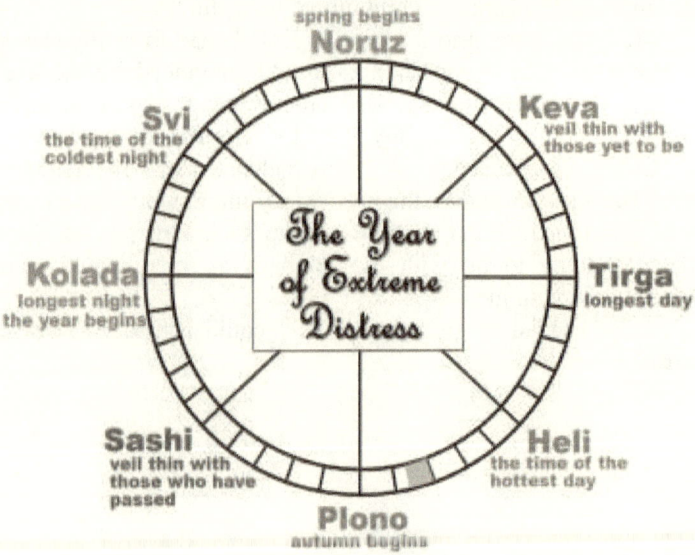

I returned to the same inn in Pilk. No musicians played so early in the day, but I got the name of the less expensive place where they stayed. I walked over and they greeted me like an old friend. Once I told them I brought important news, they sent messengers off to summon other singers and luskies in the area. Celestine wouldn't be among them, unfortunately; friends said she performed over in K'ba.

Some arrived in no time, and they poured afternoon wine while we waited for the rest.

"None for me," I said, thinking I had no lodging for the night and could ill afford to be wandering around Pilk later feeling the effects of the wine.

"Oh, have some," a singer with a pretty voice said. "We've plenty of room where we stay, you can bed down with us and be on your way in the morning."

That solved that. I took a small goblet. Some of the musicians began to entertain us until the others arrived, and I realized I was at a party. What a nice change of pace.

Before long we had eight more luskies and over twenty singers in the room; a much larger group than last time. "All the Lions in the neighborhood asked to be included if we met again," the flute player explained.

The last one to arrive was my teacher, Ewalina. I guessed we weren't strangers here so I jumped up and hugged her in greeting, happy to be able to acknowledge her and even happier when she hugged me back.

"What's the plan?" the drummer asked me. I wondered how my offer to set things in motion had morphed into my becoming the de facto leader of our luski rebellion. Well, it had.

"I've done two things. First, I sent word to my sister and grandmother that we've discovered if three or more luskies work together we can force a person to do things they object to. Hurt or embarrass themselves. Hurt others. I said it was too cumbersome a process to be used in battle, but one on one, with enough time, we could cause more harm than we thought."

"But we can't do anything like that!" one luski said.

"Of course not. And we don't want to. I lied. I told this person, someone high up in the Velka, that Hana knew about our discovery."

"So you want Velka management to ask her about it?" one singer guessed.

"Yes. Hana will be embarrassed she doesn't know, and she'll be upset we haven't told her. Then, she'll be frightened of us when she thinks about it, but excited about the potential. She'll start thinking of ways she can use it. That gives us options, so we decide how we want to play this. Do we deny it's true and then try to make her paranoid we've lied? Or do we insist it is true, and outright threaten her?"

S. R. Cronin

"Good question. If we insist it's true, she could call our bluff. What then?"

"What's the other thing you did?" Ewalina asked. She appeared less enthused about my lie than most.

"I dropped a word into a reliable part of the rumor mill that while luskies are moral and caring, our leader Hana is seeking ways to override our instincts and to force us to act in frightening ways. I let it be known how much this bothered all of us."

"Nice touch. So if she does try to get us to do things we'd rather not, we can blame her."

"She'd be the right one to blame," another of the luskies said.

"This second thing you did, Coral? I like it. I think we use it no matter what else we do," Ewalina said. "It's time the good people of Ilaria knew luskies are real. Some already know, of course, but most see us like vampires, something imaginary to be feared. We need people to know we don't live up to the myth, so if this whole Chimera thing makes it obvious who we are, we'll be better off."

"Yeah. We're like vampires without fangs," one woman said.

"We're like vampires who merely suck on the body parts of dead animals taken from the butcher."

"Ick." Several people said it.

"Okay. Enough with the vampires," I said. "I'm glad you're happy with that. I'll let the rumors run their course."

"Please do." I looked up and was surprised to see our lone male luski from Tolo. I'd never seen him without his mask, but I couldn't mistake his unruly grey hair. "The less people are afraid of us, the less reason we have to be afraid of her."

"Good point." The older luski who'd met with us last time spoke. "It's a sad fact people would rather believe a rumor that frightens them than one that calms them." She smiled. "Perhaps the touch you added about an evil leader will help perpetuate the story."

"What story?" The door opened, and Hana walked in. She smiled at the looks of surprise on our faces. "What? I'm from Pilk, and I come here often. Did you think all of you could gather together, and I wouldn't hear about it?"

No one spoke.

"I seem to have missed the beginning of your discussion. What story are you talking about?"

I could tell even the singers were frightened by her, though she'd never been anything but nice to them.

"Speaking of stories, let me tell you about a strange one I heard," Hana said. "Some of the top Velka came to me wanting to know more about an amazing discovery you made. They heard small groups of you can exert more influence on an individual than any of you can alone. Is this true?"

We hadn't quite gotten to the discussion about whether we wanted to confirm or deny this.

"Coral. I understand this story came from you. Joli told me everything; she doesn't know the meaning of discretion. She said you sought her out in the market, claiming others in Pilk had already filled me in. She said you made the discovery an ank ago when you came to Pilk to speak to your husband, and you ended up partying at a tavern without your baby. Am I right so far?"

I nodded. I couldn't talk, I was too busy trying to think.

"I assumed it was hogwash. You never come to Pilk. You never leave your baby alone. You don't go out drinking and you wouldn't even know how to find the other luskies and singers in our group. So I had to conclude you made up this bizarre story for some nefarious reason of your own."

I nodded again. I still hadn't decided how I wanted to respond.

"Then I asked around. Guess what?" she said. "You *did* come here! An ank ago, without your child. You talked to your husband, and you somehow managed to meet up with singers and other luskies. It made me wonder if the story was true? Probably not, or one of you would have told me. Right? Then I hear you're meeting again. Maybe to practice, I think. Perhaps you want to get better at this before you surprise me with it? Am I right again?"

Did she honestly believe that? Did she think we wanted to impress her? Did she not understand how much her threats made us hate her? Maybe not.

"You're right." I said it at the same time three others did. We'd all reached the same conclusion. This path was our best option, under the circumstances.

"So what are you *singers* doing here?"

"It turns out a little background music from us makes them even stronger." The man with the drum improvised. "Doesn't take much, but music focuses their energy. We hoped to test the effect out more before we got your hopes up." He gave her a warm smile I could never have managed and she smiled back. Yes, she wanted to hear this.

"I'd love to see a demonstration," she said.

Pruck.

"We can't afford to hurt anyone today, so go get any lad from the bar next door and bring him here. I want three of you, and whatever singers you need, to get him to take off his clothes. Strip completely. I think it's safe to assume that's not something he wants to do in public. Okay?"

"Good idea." Ewalina gave me an *I've got this* motion with her hand as she made her way out the door. "I'll grab the first guy I see."

I gathered together the tall blonde luski and the man from Tolo and gave them a few generic instructions. I had no idea what Ewalina would tell our chap, but I bet it would be something we could work with.

In came a young man, poorly dressed and smelling of brew. I judged him sober enough to stand and speak, but not by much. He looked at me and nodded as though he'd agreed to do something, though he wasn't sure what.

"Take off your shirt," I began. "It's so warm in here. So stuffy."

"So warm. So warm." The other two sort of crooned along with me. We'd never tried to work together before, except with the horses of course, so we fell into mimicking what we did with the animals. A couple of the musicians picked up instruments and went for some accompaniment, playing music that must have made them think of heat.

The lad shrugged and took off his shirt.

"Oh, please, your undershirt too. It's too warm for all those clothes."

He looked a little self-conscious, probably more so about his body odor than his exposed skin, but he removed his undershirt and dropped it to the floor, as we continued to encourage him to cool off and be comfortable. At this point I was throwing in a little of the timbre and so were the other two. Hana seemed pleased.

"Your shoes. They must hurt your feet."

"Hurt your feet, hurt your feet," the woman echoed.

"So help your feet. Take off your shoes," the man added. Their improvisation improved. Good. We needed this to look real.

The lad removed his shoes; deeming it a fine idea.

Next came the hard part. I doubted this poor man wore anything under his trousers. Would he drop them simply because we asked? Was there any way I could ease his decision?

Ewalina had to have told him something. What?

"Now do as we ask," I said in a singsong tone. The other two luskies followed my lead.

"Do as we ask. You must do as we ask."

"You know it's important." I went for full-on timbre, trying to find vague words that would key into whatever Ewalina had said. "Do as we ask. Take off your pants."

"Take off your pants," they echoed. "Take off your pants," a dozen singers crooned softly behind them.

This of course was the point where a normal person would look at us and say "Pruck, no. I'm not taking off my pants in a room full of people."

But the lad was a little drunk, and he was well-lulled by now. More importantly, I believed Ewalina had told him *something* to make him more cooperative. It didn't matter what, as long as it left him inclined to do what we asked.

"Take off your pants, take off your pants." We all said it and sang it again.

He did hesitate, and I watched Hana's brow begin to furrow. Then he shrugged, untied the drawstring holding up his britches, and dropped them to the floor. He was the proud owner of a fairly good-sized pizzle, which probably worked in our favor. In my limited experience, men who had something to show off were more likely to do so.

A few of the women, and a couple of the men, rewarded him with an appreciative nod. Hana could have cared less if he had two pizzles or none at all. She was just happy to see those pants hit the floor.

Ewalina hurried over to him, helping him pull up his trousers and gather up his things. She probably wanted to get him out the door before he said something awkward.

Hana turned to us.

"Impressive enough. I'll leave you to your evening of practice. Our next gathering is an ank from tomorrow and we'll have great fun figuring out how the Lions can use this to be more effective."

After she left, we made small talk for a while. I think everyone feared she lurked outside, hoping to overhear something. When enough time had passed to make her presence unlikely, Ewalina whispered in my ear.

"I told him he auditioned for a part as an actor in a play about mythical luskies forcing an innocent boy to misbehave. I said the tryouts required him to do whatever absurd thing you asked."

"So does he think he's in a play now?"

"No, I told him he didn't get the part, but I gave him a couple of coins for his trouble. I'm hoping he'll put them towards more drink and not even remember the evening.

We both laughed.

"If we have to do this again, I doubt we'll be so lucky."

"We won't," Ewalina said. "It's why we don't have a lot of choice. Next time we practice, she gets an ultimatum. We'll pretend she's in charge as long as she asks no more of us than what we agreed to do in the beginning. She can take all the credit she wants for our part in the victory, as long as she never identifies us to anyone, and never bothers us once this is over.

Several other luskies were nodding along.

"That works."

"Works for me, too."

"And who's going to tell her this and how?"

"Coral is," Ewalina said. She held up her hand to stop my objection.

"Your life is pretty much above reproach and not all of us have been so lucky. You've no real history as a luski, you get under her skin, and you're a close relative of the woman she hates most. You're perfect."

Everyone seemed to agree, probably because none of them wanted to do it, either.

I *could* come up with a plan, but I wanted the group to understand my approach.

"Let's meet at dawn, on the morning of our next practice. Pass the word to everyone who isn't here."

"Where?"

I tried to think of something outside of Pilk Central, a place that couldn't be mistaken.

"Outside the wall they're building between Gruen and Pilk. Where it meets the forest. It's easy enough to get there. We won't have much time, but we'll finalize everything before we ride over to practice."

The man from Tolo laughed. "Just seeing us all ride up together is going to scare the scump out of her."

Ewalina laughed along. "That'll be the perfect start."

~ 21 ~

An Agreement,
At Least for Now

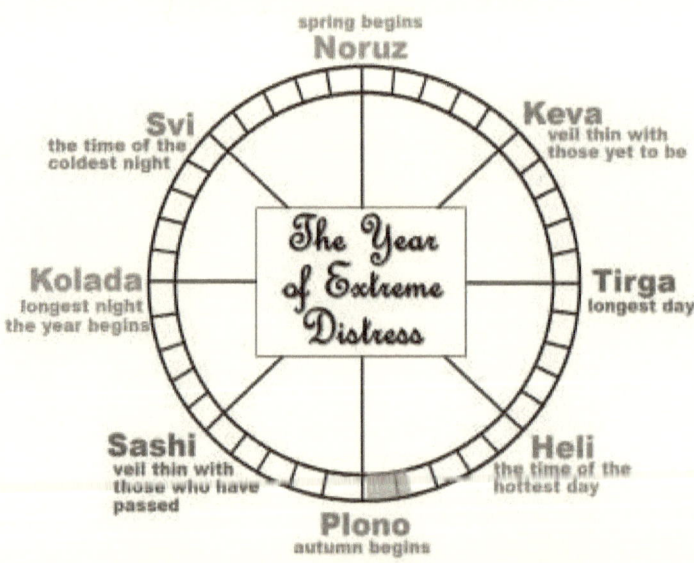

I lived the next ank only half present in my body as I cared for Votto and my home and as I continued teaching the little ones. I had Chessa come home from school and spend a night with me, but even with her I only went through the motions of what she expected.

The other half of me, the important half, rehearsed my upcoming conversation with Hana, searching for the perfect words and the irresistible tone for all I had to say.

My speech needed to leave the luskies able to move forward without fear. My words had to reassure our new allies, the singers, that Hana's future orders would bring no harm. Most importantly, Hana had to leave believing she'd acted as a smart woman, adapting to a changing scene, and not an ignorant one being played by her own minions.

It had to be flawless. I had to be perfect. Nothing could have scared me more.

I didn't sleep much the night before, fearing I'd fail to wake as early as I needed. At the first touch of light, I forced my tired body out of bed, gathered up Votto and my things, and rode over to Janx's farm.

He stirred his fire back to life as I entered, already dressed. He probably hadn't slept much either. I'd hated to ask this favor of him, but his farm was so much closer than my parents, making it easier for a predawn ride. I couldn't afford to have Votto with me and fussing on such an important day.

I didn't stay to talk but hopped back on Nutmeg. I knew she sensed my tension as she broke into a gallop without a touch from me and leapt over the dew-covered grasses as she took me to the Pilk wall.

Several of them greeted me as I rode up.

"We meet this morning to talk about what we do if she balks," I said. "She probably will. Then we've got three choices. Which one we take *has* to be a group decision."

There were nods all around. Everyone saw the wisdom in this.

"Choice one: if she says 'I don't believe you people,' we confess we lied to her and then we do what she wants."

The chorus of "no's" was overwhelming.

"Okay. Bad choice. Choice Two: We refuse to do what she wants. I tell her if she harms any of us, we'll do worse back to her. She can accept our disobedience or make good on one of her threats. I think she'll do the latter and make an example of me but whoever she picks to destroy, once she does it we have no way of retaliating."

S. R. Cronin

This option got a lot of shrugs but no enthusiasm.

"Our last choice is to put on a second demonstration."

"Surely you don't want to make another poor drunk lad drop his trousers?"

"No, I don't. And I don't think it'd work a second time either. We have to make her harm herself. Not seriously, just enough to be humiliating."

"We can't do anything like that."

I'd been giving a lot of thought to exactly what we could and couldn't do.

"Can you make her scratch her nose?" I asked.

"Of course," Ewalina answered. "Scratching feels good; most people like to do it. And the suggestion of an itch is so easy that anyone can get another person to scratch."

"Exactly. So, if we do this right, we've got the power of suggestion on our side. We do what she's been watching us do with the horses, and what she saw us do with the lad. She's already susceptible to it. We sing and croon and everyone throws in all the timbre they've got, getting her to scratch her face. We start slow, but we build up to something uncomfortable. Then I come in with the threat to turn it bloody and leave scars if she doesn't promise to leave us alone."

"And at that point, what if she looks at you and says 'pruck no'?" Ewalina asked. Others nodded in concern.

"Then we go somewhere we don't want to go. We've made sure she's in the middle of a circle, surrounded by us so she can't run. I'll take the lead and I'll look for any vulnerability. I'll seek out any uncomfortable thing she wants to do, just a little. Try to make her cry. Lose her temper and shriek. Tear off her shirt. Curl into a ball in fear. I'll keep going until she does something she *thinks* she doesn't want to do but does. I don't know what it'll be, but I'll find it and it'll scare the scump out of her when I do."

Most of the singers cheered and a few of the luskies did too, but most didn't.

Ewalina took a step back from me. "You're finding a way to turn into the monster I promised you'd never become."

The man from Tolo added, "and you'll turn the rest of us into freaks with you."

"No, I won't; you're just helping me put on a show. I need your theatrics. If we have to do this, I'll be the only real monster in the group when this is over. I promise."

"Aren't you afraid if you do something like this once, it'll be easier to do it again?" I didn't know the name of the luski who asked, but I'd already wondered the same thing.

"Right now, I want Hana's unfortunate ambitions behind us, so we can focus on defending Ilari. Ask me that question again, after Kolada."

No one said another word to me.

I noticed Celestine standing near the back of the group. She must have shown up late, probably in the middle of the most impassioned part of my speech. Well, even if she'd only heard the last bit of it, my younger sister now knew the truth about me. I couldn't imagine she'd ever look at me the same again.

"Let's go," Ewalina said to the others. "We've got serious work to do."

We mounted our horses and rode as a group towards the farm in Gruen where we'd hold today's practice. Ewalina took the lead. Whether she realized I needed to hang back and conserve my energy, or whether she did it to show her agreement with my plan, I don't know. Either way, I appreciated it.

Several luskies hung back with me, riding silently by my side like an escort. It seemed to be a gesture of respect, and I appreciated it as well.

Hana waited for us outside of the barn we'd arranged to use. She paced around with her hands on her hips, no doubt wondering why no one had shown up yet. She dropped her arms to her sides and stared at us when she realized every singer and luski she'd ever worked with rode towards her.

The group parted so I could ride to the front. We waited in silence, all of us looking down at her.

"Get off your horses," she said. "We've work to do." We all heard the shakiness in her voice.

"Not yet." I held up my hand to keep anyone behind me from obeying her. "There's no reason for us to dismount until we reach an understanding with you."

She laughed. "I believe I already have an understanding with every luski here. Do I need to reiterate those conversations?"

I'd played this scene over in my head so many times, I swear I'd done a version of every type of thing she could say. Including this.

"Those conversations don't matter anymore. As a group, we can do things to you we can't do alone. You won't harm any of us, or I'll bring the wrath of every luski in Ilari down upon you."

She looked at me, searching for a sign of weakness. I'd practiced showing none. It didn't hurt that I sat on a horse looking down at her.

She laughed. "That would be a fine show. I'd follow it up by bringing the wrath of the people of Ilari down upon each of you. None of you would have a safe life when I finished."

"Perhaps not. But the price you'd pay would be your ambitions, your dignity, and your joys. Are you willing to destroy your life to harness our power? Think. What good would it do you?"

She gave me a look I'd never seen from her before. I'd put it somewhere between puzzlement and caution.

"Why don't you put your horses up and come in the barn. Let us discuss our path forward like reasonable people."

I motioned to the group. "Reasonable is all any of us ask for." We dismounted almost as one and went inside. So far, this looked like one of the better versions I'd imagined.

Once inside, she relaxed.

"Look. We're on the same side here. We all want to save Ilari. I think you're capable of doing more, that's all. Yes, it helps me if you do more, but it helps you, too. It helps us win. It helps us save lives. Based on what I know, I thought you'd need persuasion to get past your scruples, so I gave each of you reasons to work with me. Don't be angry with me for wanting you to play a larger role."

She'd found a way to present her desires in the best light, but not an entirely factual one. I knew how to respond.

"We're not angry with you about that. We'll all do what we can for our realm. We love Ilari, too. But you misunderstand us, while other members of the Velka do not. So, if you will run your ideas by the rest of the Velka's ruling Conclave, every one of them, and if they overwhelmingly agree with your plans, then we'll participate in any way we're needed."

I heard several women behind me suck in their breath. Many in our group wouldn't use their timbre on other humans no matter who asked them to, and I knew it. But I also knew the Velka would never ask such a thing of us. Hana knew it too; it was part of why she'd kept her ideas from them.

I stood a little straighter. I was on firm ground here. "You and I will travel together and speak to my sister," I said. "I want the full story from her on who's responsible for what. I want to hear the Velka's view of using us in other ways."

Hana blew out her breath at those words.

"There is no need for such a journey. I speak for all of them."

"No, you don't." My boldness amazed me, but it felt good. "You bring Ryalgar, Aliz, and Joli to our next practice, then, and we'll agree to whatever they ask of us."

I met her gaze with a smile. I could see her weighing her options in the expressions crossing her face. One of my better alternatives won out, for now.

"Busy as everyone is, such a meeting would be difficult to arrange. Perhaps we *would* be better off focusing on our original task and doing it well. You are all still willing to coax horses into throwing riders, right?"

I glanced behind me. I saw numerous nods and a lot of relief in people's eyes.

"Very well," Hana said. "We'll concentrate on that. We've no disagreement to settle today."

Actually, we did. I could have pretended otherwise, but I wanted this crock of scump to end.

"There *is* another matter," I said. I felt as well as heard the group behind me step in closer.

"If we defeat the Mongols, once it's over, none of us want to have contact with you again. We want to go back to the lives we've chosen, ones with few if any people knowing the truth about us. You're never to ask any of us to do you any sort of favor, ever. Not in return for hiding our identities, or in return for anything else. Am I clear?"

"Oh my." She tried her best to look insulted. "I rather hoped we'd part better than that. We could become people who help each other, on occasion. That hardly seems demanding."

"Under the circumstances, it is. You hold a secret over us. We hold a power over you. We agree today to call it even and that's the end of it."

I'm sure she considered arguing with me. Perhaps she thought of telling me she wasn't sure we had enough power to compel her to make this deal. She might even have thought of asking for a demonstration. But she didn't.

"You have my word," she said. "We'll part according to *your* code. As strangers."

A sigh of relief came from most lips. It certainly did from mine.

The rest of the morning went without problems, and everyone practiced with more enthusiasm than they'd shown recently. I suspected Hana noticed it. Even if she didn't intend to honor her oath to us forever, today her acquiescence made sense.

By the time I picked up Votto around noon, I was too exhausted to visit with Chessa or Janx.

"Let Miss Coral get on home," Janx told his daughter as she pulled on my sleeve trying to get me to play with her.

I thanked him and bundled up Votto, hoping he wanted a nap as much as I did.

~ 22 ~

Adding Fire

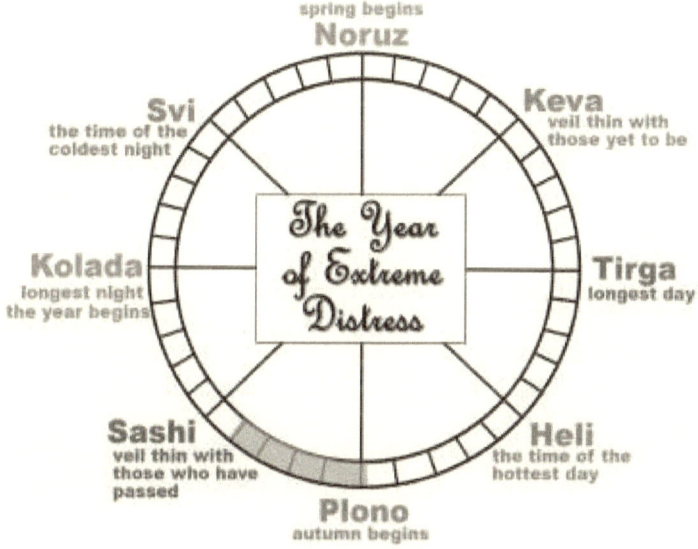

Living alone with a baby made seasonal celebrations seem less important. The Plono holiday passed with little notice from me other than remembering I was married exactly a year ago. Another couple would celebrate an anniversary, but not us.

I might have missed Plono completely, except it made the ank ten days long instead of nine. The astronomers decreed this holiday separate from the ank it occurred in, as they often did, because otherwise our years were too short to match the cycles of the earth. So, I enjoyed the day off and caught up on chores.

S. R. Cronin

The start of Plono also meant autumn arrived. I noticed the cool breeze in the mornings as I rode over to school, needing a second blanket to keep Votto warm.

Janx's farm was close enough to my cottage that I sometimes put Chessa on my mare and took her home from school. It saved her father the ride over and back. When I did, the next day he often spent the time I'd saved him over at my place instead, chopping wood for me.

As a thank you for my woodpile, I sometimes dropped off prepared food for their dinner. To repay me for the cooking, he sent me home with fresh fruit and vegetables from his wife's garden. She'd had quite a green thumb, and he'd managed to keep most of it alive through the hot summer. I had almost no garden at all.

Thus we managed to make each other's lives easier, without ever discussing the future or exchanging a kiss. I was, after all, another man's wife. He was a man who'd lost his beloved a mere two eighths ago. I suspected tongues wagged about the nature of our relationship anyway, but we never spoke of our growing interdependence. In truth, we didn't speak of much. We just did little things for each other and left it at that.

One evening in mid-Plono, after I gave Chessa a ride home, he asked if he could speak with me before I left. I noticed his table held goblets filled with wine and a plate with fruit and nuts to nibble on as we drank.

"It's a party?" I tried to sound light as my stomach did funny things. I liked our arrangement and hoped this conversation wouldn't ruin our comfortable situation.

"No, but, well, I wanted to do all I could to make you inclined to say yes to what I'm about to ask you."

My insides trembled. This didn't sound good.

He sat, gesturing me to sit also. Chessa had taken Votto into the bedroom to play. I noticed he'd closed the door on them, something he'd never done.

"I don't want Chessa to hear this conversation," he said in response to my glance. "But I'm not sure how long our children will give us to talk, so I'll be quick." He gulped his wine. Then, as he remembered his manners, he gestured to mine. "Please. Drink."

158

I didn't need encouragement. I took a gulp bigger than his. He raised an eyebrow and smiled.

"I've something very important to ask you."

Why couldn't he have waited? There was no hurry. Life was complicated enough right now.

"And this question can't wait," he added. "I think you know I've been training with the other farmers. It will be our job to round up the Mongols that you get the horses to throw. We're to secure them and parcel them out so they can be held through the winter."

"Yes. I know this."

I didn't understand why it mattered though. Did he worry I thought he shirked his responsibilities to defend the realm? Was he trying to demonstrate how he would be a worthy husband? I already knew he would be.

"Well, then you know I won't be able to care for Chessa when this happens. She's too young to help our efforts; she needs to evacuate. But she's never been apart from me for long, and she's scared of strangers."

Maybe I'd misjudged the subject of this conversation.

The metallic glint in his iron-colored eyes shown as he stared into mine. "I need your help, Coral. With Chessa."

"I can't help you. I'll be doing tasks of my own then, important tasks."

"Of course. But Chessa loves Votto." I think he wanted to add "like a brother" but he didn't. "I'm asking that whoever takes Votto to safety takes her too. If she could leave with him, she'd be so much happier. She could even help out with him. Please?"

The man was worried about his daughter during the invasion. Of course. How reasonable.

My stomach grew still. Then as I opened my mouth to answer, I felt as if someone had thrown water in my face. For all the worrying I'd done, I'd made no specific plans for where Votto would be when the invasion happened. I guess I assumed my parents would watch him, but ....

He saw the look on my face and he understood.

"You haven't thought about this yet? Of course you haven't; you've got so much family to turn to that you know it'll work out fine."

"Yes, but everyone in my family is playing some part somewhere, except for my mother. I need to talk to her about this. I'm sure she'll take Votto, and then of course she'll take Chessa, too. Votto knows Chessa and having her along would help."

He reached across the table and put both of his hands over mine. I think it was the first time he ever touched me, deliberately like that. I stared at our hands, mesmerized by how the ruddy tones of his skin contrasted with the soft pinks of mine. I liked the way they looked together.

"Thank you," he said. "We have much else to talk about, you and I, but not now. Perhaps we can agree to another conversation, once we're both reunited with our children after Kolada?"

My insides quivered one last time then calmed back down. I looked him in the eye.

"I'd like that very much."

He picked up his goblet and downed the rest of his wine. "I would too."

As the weather cooled, we practiced every ank-break in either Gruen or Vinx. Votto no longer slept through practices so I began leaving him with Janx and Chessa so I could concentrate better.

Most farmers lent us space if we asked, and I suspected they gained a certain amount of status by hosting us. The family always brought us treats to eat and asked if they could watch.

Having an audience had made the luskies nervous when we started, but by Plono they didn't object. We all donned our masks and asked the observers to keep their distance, but over time we realized we benefitted from having luskies seen as helping the greater good. If people feared us less after the invasion, we'd have easier lives.

And trust within the group grew. Many of us no longer bothered with masks when it was only us. We didn't part as strangers, even if we said we did.

To Hana's credit, she stayed focused on our task. She held no sessions for luskies only and made no further mention of using our skills on humans. Instead, she applied her devious mind to inventing obstacles we might face and to trying out ideas to overcome the unexpected.

To this end, she provided themes for the practices. She devoted one to overcoming noise. Another focused on getting the horses to run after they'd been persuaded to buck. When we woke to a heavy storm one practice day and arrived wet, each of us hoped to be sent home due to the weather. As soon as we heard the excitement in her voice, though, we knew better.

"I've been hoping for this! Let's see how the heavy rain affects the horses. Can we use the lightning and thunder?"

She noticed our annoyed expressions. "It does sometimes storm in the middle of a battle, you know."

Of course it did and we knew it. Despite mutters of resentment, we worked hard in that muck and left drenched. Back at home in front of our fires, we knew the morning workout left us better prepared.

Through Tirga, Heli, and early Plono she'd avoided practicing with the reczavy. She said she didn't want to start fires in the dry heat of summer, but I also suspected the reczavy made her uncomfortable.

The ank after the heavy rains, we showed up at practice to find several reczavy already there. They'd built two elaborate walls of dry twigs and kindling and waited for us with lit torches. It looked like time for a dress rehearsal with fire.

Once they lit the first wall, the horses could smell the smoke and became agitated. We had to coax them just to get them near. We all knew fire scared horses but were surprised at the amount of panic. I wondered if we only needed fire to get them to buck. Maybe the luskies and singers could stay home?

Hana noticed the same thing. Once we'd done a run-through with each wall of fire and put all the flames out for a second time, she gathered us together. The reczavy hung on one side, keeping their distance from us. We luskies stood behind the singers, half-hidden by our partners. We weren't a trusting group. Not yet.

"We need to make sure the horses go around the curve so they hear us. We don't want them stopping too soon," she said.

"We could wait longer to start the fire. Unless it's raining, we can get the blaze going pretty fast." One of the reczavy spoke. I looked closer at the tall slender blonde in a silver robe. It was my sister Gypsum. She saw me and gave me a little wave. I hesitated, then I gave a little wave back.

"That would help," Hana said, ignoring our waving. "The later the better, as long as it's a full-on blaze after those horses round the bend. Then they can panic, and better yet run so they can't be caught by their riders."

We nodded.

"Are we going to practice with the farmers who'll gather up the prisoners?"

"Yes, in an ank or two. I'm worried about the Mongols who manage to stay mounted. They have arrows, they have swords. We have to focus on making their horses hard to control or casualties among our farmers will be severe."

"We can help you with that too," a man from the reczavy said. "Today you just wanted fire, but we can also make smoke once the horses start to buck. You people will need to stay upwind, of course, wherever upwind is that day. And our farmers will need wet cloths over their faces. Hopefully, between coughing and poor visibility, these Mongols will have their hands full just getting away from us."

"That's the best we can hope for," Hana said.

Listening to their conversation, I understood the dangers in a way I hadn't yet.

Farmers, like Janx, would stride into this mess, hoping to corral a couple of hundred confused warriors. Even if successful, blows would be struck. Sure, we'd devised a clever way to fight, but we'd also devised a good way to get people killed.

Ilarians would die while we sang.

As we gathered our things to head home, I walked over to Gypsum, and she came towards me.

"So the mask didn't do much to disguise me?" I said.

She laughed. "I'd know that red hair of yours anywhere. Plus, I'd heard you were part of this. A luski, huh? A mother, too. Which is weirder?"

"They're both pretty strange. I've heard about you, too." I gave a vague gesture towards the rest of the reczavy. "Are you happy with them?"

"Very." She gave me a careful look. "I belong."

She didn't have to say more. I was, after all, the sister who'd comforted her as a small child when she cried because she thought my mother hated her. My mother didn't, of course, but she and Gypsum's relationship had always been difficult.

"I'm glad for you," I said.

"I can't wait to meet Votto," she replied.

"We'll make it happen soon. He's a cutie."

We hugged and parted, and all the way home I wished I'd asked her more questions.

~ 23 ~

Getting Sentimental

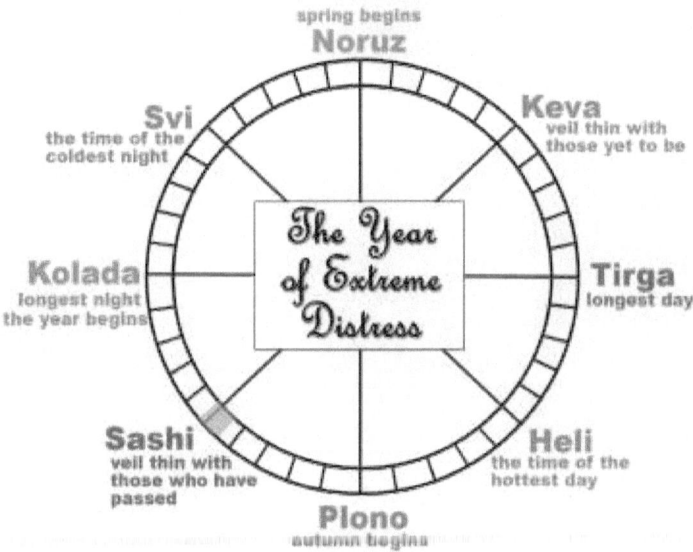

When we practiced two days before Sashi, Hana was in high spirits. At first, I figured she saw how our efforts came together and felt proud of us. But as the morning went on, I realized something else had happened. She kept looking at me as if she couldn't wait to tell me something.

I knew I wasn't going to like it.

I made it to Nutmeg's side after we finished, but she grabbed my arm before I could mount.

"Don't rush off. I need to have a little chat with you." Her nails curled into my flesh.

"We no longer chat. I thought I was clear about that."

"Oh, don't be so dramatic. This isn't about you, anyway."

When she didn't say more and didn't let go of my arm, I took the bait. I shouldn't have.

"Okay. Who do we need to talk about?"

"Your sister. I'm worried about her."

That was nice. I worried about all six of them, but Hana didn't need to know that.

"Uh, which one?"

"Ryalgar, of course. The poor dear. She is in such a precarious position."

No, I didn't like where this was going.

"How so?"

"I visited my good friend Ketevan. She's your husband's girlfriend, remember her? She's something of an item in the social circles of Pilk."

"That's nice."

"It is for you. Davor does send you money, doesn't he? You should be grateful. She's enhanced his career a lot."

"That's nice." I wondered how many times I could say the same two words before she noticed.

"She's made friends at court and she's befriended Nevik's wife. You know, the princess from the adjoining realm, alone in a strange country? They tried to pretend it was a marriage of love but everyone knows her parents forced her into it for the sake of a treaty. She has so few friends here, but Ketevan is one of them."

"'That's nice."

She still hadn't noticed.

"Not long ago, she confided to Ketevan that her husband has a lover. He's had one since before their marriage and guess what? She's a Velka. Can you believe it?"

"Leave my sister out of this."

"I didn't put your sister into anything; she put *herself* into this. It invariably becomes public knowledge, you know."

"I thought you Velka prided yourselves on keeping each other's secrets."

"Of course we do."

I felt the luski inside me growing stronger. I would not be pushed around by this woman again.

"Then you better hope news of Ryalgar's affair never leaks out of the forest," I said. "I'd hate to have to tell my sister *you* were the likely source of the leak."

Yes, I did add a touch of timbre to my speech, just enough to make the idea of being a known Velka snitch seem more unpleasant than it already did.

"Oh, I'd never do such a thing. I'm a good Velka. But my friend has become close to this poor princess, and she's trying to help the woman stand up for herself. I thought, perhaps, you and I could work together to ensure the whole situation doesn't get any messier."

A year ago, I'd have jumped in with my concern, anxious to save my sister. But I'd learned better ways to avoid problems with some people.

"Let me repeat. You and I will not work together on this or anything." I couldn't believe how rude I sounded, and I was just getting started. "Furthermore, what my sister does is her business. I'm not involved."

"I see. Well then, I'll have to take up this delicate matter directly with her. Is that what you want?"

"Yes. You do that. After Kolada."

"Exactly. After Kolada."

I left feeling pretty sure this was one of those weird conversations in which we both felt we'd gotten the better of the other.

I have fond memories of the holidays when I was a child and of the way my mother decorated the house and prepared the special foods associated with the day. Sashi was my favorite. We filled the holiday with the oranges of pumpkins and turning leaves and, even though no one said so, I thought the holiday matched my hair.

Holidays change when you get older, though. Children nearing adulthood want to be with their friends, and soon there is whispered excitement amongst both boys and girls about the freedoms coming with maturity. There is also fear and embarrassment, to be honest, on all sides, but later you realize it's all part of the difficult process of becoming an adult.

What I didn't expect was how people come full circle. Once you have your own children, you want to spend the holidays with your family again, and even with your parents. So I packed up Votto and all his supplies, and I headed over to my parents' farm the day before Sashi.

They fussed over him, of course, insisting he try the applesauce prepared for the day. It was his first taste of a fruit, and he spit it back out with a giant blubbering of his lips that made my dad laugh so hard he cried. I think the tension of the upcoming Kolada affected us all.

Later in the evening, after she'd had a few goblets of wine, my mother mentioned the surprising change in how people felt about luskies.

"So many households have watched your group practice, and they're all so impressed with how nice you people are."

"Do you think many of them recognize me as being part of the group?"

She gave a helpless little shrug. "Let's face it, if even a strand of your hair is visible, it makes you stand out and it's hard to hide every strand. But so far, everyone has been too polite to mention their theories to me."

I must have looked worried because she added "I think if this all ends well, people will either accept what you can do or be nice enough to forget about it when all is done."

"I hope so."

"There is this persistent unsubstantiated rumor afoot." She actually winked at me. "It claims a renegade in the Velka has pushed the luskies to do questionable things, and the luskies have resisted with great bravery. I have no idea where such a story came from." She looked quite pleased with herself.

"We're lucky this renegade Velka seems to have backed off for now," I said.

"Yes. Quite lucky. Well, if things change, the groundwork has been laid."

"Thanks, Mom."

The next morning Mom and I had our much-needed conversation about child care during an invasion.

"I figured I was earmarked for watching Votto," she said as we sipped our fruity morning wine. "Every other person in the family is involved somewhere, and I know your father doesn't want me to stay put here at the farm. Just in case. Of course I'll evacuate and I'll take Votto with me."

"Will you flee up into the mountains, then? Or maybe go into the forest in Zur?"

Her only other real option was to hide with the Velka, and I knew how opposed she'd be to *that* choice.

"No." She gave a long sigh, using the time to choose her words. "Your grandmother and I have had several, uh, conversations recently. She convinced me I serve my family's interests best if I take shelter with the Velka. She won't be in the forest. Believe it or not, she's part of one of these little resistance groups, too. Taking on the Mongols at her age! But, she's right; if I stay with the Velka, she and Ryalgar can ensure Votto and I have all we need. Indefinitely. For Votto's sake, I've accepted Aliz's offer."

I was impressed, and I didn't want to upset the apple cart by adding one more complication. But I had to.

"Mom, I have a favor to ask. I know it's big, but it will help me and Votto, and it may even help you."

"I know."

She put her two hands over mine in the exact way Janx had when we talked about this. The coincidence was so strange I almost withdrew my hands in surprise. I was glad I didn't.

"You want me to bring his daughter with me, don't you?"

I suppose it wasn't hard to figure out I'd ask this. "Do you mind?"

"To be honest, yes. I'd rather not have responsibility for a child who's not my kin." She swallowed hard after she said it. "But, I recognize the little girl may be your stepchild someday, and then she'll be my kin too. I wouldn't complicate your life by saying no."

I would've liked to have stayed a second night at the farm, but Ryalgar had sent word days ago that she wanted to spend the night of Sashi with me. I think she viewed it as a sisterly duty, to provide me with comfort in the absence of my husband. I wondered if she realized how many holidays I'd spent alone since my marriage? I was pretty sure she hadn't been paying attention.

Maybe, with the invasion looming only an eighth away, she felt sentimental.

She arrived before sunset and played with Votto; the last time they'd been together he'd been too little. I watched her bounce him on her knee, and my feelings softened. She wanted to be a good aunt.

Then, we kept drinking after I put him to bed.

I mentioned Hana, trying to make it clear the woman could only be trusted so far, under the best of circumstances.

"Did you know Hana has connections to Nevik's wife?" I asked after we opened the second jug.

"So she knows about my affair with Nevik? So what. Plenty in the Velka do." I remember her looking at me and asking "What is it you think she can do to hurt me?"

I'm not sure what I told her but by the time we opened the third jug, I may have gone on a bit about Hana trying to fill the wife with ideas about not putting up with things the way they were. Whatever I said, I must have crossed some line. Ryalgar finally responded by standing up on the bed and screaming.

"I! Do! Not! Need! This! Scump! Right! Now!" she yelled.

That struck me as terribly funny and once I stopped laughing I crawled up on the table and screamed back. "Let's wait and see who ends up dead before we worry about this goat scump." The liquor did the yelling.

And the liquor answered when she raised her goblet and yelled "Pruck yes. Here's to seeing who lives through this varmin pile of scump!"

I think we went on like that for a while as we started in on a fourth jug. I'm pretty sure some crying got mixed in with all the laughing and cussing, but I don't remember for sure. By the next morning, the memories were all a little fuzzy.

~ 24 ~

A Complicated Evening

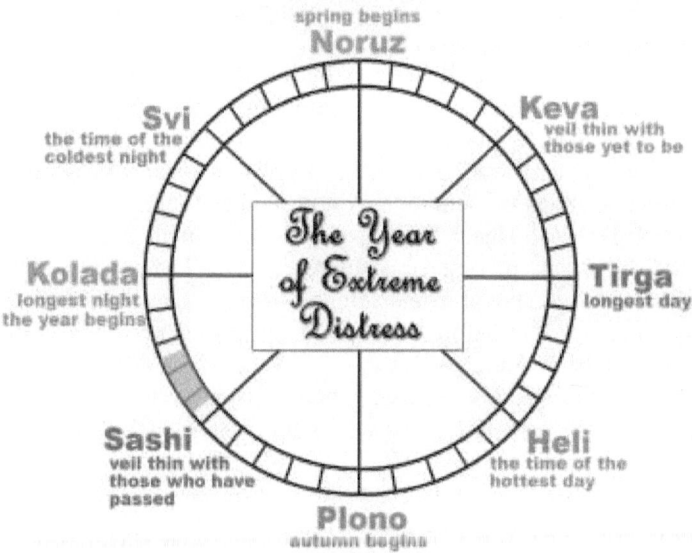

As we moved further into Sashi, people lowered their heads when they passed each other, walking faster and talking less. Schools and markets around the realm planned to close two anks before Kolada, to give everyone time for whatever they needed to do. When people did speak, they asked about each other's plans for the safety of their elderly or their children. No one wanted to talk about the past; it made us all too sad. No one wanted to talk about the future; it made us all too scared.

We had a plan. It would work. Or it wouldn't.

An ank before schools closed, Davor came to visit. He wanted to make sure I had an adequate safety plan in place for Votto.

"I need to know my little man here will be cared for."

He held Votto out at arm's length, turning the little boy sideways to the left, then to the right. Votto giggled like he was having the time of his life. I wished he would fuss instead. I didn't think Davor had invested enough time in him to be getting such a warm response, but the child thought otherwise.

I turned my attention to making one of the homemade meals I knew Davor enjoyed. He'd brought a freshly killed chicken with him, and I went outside to handle the cleaning. Being a farm girl, I'd killed and cleaned plenty of animals over the years. Most of my family handled this chore without much thought, but not me. I always felt sorry for the chicken.

I knew better than to let it keep me from doing my job, though.

Tonight, my distaste for the task faded. I hadn't had meat in a while and I craved it, maybe because of the milk I still made. I knew I had only an ank left to get Votto thoroughly weaned, and I'd waited too long for it to be anything but unpleasant for us both.

Davor watched with appreciation as I prepared the food. We both looked forward to the feast.

"Yesterday, I broke things off with the lady in Pilk I told you about." He said it as I salted the chicken, as if it was unimportant. "She's not for me, after all. Too, I don't know, conniving. I don't much care for scheming women."

Well, this one hadn't lasted long.

"Were you two living together?" I worked at keeping my voice as light as his.

"No. She thought too many would disapprove, since you and I, you know, hadn't made our split official. She didn't want to be the subject of unpleasant gossip."

When Hana crafted her threats to me, she'd relied heavily on this lady's influence. It looked like she hadn't taken Davor's short attention span into account.

"So what's the new one like?"

He gave me a surprised look. "There isn't a new one."

That amazed me. I thought there always was a new one.

"I'm giving up on women for a while. No offense to your gender. You have plenty of worthy talents." He pointed to the chicken, ready to go into the pot of water. "I just seem to have the worst luck finding the woman who's right for me. I don't know why."

I couldn't think of a single wise response.

"Do you want to know why I broke up with Ketevan?"

"Sure."

"I broke up with her because she said unflattering things about you."

Of all the answers in the world, I didn't expect that one.

"Her accusations are true, or at least I think they are, but I didn't like the way she handled it." He gave me a long, inquisitive look. "I argued with her at first, but eventually I had to admit the obvious. You're one of those luskies who are part of Ryalgar's plans, aren't you?"

The tips of my fingers felt as if they'd been dipped in a cold mountain stream. I tried to remain calm.

"I am, but I didn't know it when I met you, and I didn't believe I was one until after we split."

He nodded as if he'd concluded the same thing.

"I was pretty sure you hadn't led me on. You know, there aren't many women around with hair as red as yours. You should have worn a hood over your whole head at those practices."

"I thought about it, but it would have made it hard for anyone to hear me. Those little masks around the eyes are bad enough. Besides, people would know the hood hid something and that would just make them more curious."

"Well, before this is over everyone in Ilari will know what you can do. You accept that?"

"I do." I realized its truth as I said it. "After this is over either we're too dead to care, or a little gratitude for saving people ought to buy me some understanding."

"I hope you're right. Any soldier will tell you people have varmin-short memories when it comes to feeling grateful about being saved. It'd be nice if this was an exception."

"So why exactly *did* you leave what's her name …"

"Ketevan …"

"Why did you leave Ketevan for pointing out the truth to you?"

He chuckled. He liked my question.

"I didn't. I left her for trying to convince me to take Votto away from you. She tried to tell me your talents would make you an unfit mother, which was ridiculous. Near as I can see, you're about as fit a mother as they make."

So. Hana had tried to make good on her threats after all! Why? Had I made her that angry when I wouldn't take the bait about Ryalgar? Whatever her reasoning, she hadn't taken into account Davor's cantankerous personality, either.

It was my turn to chuckle.

"What's so funny?"

"The Velka woman running the part of the plan involving the luskies? She tried to coerce me by threatening to tell you what I was. She said you'd take Votto away from me if you knew. I was so scared."

"Are you talking about Hana?"

"You know her?"

"Heli, everyone in Pilk knows her. Worst busybody in the entire nichna, until she became the Velka's problem. Letting her join was the nicest thing those forest ladies ever did for Pilk."

We looked at each other and, for once, words weren't needed. We agreed on something.

"Here's the saddest part," he finally said. "You could have been the perfect woman for me, and I was too dumb to recognize it."

I won't lie, it felt good to hear him say it. But I didn't want to try to redo our relationship.

"But you're not the perfect woman anymore," he said, "so that's that."

"I'm not?"

"You're a luski, honey cakes. Maybe some men could handle that, I can't imagine how, but I'm certainly not one of them. Always wondering ...."

"Of course." I desperately sought a quick subject change, because I guessed where his mind would go next. I wasn't fast enough.

"Wait a minute. We saw each other plenty after the wedding .... did you ever ...."

I told him the truth because I wanted the two of us to have a clean slate as we moved forward.

"Once. I used the timbre on you once."

"Once isn't so bad. I wish I could believe you used it to get me to have sex with you, but I don't recall we ever did. Did we? You know, after the wedding."

"We didn't."

"So, are you going to tell me what you made me do?"

"Are you sure you want me to?"

We stared at each other.

"I pushed you to sponsor Sulphur when she wanted to join the Svadlu."

His eyes widened. Then he jumped to his feet and threw his hands out into the air. "Are you prucking kidding me?" he shouted, and I took a step back. Why did this make him so angry?

"She's my sister. She wanted this so bad. I knew she'd do well. I thought 'what's the harm?'"

He sat back down and put his head in his hands. When he looked up I thought I saw tears in his eyes. He was crying? No, he was laughing.

"She hasn't done well. She's done amazing. She's brought me money and prestige and saved lives. Sponsoring her was probably the best single career decision I made. I pat myself on the back for it all the time. And now you're telling me it wasn't my idea?"

"Well ... you had to be open to it to be persuaded."

"Yeah, I've heard that. I wonder if it's true. So. Smartest thing I do as a Svadlu, and I find out my wife, a luski, put me up to it."

I searched for something helpful to say.

"Not a luski. A luski who loved you at the time."

He blew out a puff of air. "I suppose that counts for something. Look, don't ever ...."

"I won't."

"But I'll never know if you do, will I?"

"No, you won't."

"Then don't you ever ... but if you do, don't tell me later. Just make sure it's a smart thing like sponsoring Sulphur, and then really don't do it again. Okay?"

I guess he was trying to be funny, in his way. He *had* handled it so much better than I expected.

I finished making our dinner, and we went on to share the meal and wine and conversation about our son. He liked that my mother was taking Votto into the forest and had been promised a place to stay for as long as she needed. I didn't mention Chessa who'd be traveling with them. The evening had been complicated enough.

Then three of us shared the bed, with Votto in the middle.

The next morning before he left, he kissed his son on the forehead, and then took my hand and kissed the top of it as he looked me in the eye.

"Stay safe."

"You too."

I knew it was a dumb answer, given his occupation, but I didn't know what else to say.

The Svadlu had been sending soldiers to train the farmers, but now, with under three anks until Kolada, they came to speak to all of us at our practice. I sat on a bale of hay off to one side, with the other masked luskies. In the middle were more singers than I'd seen before. It looked like entire choirs from around the realm had joined us here at the end. Several reczavy sat on the other side of the singers, and for the first time, I considered how they could be as scared of us as we were of them.

A few dozen cow-herders sat on the ground in front of us. They'd been selected to handle any unexpected issues with the animals while we were doing our part. Behind all of us stood the farmers of Vinx who planned to step in and capture Mongols after we were done.

"You know what the biggest problem is in battle?" an older man with a deep voice asked us all as he stood on a bale of hay. We'd been told he was a retired Mozdol from Kir who'd volunteered to help us with our planning.

We stared back at him, our hundreds of faces blank.

"The problem is what I'm seeing now. Confusion. As soon as things don't go according to plan, no one knows what to do. It's a mess."

We nodded. That made sense.

"How often do you think things don't go according to plan?"

"All the time," Ewalina answered, loud and clear.

He laughed. "You're a woman who's seen a thing or two. She's right, people. Nothing ever goes exactly according to plan. So, does the biggest army always win?"

We shook our heads. We knew better.

"Does the smartest?"

No, probably not that either.

"How about the luckiest?"

"Sometimes the luckiest," one of the singers yelled out.

"You're right, young man. Don't underestimate dumb luck. But, we can't do much about it. So if you take out luck, which army wins?"

I took a guess. It wasn't hard; he'd given us plenty of clues.

"The one that deals best with whatever really happens." I shouted it out.

He squinted at me. "Bonus points to the lady luski with the red hair. So, let's get ready for the unexpected."

We didn't practice at all that day. Instead, we talked about "what ifs?"

What if it rained? What if it snowed? Could we sing through thunder?

What if the Mongols came days early? How would we assemble? What if they came anks late? What if instead of an army, more envoys showed up to offer us a second deadline? We talked about how decisions would be made and communicated in the most bizarre situations we could imagine.

It was the only time we gathered together like that, but I think it mattered. It gave us a sense of the enormity of what we planned to do.

Hana remained subdued throughout, standing far off to the side. She accepted she wasn't in charge today. I kept my distance from her, angry at the way she'd worked behind the scenes to cause me such trouble with Davor. Angrier at the way she'd done it merely out of spite.

I kept glancing at her, but she avoided my eyes. She must have figured out I knew what she'd done. She was probably angry, too. Not at me, but at Davor and at the fact that people didn't always act in the predictable way she hoped. She had to be angry with Ketevan, too, for failing to deliver.

Now, with Kolada so close, few would have patience with her rumors or nonsense. If she still wanted to get her revenge with me, she'd have to wait until after the attack.

~ 25 ~

The Wind on My Face

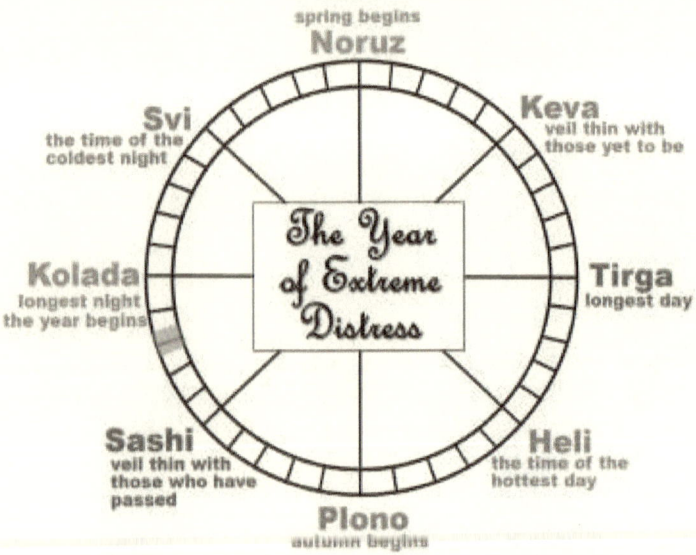

A few days later, the woman who ran our little school asked if she could speak with me when I finished teaching. The day already overflowed with emotion, as tomorrow would be the last day of classes until after the invasion.

Her request unsettled me. All basic schools in Vinx existed under the patronage of our royal family, but the Royals seldom got involved. My country school ran with a surprising lack of management. By custom, the eldest of the teachers enforced the few rules, so a conversation with her usually meant behavior needed to be corrected.

My breasts ached with unused milk from my too-little-too-late efforts to get Votto weaned before he left with my mother. I needed to get his things packed up tonight, and I'd spent most of the morning on the verge of tears. I didn't need a reprimand today for some minor infraction.

She greeted me with enough warmth to signal the subject of the conversation wasn't dire.

"I'll get to the point," she said. "Many of us were nervous about you returning part-time after you had a baby, but this has worked out well for all, especially the children. Even the people who objected the loudest agree."

"I'm glad. I hope you know I want to come back after the invasion and work full-time now that Votto is older."

"It's a discussion we'll have later. That's not what we need to talk about today. Some parents have approached me, and a few have even approached the royal family, expressing concerns about you."

"Me? Why?"

"Because of your potential influence on their children. Preparing for the invasion has made it obvious the somewhat imaginary creatures known as luskies not only exist, but we have many here in Ilari. True?"

"True. My sister with the Velka turned to the luskies for part of our defense."

"That's what I heard. They've practiced various places around Vinx, and some have observed a young luski with hair quite like yours. I'll ask directly. Are you that luski?"

"I am. I could have hidden it better, and perhaps I should have, but I was more concerned with learning how to do what I needed to do. I use my gift as part of Ilari's defense."

"I understand. It's why I counseled patience concerning your situation. But Coral, what do I tell parents who are worried you'll coerce their children to do something wrong?"

"I'd never do that. I have a personal code of ethics, and the luskies have one as well."

She laughed. "Plenty of people violate codes of ethics every day."

"And far more do not. Are you capable of hurting one of the small children in my class?"

"What a horrible thought."

"Yes, but you *could* do it."

"I suppose, but ..."

"But you wouldn't, even though you can. And no parent needs to worry about it, right?"

She could see where I was going with this.

"Yes, but everyone would know what I'd done. My understanding is your talents are so subtle, you'd never be found out."

"Is the *only* reason you wouldn't hurt a child because you think you'd be caught? Of course it isn't."

"I'm not sure this line of reasoning will bring comfort to a parent."

"Then tell them this. I have constraints, too. On what I'm capable of and how much I can do without being detected. I'll give a full accounting of the controls on my behavior. After."

"That will help. Those who try to chase away their fears over the next two anks by causing trouble for you will get that answer from me. We'll have a more in-depth conversation. After."

I turned to go. I had so much I needed to do before this day was over.

"One more thing, Coral. I know every one of you will be risking your life out there. I just want you to know, it means more than I can say, that we could have Vinx to come back to."

I'd already decided to have my mother come get Votto while I was teaching. Otherwise, I'd probably break down and cry so hard he'd be unmanageable for her. I'd heard Ryalgar would personally escort Mom into the forest and get her settled. I silently thanked my sister, knowing how difficult a journey this would be for Mom.

In the morning, I allowed myself one last time to nurse him, and I played with his hair and tickled his toes while I did. He squirmed and laughed. He didn't nurse as hard as when he was younger; at nearly a year old the smells and tastes of food intrigued him more. He'd be fine without me.

My most dependable babysitter had agreed to watch him for the morning, so I could have a last session with the little ones. My eyes teared up thinking of them, too, and I thanked the girl for doing this on her last day of school.

"Do you know I'm going to be part of a team to capture Mongols?" she said.

"What? You?"

She and I seldom spoke about anything besides Votto, so I hadn't expected this. She was a tiny thing; I couldn't imagine she could hold her own against a man of any normal size and strength.

"It's the plan your younger sister devised. The one with the short gold hair."

"Sulphur?"

"That's her. Each team needs people who are small, quick, and limber. That's me!"

I felt my heart clench at the thought of this sweet girl dying at the hands of our enemy.

"Please be careful."

"You do, too."

I can't be worrying about my safety. Not yet. I have too many sad good-byes to survive first.

"Janx should be here soon with Chessa. Remind her she promised to be strong for me. Tell her I'll see her again soon." *That was another good-bye I avoided.* "And be sure and give my mother and sister my love. I think they'll understand why I couldn't be here. I hope they will."

I turned and left before she could see either the sorrow or the fear on my face.

We held the last practice at our farm a few days later. I planned to stay there with my dad until I had to be in place for Kolada, so before I left my house, I loaded poor Nutmeg down with sacks holding as many of my things as she could carry and then I added whatever food and drink I didn't wish to leave in an empty home. Burdened as she was, I rode her slow, and twice I got off and walked to give her a break. While on foot, I made an important decision.

I hadn't planned for life to go this way, but everyone who mattered to me now knew I was a luski. Except for Janx and Chessa. I couldn't do much about Chessa, but I needed to tell Janx. Tomorrow. Too many other people knew and he'd find out soon. If we were going to have any sort of a life together, it needed a foundation of honesty.

Then I had a horrible thought. What if he knew already? Maybe he'd heard since the last time I'd seen him. What if our foundation already contained my lies? Which would bother him most? My talents? Or my lack of candor? I had to get over there tomorrow.

I arrived at the farm early enough to unload my things. Before I put Nutmeg in the stable, I gave her an apple as a thank you for the extra burdens she'd carried. My parents' other horses whinnied their happiness at seeing her. I knew horses made friends much like humans, so I supposed they'd missed her, and she'd missed them, too.

Once I unpacked my belongings, I headed to the barn seeking Celestine. She and I seldom talked at practices, not wanting to draw attention to my identity, but today I'd taken off my mask. The wind on my bare face felt good.

Celestine saw me and pointed to her eyes and opened her hands palms up as though to say "what gives?" I ran to her, laughing.

"Davor was good about it, the school doesn't care, at least not much, Mom knows and I just have one more person to tell. Then I could give a scump who else finds out. I'm done hiding. I've decided I'm going to be Ilari's first public luski!"

She hugged me, sharing in my glee. "I'm so glad. I'm sick of pretending I don't know you!"

We walked arm in arm over to the rest of the group.

"So what do you think today is about? Another pep talk?" I asked her.

"Part of it is the stuff I've been working on with Ryalgar. Communication ideas. How we'll get everyone where they need to be when. It's pretty cool."

"You worked on that?" I didn't mean to sound surprised.

"Yeah. Me and a friend." She probably didn't mean to sound defensive, either.

"Okay, everyone. Get comfortable. We've got lots to go over." Hana oozed confidence and leadership as she took center stage. As Celestine predicted, we talked about logistics. Local inns and various families had offered lodging to those from other nichnas. Everyone, including the singers, were to be in Vinx within five days. Our small group of reczavy fire makers already camped just inside the forest. I guessed they preferred living under the slightly more tolerant auspices of the Velka until they were needed.

As Celestine said, elaborate methods of communication had been devised to keep us in touch, and we were required to sit through a lengthy explanation of each.

"Okay, everybody get up and walk around. Get some water, pee if you must. We go over assignments next." Hana's good humor kept everyone's fear at bay. You'd think we discussed arrangements for a complicated party.

"Assignments? I thought we all were working together? What's to assign?" The person who asked wore a mask but I knew she was Ewalina. She and the other luskies remained disguised, but by now I knew who each of them were. They were all too polite to ask why I'd removed my mask; maybe they figured I didn't mind showing my face because this was my home.

I wondered if any of the others would adopt my open approach after Kolada. Each of them had said they led complicated lives. Perhaps my decision was easy compared to what theirs would involve.

"I've decided we'll work in five teams," Hana said as the group began to gather back together. "It will make it easier for us to move around. We'll start with two teams on either side of the fire and adjust as the smoke gets thicker. Luskies, all twenty of you have been given a number. Singers, you're being assigned by your performing groups. So team one is luskies one through five, Celestine's performing combo, and the entire choir from Zur. The large gong goes with them. Team two ..."

I stopped listening so I could do the math. There were twenty-one luskies still involved, including me. The other twenty were holding numbers. I was not. I didn't like where this was going.

"Team four." Hana kept talking. "You're obviously luski numbers sixteen through twenty, the drummers from Faroo, the three singing duets here from Lev, and the kids choir from Pilk. Older kids only, right?"

"Yep. We sent the little ones on," an older man assured her.

"Great. Have I missed anyone?"

She looked in my direction daring me to say something.

"You said five teams," Ewalina yelled out. "Where's the fifth?" I could have hugged her.

"Ah yes. Team five will be a special assignment team, a mere duo handling emergencies as they arise and then joining whichever team appears most in need at the end. It will consist of me, and one of our stronger luskies. The one who looks like she has nothing to hide today."

Hana made a grand gesture towards me, inviting everyone to see my exposed face as it turned a deep shade of pink.

"Her confidence will be an asset." I couldn't tell if she was being sarcastic or not.

"Your team has no singer," Celestine shouted. "I'll join you two if you like."

A look of surprise crossed Hana's face. She'd forgotten she didn't have a singer. Perhaps she knew she didn't need one.

"Thank you, Celestine, but I'll manage that part myself. Your considerable singing talents are best used elsewhere."

She turned away from Celestine and addressed the crowd with a few words of encouragement. Everyone began to disperse. Everyone except for me. I walked right towards her.

"What kind of scump is this?"

She looked around to see if anyone had overheard my disrespectful tone. If they had, they were looking away now, pretending they hadn't.

"I'm in charge," she said. "I want to be able to handle any emergencies that arise in the days before the attack, and I may need a luski at my side. You'll do nicely. Do you have a problem with your assignment?"

"Keta what's-her-name tried to get Davor to make me give up my child." I spat the words at her.

"Yes, I heard. Unfortunate. She and I had a misunderstanding, and her enthusiasm got the better of her as she tried to prove her worth to me. No harm done though; I understand Davor defended your mothering skills and broke off his relationship with Ketevan instead. Something of a victory for you. Is that what inspired your nude-faced look today?"

"That and the fact that my school is willing to consider having a luski on staff."

"Oh dear. My options for influencing you have dwindled, haven't they?" She seemed amused, not concerned. "Well, as I remember, you and I have an understanding all our own. I'm on good behavior and so are you."

I replied with what may have been the single boldest thing I'd said in my life.

"Pick another luski for your contingency team. I don't want to work with you."

Fat bit of difference it made.

"I don't care if you do or not. You won't be so foolish as to try to destroy me before the invasion, and I insist you aid me as necessary for the next two anks. It's a reasonable request Coral. Get over your dislike of me."

How could I refuse to help her if she needed me? My best bet was to hope she wouldn't.

~ 26 ~

Unnerving Good Cheer

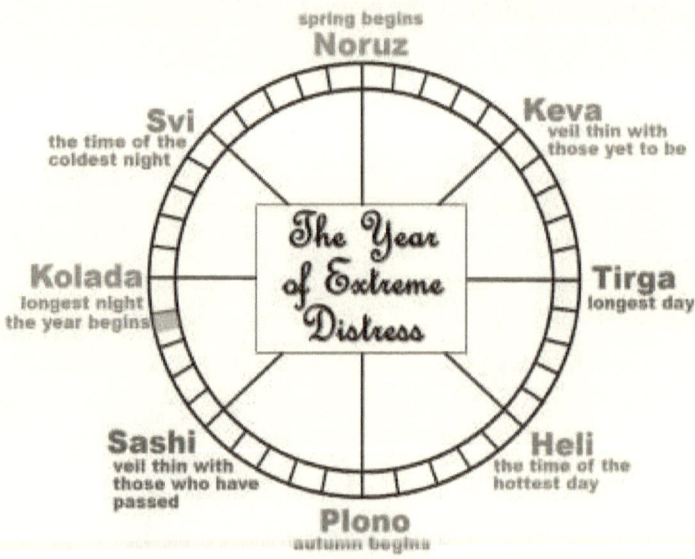

Celestine opted to stay elsewhere, so only Dad and I were at the house that evening. With Mom gone, I figured he could use my company. With Votto gone, I knew I could use his.

I learned he planned to spend the next twelve days dousing the buildings and fields in Bisu with water. He didn't want the Mongols to be able to set fire to the entry to our realm.

"Won't everything just dry back out before the invasion, Dad?"

"We're soaking it in an uncommon amount of water, dear. I designed this wonderful pumping device to make it possible. Then the Velka, they've never been able to make rain for us, but they can keep things misty. They'll do their best in the few days before the invasion. You see, Bisu doesn't have to be inflammable, just unexpectedly hard to ignite."

I understood. We'd found a dozen ways or more to confound these invaders by reducing the effectiveness of their techniques. Or at least every technique Ryalgar's research had revealed. Maybe they'd give up on us in aggravation. Under circumstances less dire, the idea would have been comical.

"When I'm finished watering down Bisu, I'll take my crew into Zur," Dad said. "We'll be on call there, waiting to provide any last-minute alterations to the landscape anywhere it's needed. You'll be okay here alone those last couple of days?"

"I may not be here either, Dad. The woman in charge of my part ..."

"Hana ..." he interrupted.

"Yes, her. I found out today she wants me to assist her. I could end up traveling around with her dealing with unexpected issues."

"I don't mean to give advice where it's not wanted ...."

"It's wanted..."

"I wouldn't trust that woman ..."

"I don't. At all. I just wish I could figure out what she had in mind by asking me to do this."

He looked thoughtful. "Then ask yourself, what is it she's after?"

Good question. "World domination, I think."

He laughed. "Seriously, Coral ..."

"I am serious. At first, the woman just wanted to use us luskies to gain a more important role in Ryalgar's plans. When that didn't work out, she tried to coerce us into being on permanent standby to help her control everything."

"Okay. Well, if she's like most people, her immediate world *is* her everything, so she probably just wants to run the Velka."

"I didn't think anyone ran them."

Dad winced. "They have their ways. I believe they've opted for having a leader of sorts and, if I understand the situation correctly, I'm pretty sure their current leader is your grandmother."

"Really? Ryalgar said Grandma was important. Everyone sure acts like she is. So you think Hana might want to eliminate Grandma so she can take over her spot?"

"Well, that would be the equivalent of world domination for Hana, wouldn't it?"

I worried about Dad's theory all night, as I tossed in my old bed, my breasts still heavy with unused milk three days after Votto had left. I liked my grandmother, and I didn't want her replaced by Hana. I missed my baby. I missed my little house and teaching and my life, and there was a reasonable chance I'd never get any of it back. Ever.

I felt the tears coming. Then I remembered that tomorrow I planned to ride over to Janx's farm and tell him I was far from the sweet woman he'd come to trust.

My tears froze inside my eyes, turning into an icy snowdrift of dread.

A messenger arrived on horseback the next morning as I readied myself for the day. It surprised me messengers still worked this close to the invasion, but I supposed we needed them more than ever. I assumed he brought news for my father, but he sought me out instead.

"You are hereby requested to be prepared to leave your home eight days hence," he began in the traditional singsong tone of the messenger. "Dress warm and bring extra clothes, as you will be camping on high ground. You are to meet your leader Hana at the forest's opening where Vinx, Bisu, and Scrud all touch."

"What the Heli kind of problems could they be having in Scrud?" I demanded to know.

"If you respond with any question I am to tell you that the two of you will be riding into Eds to handle problems that have arisen there."

"What the Heli kind of problems could they be having in Eds?"

The poor messenger gave me a helpless shrug. "This is all the information I have. Hana will expect you at the agreed-upon location mid-morning eight days hence. She will have food, water, and other necessary supplies."

I thanked him, gave him the customary extra small coin, and sought out my dad.

"I'm sorry to hear it," he said. "You'll be leaving before I will."

"I know, but I should return before you leave. Hana and I need to be back in Vinx well before the invasion. At least this way we know she's not going after Grandma. Aliz and all the other oomrushers are staying close to the grasslands of Bisu, in case the Mongols show up early. And Bisu is nowhere near Eds."

"True. That's some comfort."

The question of why anyone, much less Hana, would want to go to Eds seven days before Kolada vexed me all the way over to Janx's farm. It was just as well, as it distracted me from the conversation Janx and I were about to have.

He must have seen me in the distance. By the time I arrived, he'd poured morning wine for both of us and found an apple to slice so it could be shared. He smiled at me from the time I dismounted till I sat in the chair he offered me.

"You seem happy this morning." His good cheer unnerved me.

"We've plenty to be worried about, that's for sure. And yet …" He took a sip of his wine.

"And yet what?"

The question came out sharper than I meant it to, but my conversation with him held enough difficulties without all this unexpected glee on his part. Whatever had gone so well for him, I'd no doubt destroy his good mood and that only made me feel worse.

"I feared you wouldn't come see me now that Chessa had left. And here you are. Tell me why you came."

"Surely you realize I enjoy your company as well as hers?"

"I do, but I think your visit has a special meaning today. Or at least I hope it does."

Screaming skunk scump. He would not be dissuaded from his jubilance. Enough was enough.

"Janx. Listen to me. I'm a prucking luski."

"I know. And I am so happy you rode over here to tell me when it would have been so easy to keep your secret instead."

"You know?"

189

"Coral, the first farmer who thought she recognized your hair under your hat came to warn me about you anks ago. Seven others have been kind enough to do the same since. Not to mention, despite my grief and struggles to raise a child, I can draw conclusions as well as anyone."

"Aren't you scared of me?"

"Not unless you give me reason to be. So far you haven't. I do have questions, but the fact that you're here makes me think you're willing to answer them."

"Wait. You're so happy *because* I came to talk to you?"

"Yes! I decided if you couldn't trust me enough to tell me the truth before Kolada, then you and I had no future together. On the other hand ..." His smile hadn't diminished a bit. "... when I recognized you in the distance, I realized perhaps we did."

I guess I *wasn't* going to destroy his happy mood. I'd caused it.

"I wanted to tell you sooner, but ..."

"Believe me, I understand ..."

"You do?"

"Coral, there are things you need to know about me too. Not things like yours, but difficult truths none-the-less. Like why my wife and I left Faroo, and why it wouldn't be wise for me to ever set foot in my home nichna again."

I reached out and took his hand in mine. I'd always liked men's hands, but today I noticed how strong his were.

"I'd like to know your secrets too," I said.

He touched my arm in response, just below the elbow, and then he ran his hand up to my shoulder and left it there. Those eyes, with their intensity, bored into mine.

"She and I grew up playing together, childhood friends because our parents were business partners. We married young, had a child, and then our story took a sad turn. My wife, she had skills with numbers so our parents put her to work with the coin handling. They didn't realize how smart she was. When she discovered our families shared dishonest secrets she confronted them and it went poorly, to say the least."

"She sounds amazing," I said. Odd perhaps, but I admired a woman who would do this.

"We moved to the other side of Faroo and tried to make a life apart from our kin. We thought they'd leave us be, but when others uncovered their thievery, my brother and her father conspired to lay the blame on me."

I saw the grief creeping into his face and heard it in his words.

"She blamed herself for my troubles and not a single person in either family came to my defense. We fled in the night with Chessa and the little we'd saved."

I touched his face, wiping at a trace of a tear. He leaned towards me as I did, and I have no idea who kissed who first, but once it happened, we kept kissing as the passion of that first embrace washed away the conversation.

The heat between us had increased considerably when he said, "If this morning is all the time you and I will ever have together, then I choose to spend it enjoying each other, not talking of our troubles. What do you think?"

I smiled and reached for him as we both forgot about everything else in the world.

It wasn't our only time together. Despite his rather dramatic proclamation, I didn't need to meet Hana for another eight days. My father left every morning to dump more water over Bisu. Chessa and Votto were being well-cared for deep in the forest. Janx and I? We had our minor chores and practice sessions, but we also had more free time on our hands than we'd had in a long time. It made no sense to sit alone and worry.

At least, that's what I told myself when I showed up the next morning at his farm with a freshly made cake. He was more interested in me than breakfast, but we enjoyed the cake, too.

He came to my farmhouse the next day, awkwardly catching my father as he left. Dad seemed amused, and that evening he told me how much he liked Janx.

I brought Janx dinner the day after that, and I stayed the night and half the morning, too.

The following day we took a break. By then we both needed it. Then the next morning I went over to his house to say my real goodbyes. I told him I'd need the following day to pack. Our farewells lasted most of the morning and ended with a promise to discuss marriage when Kolada passed.

He showed up at the farmhouse the next morning anyway.

"You don't need a whole day to pack," he said. He was right of course, so we spent the morning saying good-bye again. We knew this time it was for real, though. I had to leave shortly after dawn the next day to meet Hana.

I rode Nutmeg and found Hana on her excellent mount with two donkeys in tow. They both carried provisions.

"What to do we need all those supplies for?" I asked.

"Have you spent much time in Eds?" she answered. "Me neither, but I understand there isn't much there under the best of circumstances and most of the population has either been evacuated by now or relocated to nichnas where fighting is expected. We need camping gear, food, and water for up to an ank, in case this all runs slow."

"What the Heli is in Eds that concerns you so?"

She gave me a grin. "An exceptional opportunity."

I hoped Hana would become more talkative, but she remained unusually close-mouthed about our mission as we rode through the desolation of Scud. As we entered K'ba we kept to the road which skirted north of the reczavy campsites. I knew how much she liked to brag, so I kept prodding, putting the most delicate bit of timbre into my questions. She deflected every one.

I decided her demeanor towards me had changed. She'd never relaxed this much in my presence, not even when she showed up at my house half a year ago to tell me Ryalgar had put her in charge of me. She'd lost her fear of me.

"What makes you so sure I'll help you with something you're not even willing to discuss with me?" I finally asked.

"Hmm. Maybe I have my reasons."

Good. I had her on comfortable bragging ground now.

"I thought you and I had an understanding. Don't we?" Only a hint of encouragement.

"Oh, we do," she said. "We do. You will do as I say, and I will not expose you as a luski. Not much of promise on my part anymore, though, given you've decided to expose yourself. But that was your choice."

"I rather thought our agreement involved a broader promise to behave ethically towards each other."

She laughed. "As long as you do what I ask, I'll be ethical as the day is long."

"And what do you intend to ask of me?"

"I'll need to know more about the situation before I can answer that. Of necessity, there will be a lot of improvisation."

"I see. Yet, I can't imagine you have any way to hurt me if I refuse. As you said, I have nothing left to lose."

"Oh don't be ridiculous," she said. "Of course you do. You have that lovely son you adore. You'd do anything to keep him safe, wouldn't you?"

I sat up straighter and slowed Nutmeg down. "My son couldn't be safer. He's with my mother and the Velka."

"He certainly is. Your mother hasn't a friend among them, you know, and your grandmother and sister are far away saving the realm. Tell me, what makes you think the forest is such a safe place for them?"

I'd never considered it anything but.

"Because the Velka are people of honor. They … they have a code. They'd never hurt a child." My fear grew and I knew she could tell. Worse yet, I knew she enjoyed watching it grow.

"You know, Coral, one doesn't have to be a luski to get someone to do their bidding. Sometimes friendship does the trick. No magic needed."

My mind raced. Friendship? Ryalgar had spoken of Hana's two closest friends a few times. The two of them and Hana had given her grief during her early days among the Velka. I searched for their names or anything else about them I could remember.

"Idris." Her name popped into my head. I remembered a skinny, angry young woman. From Eds, I thought. Was *that* why we were going to Eds?

"Very good. I once had a close friend named Idris. I'd still have her, but your prucking sister put her in touch with another prucking sister of yours – the one in the reczavy – and now Idris has run off to have sex with multiple men or whatever it is the reczavy do."

Oh wait. I had heard about Idris. She worked with Gypsum on the Goat. So Idris wasn't part of this.

"But the other one, she's still loyal to you?"

"You bet your arse she is. Ryalgar tried to take her away from me too, by sending her off on that horrible mapping mission where poor Natia saw things no one should see. She still has nightmares about it."

Natia. That's right. Ryalgar thought she'd won Natia over by teaching her to make maps and by giving her an important assignment. Guess Ryalgar had only seen what she wanted to see.

"Natia isn't a fan of my sister?"

"Natia hates your sister. But she knows how to hide it well. She's been nice to Ryalgar and Aliz for half a year now, so she'll be in charge during the invasion. Much of the Conclave will be off doing important things and, of those who aren't, Natia is the most informed about the Chimera. All that mapping she did."

I stopped my horse.

"Let's keep moving. We need to be in Eds by nightfall."

We rode in silence for a while, me turning every bit of information over in my mind.

Finally, Hana broke the silence right where she'd left off.

"Natia doesn't have to be in charge to do my bidding though. You don't know this woman. Trust me, she'd enjoy arranging a fatal accident for Ryalgar's little nephew. That's how much she hates your sister. And that's how desperately she wants to see me, her best friend, in charge of the Velka."

"Fatal? Fatal accident?"

"Oh, everyone will feel just awful about it. Yet, it is true. The world is such a dangerous place for a curious little one year old, isn't it?"

I knew every bit of color had drained from my face, giving Hana the satisfaction of seeing my deathly-white panic.

"So. We have an understanding. You will use your luski talents in whatever way I command, and your son will remain safe. Anything less than a report from me about your full obedience will result in an accident happening before anyone can prevent it."

~ 27 ~

The Executioner's Advice

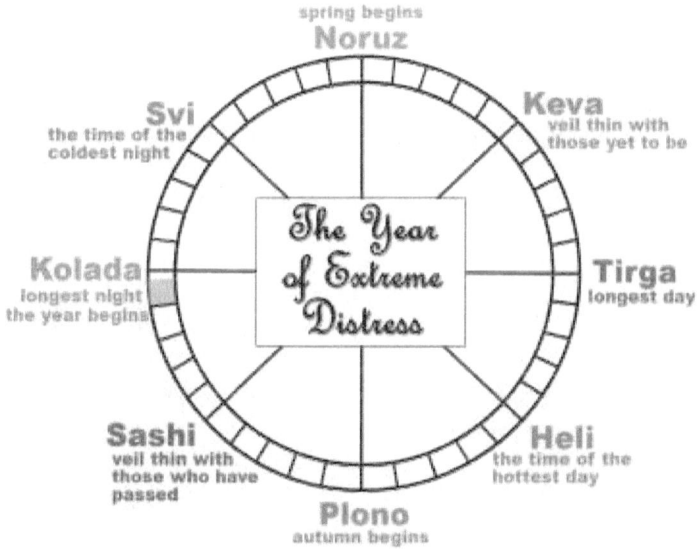

It's one thing to make a bizarre threat like that, and quite another to be able to carry it out. I understood that. But Hana knew I'd take no chances with the life of my son, making this the perfect coercion for me. Also, based on her assessment of me, she thought her threats would leave me too paralyzed with fear to stop her. Not a bad guess, but not necessarily correct. Not anymore.

The donkeys slowed us down and that first night we made a meager camp just inside the barren hills of Eds. Night came early and we opted to eat a cold supper by a small fire. As we huddled close to it, I shuddered at the sound of a wolf howling. I saw her smile at my reaction. She loved seeing my fear, seeing anything that confirmed her opinion of me.

My first instinct was to prove her wrong. Laugh at my nervousness.

No. I stopped myself. The more scared I appeared, the better. I gave a fearful look around and held my arms tight around my chest. I *was* cold and miserable; it was only a small step to add the appearance of being terrified into the mix.

We had wine with our food. Hana drank little, but even the small amount loosened her tongue.

"My mistake was thinking fear is the best way to coerce everyone," she said as she handed me a hard biscuit and some smoked meat. I marveled at how she shared the information with no shame. She believed her scheming impressed others more than it repulsed them.

"Seems to me fear works well." I wanted her to keep talking.

"It does with you. It compliments your nature. But I forgot how even luskies are motivated by different things."

Yes. Keep her bragging. Let her show me how smart she was.

"I can't think of another powerful motive," I said, though I could think of several.

"Oh, there are many," she corrected me. "Greed is one of the best."

"You paid off a luski to do something?" My tone held a little more shock than I would have liked.

She gave me a sly smile, pleased with herself.

"You people gave me the impression you had such a moral code. Silly me for forgetting that someone will always develop flexibility for the right amount of coins."

"Who?"

"I'm not telling."

"Come on, there's only twenty to pick from. I can guess. Was it the guy?"

She shook her head. "No, He's an odd duck, alright, and I might have gone after him, but I needed someone who could go into the forest and spend time with the Velka."

"You used a luski on the Velka?" I tried to sound impressed.

"Why not? You all threatened to use your timbre on me and I'm a Velka. We're not immune."

Right. I didn't mean to bring that up.

"And it wasn't a problem," she said. "In both cases what I needed done made complete sense anyway. That's how I persuaded Ewa …"

I ignored her misstep. I'd already worried that the luski she recruited had to have a strong relationship with the Velka and not many did. My teacher and friend Ewalina was the most likely candidate. Why had Ewalina sold out? Did she need the money? I put those questions aside and tried to continue my subtle questioning.

"You got her to do it not once but twice?"

The sly smile again.

"On anyone significant?"

"Oh, only on Aliz herself and on that self-important Zurian Joli who thinks she runs things whenever Ryalgar isn't around."

Bat scump. Hana had warped the decision making of two of the top Velka leaders? Forcing them to do what?

"They were little things." She answered without being asked. "That's why they worked. I have been listening to you people, you know."

Great.

"We persuaded Aliz to let your mother bring Votto into the forest to hide. It was absolutely the right thing to do, and the safest place for her and the baby, but Aliz resisted the idea. Ewa … my luski had no trouble rationalizing using her timbre to get Aliz to do the right thing. She didn't think to question why I cared."

This made more sense. Ewalina could have been willing to pocket a few coins, maybe to help get her own kids to safety, if all she had to do was persuade Aliz to get past her decades-old anger at my mother.

And now I knew why Hana cared.

"You had to have Votto in the forest to be able to threaten me like this?"

"You may be timid, Coral, but you do catch on quick."

"Well done," I acknowledged. "Now, what sensible thing did you nudge Joli into doing?

"Enough shared confidences for tonight," she said. She wrapped her blanket around her as she stood, and I knew further revelations would have to wait until morning.

On our second day, we headed north. Eds was sparsely populated and most people clustered towards the east side of the little river, which ran along Eds' northwest border below the cliffs of Tolo. Hana told me Joli had arranged for a group of Edsers to stay behind, and they waited in this area. We'd spend this evening and tomorrow with them.

"I should tell you," she said as we rode, "because you're soon to find out. Your sister worried that a second group of invaders might enter Ilari through the northwest corner of Eds. She sent Natia to scout the area last summer."

"That's when Natia saw the horrible things?"

Hana stiffened. She remained angry about this.

"Yes. She did. What no one else knows is she rode off on her own while they were there, and she saw something she didn't report. She confided in me, and me alone, that the Mongols did more than burn the land, the people, the crops, and the animals. Once they finished, they erected a big permanent tent and filled it with their supplies."

"Why wouldn't she tell her group this? They should have investigated it. And Ryalgar should have been told."

"Probably." The sly smile again.

"Natia had to realize this discovery makes it far more likely the Mongols will send some of their people into Ilari thru northwest Eds."

"Oh, she realized it. Natia knew then how important the information was, but she also understood the importance of me following in your grandmother's footsteps. Me, not your sister. She thought I could find a way to use this information, and I have."

I felt nauseous. These two women were so embroiled in a power struggle that they'd put all of Ilari at risk to gain an advantage over Ryalgar?

I took a stab at the truth. "So Joli wanted to send oomrushers and archers up here to defend against a second attack, and you got Ewalina to talk her out of it?" Scump. Hana could have sold out the whole realm for some varmin chance of running the Velka! What was wrong with the woman?

She laughed out loud.

"Oh no. Just the opposite. Joli didn't want to waste an oomrusher/archer team on this low probability. At least she thought it was a low probability. If she was going to send people, she knew they had to be good enough to handle the problem. Her best choice was her second-strongest team, but she hated the idea of not having them in Bisu, where she needed them. And she knew how badly they wouldn't want to be sidelined."

This confused me. "Why would you want to get Joli to send a team up here?"

Hana looked at me, and I don't know if I have ever seen anyone more pleased with themselves.

Then I got it. Of course. That was exactly why I was here.

"Ewalina convinced Joli to send Aliz and Ryalgar up here to Eds?" I said.

"It was the right choice. Joli knew it. She just had to overcome her irrational desire to please your sister. We helped her with that."

"So now …."

"So now you and I are going to spend some time making friends with the Edsers. You will do everything in your power to make them trust me and accept that I speak for those running this Chimera. You will ensure that by the time we leave they are prepared to take direct orders from me. In return, I will send word back to Natia that all is well. She'll be expecting my message."

My father had been right. All that stood between Hana and world domination was the lives of my grandmother and my sister. If Hana had warring Mongols on one side and a small group of obedient Edsers on the other, it wasn't unreasonable to think she could craft a way for Aliz and Ryalgar to end up dead.

That night, we made camp with the hundred or so Edsers who'd been left behind to assist Ryalgar, Aliz, and their long-eyed archer Nikolo. They were a friendly group, at least by the standard of Eds, and our warm welcome was helped by their perception that we were all on the same side.

I played the role of Hana's meek assistant, dropping plenty of small references to her importance, knowledge, and wisdom. I put in enough timbre to elicit the respect she craved, and I got several approving nods from her.

I held back a bit, though. Enough, I hoped, to better allow some of the Edsers to reconsider any order she gave that didn't make sense to them.

We spent the next day discussing plans. They were kind enough to tell Hana absolutely everything they knew, and every contingency they'd discussed with Joli and others over the last several eighths. By late afternoon I had no doubt Hana had all the information she needed for a reasonable chance of orchestrating the tragic set of events she craved.

Before we left the next morning, I helped Hana convince two young Edsers to make their way south to the open forest to get word of our well-being to the Velka. I knew their message would keep Votto safe for a few more days. Then we began our slow journey north along the river to where the U-shaped cliffs of Tolo began.

It was four days until Kolada.

Hana confided she planned to spend the remainder of today and all of tomorrow in Tolo, on top of the cliffs, scouting Eds and its narrow entrance from this vantage point. The better for her to manage any contingency in the heat of the moment.

She actually complimented me on my behavior with the Edsers as we rode, and she spoke of the various ideas she considered. I wondered what sort of disconnect in her mind allowed her to ignore how she discussed the deaths of people I loved. She didn't really get the implications for me, only how this would benefit her.

As we rode, I mulled over my options.

We made it to where the cliffs began and started our ride along the crest. I'd never been up here. The steep rise and sheer vertical drop impressed me with its beauty and its danger.

"We'll be camping up here tonight?" I asked.

"Yes, I don't want to rush this part. We have plenty of time to do this right."

"Good. It's pretty up here. I'm glad we'll get another day."

Up until then, I'd thought I had two bad options. One. Assist in the possible if not probable death of my sister and my grandmother. Two. Set in motion events leading to the possible if not probable death of my child. Neither tragedy was a sure thing, and part of my decision involved weighing the relative likelihood of each horrible outcome.

Tonight, in the dark, I had a third bad option. I could take a walk and jump off a cliff.

Hana would have a rougher time manipulating the Edsers without me, though she might still manage it. Natia could cause Votto's fatal accident anyway out of spite, though she might not bother. And while the other deaths weren't a certainty, if I jumped off the cliffs of Tolo, my death was.

So option three had some problems associated with it, other than the obvious issue of my being terrified of it and not wanting to die.

I shivered in my blankets on the hard ground, but finally fell asleep, and woke at dawn to the memory of a dream. I'd been locked in a cold room with stone walls and almost no light, while a hooded executioner yelled at me. I had no idea what he was doing in Ilari; we'd eliminated executions long ago. But he was angry at me because I would not choose.

"I must kill you. Or your baby. Or your sister. Pick one or I will kill all three."

"I can't. I can't choose. Who could make that kind of choice?"

His exasperation grew. "Then pick the other."

"What other?"

"The other one. Pick the other one, and she dies instead."

"That's no less right. I can't send anyone to their death. What's wrong with you?"

"What if I told you the other one put you here? It is she who insists you make this choice."

I woke up and I understood what the executioner meant. There was a fourth option, though I hadn't wanted to think of it. I knew what I needed to do.

I found it sad that Ewalina had been persuaded to help Hana. No matter how much the requests seemed reasonable, she must have known Hana would not use the outcomes for the greater good. Yet she'd done it anyway. I felt betrayed by this teacher and friend who'd found a way to justify actions leading to the mess I was in.

But Ewalina had taught me well. Extremely well. And right now I had to put my frustration with her aside and focus on the wisdom in her instruction, so I could find a way to do something that made *her* crimes pale in comparison.

What did Hana want? She didn't want to die. She did want to impress everyone. This morning, she and I would go for a walk.

"You're right. You do see things on foot you'd miss on horseback." Hana had been happy to accept my suggestion to walk the last part of the cliff that headed out of Ilari. We'd gotten further than we expected yesterday and left our camp this morning with the horses and donkeys tethered to a lone tree so we could cover this important piece of ground with care.

"I thought about jumping off these cliffs last night," I said, surprising her. I wanted her off balance in every sense of the word.

"Well, I'm glad you didn't." She laughed but she didn't seem amused.

"I don't want to die, and I was afraid you might kill Votto anyway out of spite."

She liked my reasoning. "Good."

"Are you afraid I might make *you* jump off?" More lack of balance.

"Certainly not. I know how this works. I've no death wish, and I'm sure of it."

"You do have a lot to live for," I agreed. "Do heights bother you?"

"Oh no. Not a lot scares me, Coral. I'm a different sort of person than you."

"I suppose. It makes me nervous to be anywhere close to the edge."

"You shouldn't be so cautious. These rocks are solid." She stepped closer to the edge and kept walking. "See. There's no danger, even in walking right along the lip."

She strode along the outer rim, showing me how brave she was.

Yes. You are so courageous. So impressive. So admirable.

"I can't believe walking on the edge doesn't bother you at all."

How I wish I could be as daring as you. You are so fearless.

She flashed me a smile filled with pride. "I can walk right along this drop off all day if I like."

"I can't imagine being so bold."

I took a deep breath. *Do what you must.*

I'd stayed close enough to startle her when I turned towards her suddenly, with my palms out as if to shove her backward. She did the instinctive thing as I lunged. She took a step back; I didn't even have to touch her.

I counted to seven before I walked to the absolute edge and looked down.

Her body lay crumpled; there was no movement. If she wasn't dead now, she soon would be.

What have I done? One voice in my head asked the question. *What you had to,* another voice answered.

I hurried back to our camp, shutting everything but haste out of my mind. I didn't know how long I had until Natia expected the next update, or how much wiggle room she'd allow.

My mind raced. I'd ride Nutmeg, of course, and leave behind the small tent and much of the supplies. I'd need water, though, and some food, and a little firewood and some blankets just in case. So I needed one of the donkeys to carry things even though it would slow me down. Wait. If I brought one, why not bring both. Two was no slower and I could split the load.

I turned towards Hana's beautiful horse. I certainly didn't need a second horse with me, but this creature didn't deserve to die out here, tied to a tree. She'd miss Hana. I felt a pang of guilt as I untethered her and sent her on her way, hoping she'd survive.

Then I and other the three animals retraced the path Hana and I had followed along the cliffs. I knew this would lead me to the Little River, which would lead me to the forest. Good. I needed landmarks. I didn't know this part of the realm and I couldn't afford to get lost. Not now.

By the time the sun shone high in the sky, I became angry. Hana had forced me into this. She'd chosen to give me horrible options, turning me into what I swore to never become. I ranted at her in my head as I made my way back to where the cliffs began.

Once the animals and I began to follow the river, though, I shoved my anger aside just as I had my remorse. I needed to focus on keeping us safe as we picked our way along the rocky river's edge and on keeping us hidden from any Edsers near the river. At our slow pace, I'd never get to the Velka before dark. Where should I stop for the night?

I could tell I'd reached the border between Eds and Zur when the trees went from sparse to plentiful. I needed to turn right and follow the forest's edge. I noted how Zur's border differed from that of the open forest. The Zurians lacked the Velka's talents with plants, and couldn't reinforce their border with the thick shrubbery and thorny vines the Velka used to discourage intruders. Instead, the Zurians had erected a stone wall to establish the boundary between them and Eds. Good again. I could ride outside of the wall until dusk and then camp with the wall at my back. Tomorrow I'd know I'd reached the open forest when the wall ended and the vines began.

So. All you had to do to avoid being forced into becoming a monster was to act like one.

I pushed the uncomfortable thought out of my head as I made camp. I'd moved beyond shock, and I'd run out of anger, at least for now. Sadness threatened to engulf me as I built a small fire, but I didn't want to reflect on my deeds alone in the dark. I turned to the animals, thankful for their company, and I talked to Nutmeg all evening to keep my thoughts from wandering back into the darkest corners of my mind.

The night turned cold, but eventually I slept and at least no winter storm blew in.

~ 28 ~

Living With It

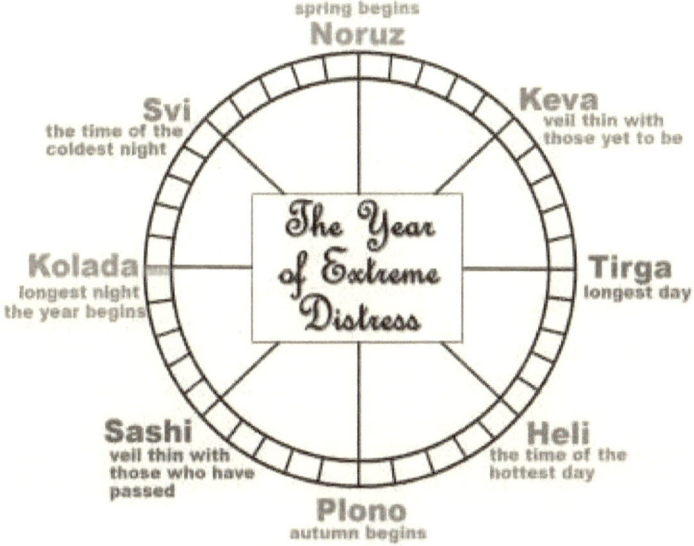

I awoke in a panic when I saw the sun high in the sky. Exhaustion had overcome my urgency to get to Votto. What day was it? I hoped I'd counted right and Kolada was the day after tomorrow.

I took care of my small personal needs, handed out a bit of the food Hana had brought for the animals, and smothered the fleeting thought of how, for all her faults, Hana had always been kind to four-legged creatures. This was no time to eulogize her. She'd put me in this predicament.

I hadn't gone far before the stone wall of Zur crumbled into disarray and the plants along the forest's edge took a turn for the nasty. I'd made it to the overgrown home of the Velka. Now I just had to find the entrance hidden in this corner.

It didn't take long, given my knowledge of what I sought. I could manage to get through, but then what? How did one make their way through this forest? I wish I'd paid more attention when Ryalgar learned to navigate the twisted and poorly marked paths.

One sad fact was certain. I couldn't possibly bring my beloved Nutmeg in with me.

I wrapped my arms around her neck and held on tight. I hadn't given this sad goodbye much thought, yet I'd probably never see her again. Worse yet, would she find the food and water she needed to survive in the winter? Would she manage not to freeze to death?

The tears I'd held back for days finally came and, when they did, they didn't just flow for Nutmeg. They flowed for me, for being forced into becoming something I never wished to be. They flowed for Janx, facing death somewhere out there as he captured Mongols, and for Ryalgar and Grandma, and my father and his road crew and my mother hiding in the forest and my baby in danger and all my sisters out there doing I-wasn't-sure-what. I even cried for Davor, my flawed prince likely to die in a battle that few armies won. The only one I didn't cry for was Hana. I decided I wouldn't waste tears on her.

I probably didn't stand there sobbing for all that long, but it felt like I did. For the first time I could remember, I let myself cry till I was done. What a relief. Maybe I'd cry less now that suppressed old tears didn't struggle to escape.

I kissed Nutmeg on her neck, then patted her on her flank to urge her to go. I turned to enter the forest. I could do this. I'd somehow find my way.

I consolidated the most necessary gear onto one donkey and mounted the other. My feet ached from the unaccustomed amount of walking I'd done, and I couldn't let blisters or even fatigue slow me down. As I sat wondering what direction to go, the donkey tired of waiting for me to decide and started to pick her way along a path.

Didn't these creatures spend their lives traveling these unkempt trails? Of course they did. This animal knew where she was going. Even if it wasn't to the main lodge, we'd end up with someone somewhere who could direct me there. I didn't have to know my way around at all.

The donkey stopped a while later in a part of the forest at least as overgrown as where I'd started. I saw no cottages. Yet, the donkey stood firm, waiting for me to dismount. She knew we'd arrived. Stupid varmin thing. I'd thought she was taking me somewhere worth going.

"Hello!" I shouted into the trees. "Anybody around?"

Silence.

"Please! Come out if you're here!"

I caught a motion out of the corner of my eye and turned. A good-sized rock, at least as big as my fist, hung in the air inches from my eye. I'm sure my mouth dropped open.

"Well, that was a close call, girlie, wasn't it?" A woman as ancient as any I'd seen stepped out from between the trees cackling with amusement. "Scump. I thought you was another one of those oomrushers come to talk me into helping you out with your cause. You people just keep coming."

"I'm no oomrusher."

"I got that, and just in time before that rock hit you in the face, too. Heli, I already hit another one of you yesterday when she come to give me a message."

She seemed far more amused than apologetic. Then she looked at my donkey.

"Goose Feather. You came back. I knew you would."

"She's yours?"

"She's no one's." The old woman cackled again. "Donkeys don't belong to no one in here. But she takes me places more than the others. Here." The woman pulled a carrot out of her pocket and offered it to Goose Feather, who chomped it down in appreciation. "You're related to that dark-haired one who's in charge of this invasion, aren't you? I see a resemblance."

She had to be talking about Ryalgar. "No one's ever said we look alike. But yeah, she's my sister. Look, I'm in a hurry to get to the big lodge. My son is there, and I think he's in danger. Can you help me?"

"I can but I won't. I don't ever go near there."

When she saw the expression on my face, she cackled again. "It's okay, sweetie. You don't need me. Goose Feather's pal here spends most of his time at the main lodge. Get on him, he'll take you straight over there."

I thought my situation was too desperate to be trusted to the whims of a donkey, but I didn't have a better plan.

"Besides," she said "I just got word yesterday about where your sister needs me. That girl is out there guarding the Eds entrance into Ilari!"

"Yeah. I heard."

"I planned to stay out of this nonsense, but seeing how you brought Goose Feather back to me, I think I'll ride her up along the Zurian forest line and see if I can help."

It seemed to me this tiny elderly woman shouldn't be anywhere near an invading army.

"With all respect, perhaps it's too dangerous to head up that way right now."

She cackled so hard she started to cough.

"With all respect back, girlie, I'm pretty varmin good with rocks. I'll be fine."

I looked overhead. It was impossible to judge the time of day this deep in the forest.

"Will I make it to the main lodge before dark?"

"Well before."

Despite what she said, the ride took forever. I left behind all but a jug of water, a biscuit, and an extra blanket so I wasn't prepared to spend another night alone. I wondered if this donkey was less adept at pathfinding than the other. Then, I saw the clearing ahead.

My mother. My mother sat on the huge porch in front of the main lodge holding Votto on her lap. Chessa sat next to her. I screamed when I saw them. Mom jumped up, Chessa screamed back, and Votto reached his little arms out in my direction. A few other women looked up from their chairs while others came out the front door to check out the commotion.

I ran to mom and grabbed Votto and held him tight.

"Coral! What are you doing here? I thought you were …"

"I am, Mom, I am. But, uh, I bring word. Important word. For the Velka. Conclave. I have to speak with them now."

A woman with soft blonde hair and a pleasant face approached us. I guessed she was Natia.

"Coral? What a surprise. I represent the Conclave now as many of our leaders have bravely positioned themselves around the realm. What can I do for you?"

"Gather the rest of the conclave. All who are here. I must deliver this message to every member of the conclave at once."

"I hardly think that's necessary. Those who remain are the more elderly in our group who shouldn't be rushed. Others are far from the lodge and can't be summoned quickly. Tell me what it is you have to say, and I'll call them if I think it's required."

"I can't do that. It has to be all of you." I made this up as I went, but now that I stood on the front porch of the Velka surrounded by people, insisting on a large audience seemed best.

"I'm part of the Conclave, and I'm right here," a woman behind me said.

"And Boyanne is in the dining room," said another. "She's part of the Conclave. I'll go get her."

Natia didn't look pleased. "Very well. Gather the others who are close by, and we'll meet inside. In private."

The look she gave me could best be described as a glare. I ignored it, focusing instead on what I would say when I got the audience I'd asked for.

Votto cried when I gave him back to Mom, and Chessa didn't want to let go of my hand, but I had to go.

Once I was in a room with five other women, I figured I had their full attention for a few minutes. I didn't waste time.

"Hana is dead." There were several gasps. "She took me along on a special mission to Eds and she fell while we were scouting along the cliffs." If more explanation was needed, it didn't have to be given now. I saw the clouds gather in Natia's eyes. She didn't know how lucky she was. I intended to give her a way out of this if she wanted it.

"Hana made some rather unbelievable claims before her death," I said. "She wished for me to do things, as a luski, which I found questionable. So to persuade me she told me she'd have Natia see to the death of my child if I didn't comply."

The other four women looked at Natia and me in confusion.

"I ..." Natia began but I cut her off.

"I didn't believe her. I mean, how could she even get word to you? And you'd never do such a thing, of course. It was an idle threat, desperately made, for reasons I'm sure Hana considered to be justified. Now that she's gone, I forgive her."

It was quite the act, I knew, but I thought Natia could be extremely dangerous if cornered. I wanted her to have an exit.

"I suppose," she said, "that Hana could have said unwise things to you because she thought she had to, though I can hardly imagine her saying such a thing as that."

The other women exchanged looks.

"I am worried though. Hana could have another ally," I said. "Perhaps someone in the Velka she persuaded to harm Votto if, well, things didn't go as she wished." I gave Natia a pointed look. "I think she may have wanted her threat to have some teeth." I paused, hoping my worries would seem reasonable. "I wish to leave, to go do my part as a luski to help save our realm. But I'll only go if you promise to station at least two Velka at all times to stand guard over my mother and my child while I'm gone."

"Of course we will. I'll take a shift myself," Natia said.

"No." I barked it out, and the vehemence in my voice caught the ear of more than one woman in the room.

"Don't be ridiculous, Natia," one of them said. "You're part of what was used to scare this poor young mother. I think it'd be best if you recused yourself over to the Southeast lodge for now. You can run things from there."

"There's no way I'm leaving."

The women exchanged a glance. "The vote is four to one. Given these accusations, you need to leave here for everyone's sake, including your own. We can convene the rest of the Conclave if we have to."

"Go peacefully," another said. "You're still in good standing. Don't jeopardize that."

I saw the light dawn on Natia's face. These women knew how devoted she'd been to Hana, and how desperately Hana had wanted to succeed Aliz. They weren't sure of Natia's role, no matter what I said. They were giving her some room, but they had concerns. Good.

"I'll help you pack," one of the women said as she took Natia by the arm and led her out of the room.

As soon as the door closed, the other three turned to me.

"What exactly did Hana wish for you to do?" one asked pleasantly.

Heli. I'd stick to all the truth I could.

"She wanted me to ensure the Edsers would obey her orders without question."

"These were the Edsers left in place to protect Ryalgar and Aliz?"

"They were."

The women looked at each other.

"How did Hana manage to fall off a cliff? She's hardly a clumsy woman."

"She isn't. But she showed off her boldness by walking along the cliff's edge."

"I see. Did you push her?"

"I didn't touch her."

The woman smiled. "That's something, I suppose. Well then, whatever you did will be between you and your conscience. I hope you can live with it."

"I hope I can too."

It grew dark, and the women suggested I spend the night. I took them up on it, eating a glorious meal of hot food as I told my mother much of what had happened since we parted. I let Chessa sit on my lap that evening and the rest of the time I held Votto so tight he squirmed to be set free.

I rose after a decent night's sleep in a bed and by mid-morning, I'd readied myself to leave. The Conclave member named Boyanne offered to escort me to where one exited the forest into Vinx's main market.

"The luskies and singers have gathered near there," she said. "You can walk to the place."

I stepped out of the forest to see a clear noon-time sky above and the most unexpected sight in the world in front of me.

Nutmeg, not a hundred paces away, whinnied with delight.

"What are you doing here?" I yelled as she trotted towards me.

"Is this where she often saw you go into the forest?" Boyanne asked.

"Well yes, a few times but …"

"Smart horse. She figured it was where you'd come out as well."

As I hugged my mare, I asked Boyanne "It is the day before Kolada, right?"

"Right."

She looked away and I followed her gaze. A tall flagpole now stood near the market, and a red square flag flew from the top.

"They've been sighted," she said. "That flag means the horde comes from the east and will be here soon."

My whole body shuddered. It was happening.

I meant to go join the luskies right away, I really did, but once Boyanne left me I recoiled at the prospect of discussing Hana's death with a group that would be wildly curious about the event. And with a group that would undoubtedly contain my disloyal ex-friend Ewalina.

I considered other options. Nutmeg's presence gave me the freedom to ride out to the cliffs of Vinx and see the oncoming horde. Why not? A thousand horsemen galloping towards us had to be a sight to behold.

Then maybe I could face the others.

There was a hint of fog on the horizon as I left, but it grew as I rode, rising off of the Southeast Lake and up out of the adjoining marsh. I remembered a group within the Velka created this fog to slow the Mongols. They did their job well. Even upon Vinx's high plain, visibility became poor. I needed to turn back.

Then I saw the house I'd heard about. It had been built for a local man who spoke Mongolian and had agreed to train the farmers taking captives. He'd vacated it now so it could be used as a watchtower.

A dark-skinned woman with unusually long dark hair rode out to meet me.

"You're Coral, Celestine's sister?"

She knew of me?

"I'm a friend of Celestine's. I run this lookout. Are you trying to find the luskies? You've passed them. I can take you back."

"No, I thought I had time to peek at the invaders first. Before it all happened."

"You do." Her warm smile reassured me. "You can't see anything with this fog, but ride with me. I've been coming out all day to check on them."

She turned her horse towards the edge of the cliffs, motioning for me to follow. An eerie feeling overcame me, and I hesitated. Was this some apparition, sent from the netherworld by Hana to seek her revenge?

"Come on. It's safe."

Of course it was safe. Was I going to be afraid of cliffs for the rest of my life? No. I wasn't. I nudged Nutmeg towards the woman.

"It doesn't look like we'll be able to see anything," I said as we rode.

"We won't. But they can't see us either. And we can listen."

As we rode north along the cliff's edge I heard horses in the distance. Lots of horses.

She lowered her voice. "Early this morning they came galloping in, looking for their tribute. We heard them come to a halt once they hit the fog and a lot more marsh than they remembered. They've spent much of the day moving slowly, puzzled. You can hear it in their voices."

Sound carried well out on these plains. She was right, I could hear faint shouting between men. The words made no sense, but they spoke in tones of anger and confusion.

"Soon the first of them will hit the extremely lush grass the Velka worked so hard to grow.

We moved a little further northward in silence. Fewer horses walked down there now. Men urged them on. Others argued. We waited.

"This is *really* the first part of the plan," she said. "It was always the part we had the least control over. We need them to stop for the night."

Most of the sounds of hoofs had ceased. We heard the clanging of metal. Pots? Camping gear?

Argument stopped. Tones turned more jovial. A decision had been made, and it wasn't hard to guess.

Let the horses graze in this wonderful grass. Open a jug or two and relax. Perhaps tomorrow this horrible fog would be gone and it would be just as good a day to deal with these troublesome Ilarians.

And it would be.

Archers and oomrushers had taken their places already, hidden by the fog and soon to be hidden by the darkness. Then the mist would lift in the night.

"I need to go," I said.

"Of course. I'll ride with you until you're out of the fog. Tell the others that we've made it through the first part. Perhaps the hardest part. At the first hint of light, the snakes of the Chimera will strike."

I found the various camps not far from the abandoned market stalls. The singers made up most of our numbers, but the few fire-wielding reczavy had carved out their spot, as had the herders trained to work with the runaway horses. The luskies camped furthest off to the side.

I knew the first question I'd be asked. I'd prepared for it.

"Coral. There you are!" Ewalina dared to greet me. "What took you so long? And where's Hana?"

"Dead."

The luskies went silent.

"She fell off a cliff. I hope there's someone else here to coordinate things." Ewalina's cheerfulness left me in no mood to soften anything.

"Is Ura with you?" another asked me.

Ura was a young luski from Pilk who'd hung out a lot with the singers. I had no idea why anyone would think I knew her whereabouts. "No. Have you asked the musicians?"

"Yes, and they said she's acted strange for days. Spent all her time with Hana in the forest, so we thought maybe she ended up with you and Hana."

A suspicious thought crossed my mind. Would Hana have *pretended* Ewalina helped her? Why? To upset me, probably. My feelings of betrayal could make me easier to manipulate.

I turned to Ewalina.

"When's the last time you were in the forest?" I demanded. Whoever had nudged Aliz and Joli in their decision making had done so in the last few anks. Ewalina looked puzzled and hurt by my tone.

"Sometime before Sashi. I've been so busy getting my kids ready to go with my mother ..."

I blew out a puff of air. "Hana tried to leave me a parting gift by telling me you'd betrayed me."

Ewalina's eyes grew wide. I spoke before she could respond.

"I'm sorry I believed her. I really am. She was varmin convincing, though, and I was pretty agitated after she threatened Votto's life."

The luskies went from silent to talking at once. Ewalina held up her hand to hush them.

"If Hana's not coming, we've got to put this nonsense aside and think. There's a hundred people here who need direction, and most of them are restless already because Hana hasn't shown up."

"Coral. Do you think you can take over?" the man from Tolo asked.

I shook my head. "It needs to be someone who's not a luski. This plan needs every one of us."

I gave Ewalina a questioning look. She was in many ways our leader and a logical choice to replace Hana. She nodded at me. "I agree. Not a luski."

"I have an idea," I said. "Celestine is not only uncommonly good at communicating, but she's responsible for gathering most of these singers. I think she could handle the job."

"Yes. She could do this," several said it at once.

You want to talk to her?" Ewalina asked.

"Sure."

As I walked over to the singers' area, I thought of Ryalgar, somewhere in Eds. Thanks to me, and to what I'd done, she now had a chance to make things right there.

I thought of Olivine, already hidden in the fog, ready to shoot poisoned arrows off in the hour before dawn. Of Sulphur, taking her position with our soldiers, willing to die tomorrow for her realm. Of Gypsum, coordinating a circus of illusions designed to push our enemy over the brink. Of Iolite, somewhere unknown, but no doubt playing a part I might never know.

Now, I needed to convince my remaining sister that she was capable of coordinating this rowdy crowd as we tried to persuade two hundred horses to throw their riders into the waiting arms of our farmers.

Could she do it? Could we do it?

After what I'd done to get us this far, I had to believe we could.

Thank you for reading my story of how I saved my entire world from oblivion

-- Coral Renata Glonti

What's Next?

The War Stories of the Seven Troublesome Sisters consists of seven short companion novels. Each tells the personal story and perspective of one of seven radically different sisters in the 1200s as they prepare for an invasion of their realm.

Which sister saves Ilari? That will depend on whose story you are reading. For while each of these historical fantasy/alternate history books can be enjoyed as stand-alone novels, together they tell the full story of how Ilari survived. Each sister offers new information about why this didn't go as anyone expected.

Book 2, *She's the One Who Cares Too Much* became available in February 2021. Book 3, *She's the One Who Gets in Fights,* followed in May 2021. Book 4, *She's the One Who Can't Keep Quiet,* was released in August 2021.

Want to make sure you don't miss a release? Go to my landing page at *https://mailchi.mp/11db23804c68/tell-me-about-new-books* to be notified when each book is ready for purchase. I promise you'll only get notifications about the release of these books.

If you enjoyed this story, please leave a review somewhere. If you enjoyed it a lot, please leave a review in many places.

She's the One Who Gets in Fights

Sulphur, the third of seven sisters, is glad the older two have been slow to wed. It's given her the freedom to train as a fighter, in hopes of fulfilling her lifelong dream of joining Ilari's army. Then, within a matter of days, both sisters announce plans and now Sulphur is expected to find a man to marry.

Is it Sulphur's good fortune her homeland is gripped by fear of a pending Mongol invasion? And the army is going door to door encouraging recruits? Sulphur thinks it is. But once she's forced to kill in a small skirmish, she's ready to rethink her career decision.

Too bad it's too late. The invasion is coming, and Ilari needs every good soldier it has.

Once Sulphur learns Ilari's army has made the strategic decision to not defend certain parts of the realm, including the one where her family lives, she must re-evaluate her loyalty. Is it with the military she's always admired? Or is it with her sisters, who are hatching a plan to defend their homeland with magic?

Everywhere she turns, someone is counting on her to fight for what's right. But what is?

She's the One Who Doesn't Say Much

Olivine, the fourth of seven sisters, has been hiding a secret as she travels to K'ba to meet her artist friends. Others assume she has fallen in love with another artist, and it's not a match Mother would consider suitable. But it's much worse than that. For on the way to K'ba is the dirt poor nichna of Scrud, a place scorned by other Ilarians. And in Scrud is the one man who understands her.

However, Bohdan is also a man who recognizes the dangers posed by an impending Mongol invasion. When he learns of Olivine's unusual visual powers, he convinces her to pick up her bow and start practicing.

She does, though she's more concerned with producing enough art to raise the funds to run away from home and live in K'ba, where she can paint all day and see Bohdan as often as she wants. If only her sister Ryalgar hadn't learned of what she can do and decided Olivine and her fellow long-eyes held one of the keys to defending the realm.

Then, as if life wasn't complicated enough, Olivine learns the artist community she yearns to be part of has developed a different take on the invasion. They feel certain the only way to survive is to capitulate completely to the Mongols' demands. Artists who feel otherwise are no longer welcome.

Where does her future lie? The supposed invasion is coming soon and Olivine doesn't have much time to decide.

What About the Other Sisters?

Look for more information on the adventures of the remaining three sisters in the next book.

About the Author

Sherrie Cronin is the author of a collection of six speculative fiction novels known as 46. Ascending and is now publishing a historical fantasy series called The War Stories of the Seven Troublesome Sisters. A quick look at the synopses of her books makes it obvious she is fascinated by people achieving the astonishing by developing abilities they barely knew they had.

She's made a lot of stops along the way to writing these novels. She's lived in seven cities, visited forty-six countries, and worked as a waitress, technical writer, and geophysicist. Now she answers a hot-line. Along the way, she's lost several cats but acquired a husband who still loves her and three kids who've grown up fine, both despite how eccentric she is.

All her life she has wanted to either tell these kinds of stories or be Chief Science Officer on the Starship Enterprise. She now lives and writes in the mountains of Western North Carolina, where she admits to occasionally checking her phone for a message from Captain Picard, just in case.

Find her at:
Facebook: facebook.com/46Ascending
Goodreads: goodreads.com/author/show/5805814.Sherrie_Cronin
Amazon: amazon.com/Sherrie-Cronin/e/B007FRMO9Q
Twitter: twitter.com/cinnabar01
Author Blog: sherriecronin.xyz/
Book Series Blog: troublesome7sisters.xyz/

Information About Ilari

Words Used by Ilarians

Ank: A nine-day period. Business is conducted during the first six days while the last three are intended for family life and relaxation.

Heli: The hottest time of the year, but sometimes also used as a cussword.

Luski: A feared, possibly imaginary creature who can control others with her voice.

Mozdol: A member of the Svadlu who has been made into an honorary prince due to brave actions defending the realm.

Nichna: One of the twelve principalities of Ilari. Each has its own royal family and is ruled by a prince. All twelve coordinate as regards the Svadlu and other matters pertaining to the common good. There is no king, therefore Ilari is not a kingdom.

Oomrush: telekinesis.

Pruck: An extremely rude word sometimes referring to copulation and other times merely expressing disgust or dismay.

Pruska: An extremely rude word referring to a female possessing any number of undesirable qualities.

Rantallion: A man who is being disagreeable, dishonest, or disgusting.

Reczavy: a group of free-spirited people living in the open forest who choose to continue and extend the sexual freedom permitted to tidzys.

Scump: a rude word referring to excrement.

Svadlu: The Ilarian army and police force. A member of the Svadlu is called a Svadlu.

Tidzy: A young adult who is searching for a mate and is allowed a great deal of sexual freedom around holidays.

Velka: A group of women who live in the open forest, possibly performing magic. A member of the Velka is called a Velka.

The Ilarian Calendar

A year in Ilari is divided into eight parts based on the seasons. Each eighth lasts for 45 days and is named for the holiday at its start.

Each eighth is subdivided into five anks. An ank is nine days long. Businesses and schools are open during the first six days of an ank while the last three, called the ank-break, are intended for family life and relaxation.

Every year astronomers consult the stars to decide which of the holidays will be inside their eighth and which will be treated as extra days. Most years, five or six holidays are ruled to be extra days.

Holidays Marking the Beginning of Each Eighth

Kolada: The winter solstice, the shortest day of the year, and the start of a new year.

Svi: The coldest time of the year, halfway between the winter solstice and the spring equinox.

Noruz: The spring equinox, the start of spring.

Keva: A celebration of those yet to be, held halfway between the spring equinox and the summer solstice. More babies are conceived at Keva than at any other time of the year.

Tirga: The summer solstice, the longest day of the year, the halfway point of a year.

Heli: The hottest time of the year, halfway between the summer solstice and the autumn equinox. Ilarians are not fond of the heat and sometimes use "Heli" as a cussword.

Plono: The autumn equinox, the start of autumn.

Sashi: A celebration of those who have passed, held halfway between the fall equinox and the winter solstice.

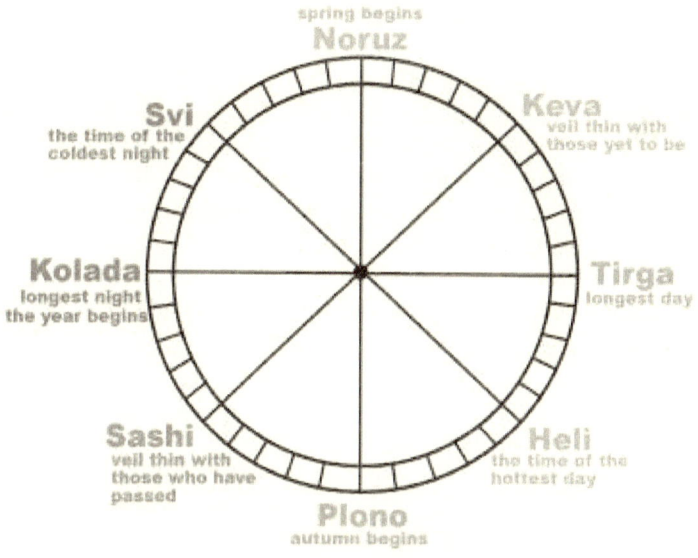

The Twelve Nichnas

Bisu: These low grasslands at the eastern entrance to Ilari supply coveted beef and cows' milk to Ilarians.

Eds: These dry hills leading up to the mountains are sparsely populated with independent-minded goat herders.

Gruen: The fertile soil along the river makes for easy farming of fruits and vegetables and makes Gruen home to one of the two more densely populated areas outside of Pilk.

Faroo: This flood-prone nichna in the rivers bend struggles during heavy rains, but is known for fishing and the boating prowess of its residents.

K'ba: This drought-stricken nichna has survived by becoming home to artists, entertainers, and those seeking more freedom of choice. It is also a playground for the richest Ilarians and boasts a densely populated area known for its spectacular food and lodging.

Kir: Ilari's oldest farming region nestles between Pilk and Lev and grows specialty items for the connoisseurs in both of its neighboring nichnas.

Lev: This nichna is home to the realm's famed vineyards and supplies Ilarians with wine, their most important beverage. It also leads the fashion scene and sparks trends within the realm.

Pilk: As the informal capital of Ilari, Pilk is home to the Svadlu headquarters, most of the institutes of higher learning, and much of the commerce in the realm. The ruling prince of Pilk coordinates cooperation among the twelve ruling princes. The Pilk Palace outshines any other building in Ilari.

Scrud: Rain-deprived Scrud is the poorest and least populated of the nichnas and the most lacking in natural resources. Most Scrudites survive by taking menial jobs in adjoining Bisu or K'ba.

Tolo: Home to the highest mountains in . Ilari, independent Tolovians mine for ore, produce lumber, and serve as a gateway to the even higher mountains to the north.

Vinx: With incredibly flat land sitting above cliffs, the high plains of Vinx provide the wheat, oats, rye, and barley that are the staples of an Ilarian's diet.

Zur: As the only nichna inside of Ilari's large central forest, Zur shares the woods with occupants of the Open Forest including the Velka, the reczavy, and scrounger Scrudites.

Map of Ilari

Meet the Ilarians in this Book

Aliz: Coral's grandmother
Celestine: Coral's sister
Chessa: One of Coral's young students, Janx's daughter
Coral: the second of seven sisters
Davor: Coral's husband
Davot: Coral and Davor's son, more commonly called Votto
Ewalina: an older luski who mentors Coral
Gypsum: Coral's sister
Hana: an ambitious Velka from Pilk
Iolite: Coral's sister
Janx: Chessa's dad, farmer originally from Faroo
Joli: a Velka oomrusher, Ryalgar's best friend
Ketevan: Davor's girlfriend from Pilk, Hana's friend
Markita: Coral's mother
Nevik: a Prince of Pilk, Ryalgar's secret lover
Nutmeg: Coral's mare
Ryalgar: Coral's sister
Sakina: Coral's co-worker & friend
Sulphur: Coral's sister
Votto: Coral's nickname for her son
Yasen: Coral's father

www.ingramcontent.com/pod-product-compliance
Lightning Source LLC
Chambersburg PA
CBHW022013170626
46808CB00001B/384